FALLEN ANGEL OF PARIS

HANS M HIRSCHI

Beaten Track
www.beatentrackpublishing.com

Michel – Fallen Angel of Paris
First published 2022 by Beaten Track Publishing
Copyright © 2022 Hans M Hirschi

Paperback ISBN: 978 1 78645 534 5
eBook ISBN: 978 1 78645 535 2

Beaten Track Publishing,
Burscough, Lancashire.
www.beatentrackpublishing.com

CONTENTS

NOTE FROM THE AUTHOR

Gothenburg, early in 2022

Thank you for picking up this story. I hope you will enjoy reading or listening to it. Be warned that this is not a light-hearted tale. I began writing it at the onset of the COVID-19 pandemic and finished it as the world was entering the latest, Omicron-induced wave. I wonder how many more Greek letters we will need to learn before we finally tire of it and other news takes over the airwaves.

The AIDS pandemic on the other hand has been ongoing since 1981 and is in its fifth decade. It long ago left news cycles and people's general interest—if it ever held it. While we now have great medications to keep those affected alive, and we have enough knowledge to stop transmission, HIV is still killing almost 800,000 people every year and infecting millions. Ignorance, dogma, and lack of adequate healthcare are the main culprits. The stigma is unbroken, especially in places where the disease rages on. There is still no vaccine, even though the mRNA technology used in two of the most successful COVID-19 vaccines offers the most promise yet. There is hope that we may not see a sixth decade of this pandemic.

I first heard about AIDS in May 1983, from a young American college student I had met in the Caribbean. He wondered if I was "safe" to be with before we engaged in harmless and (unknowingly) safe sex. Later that year, he was raped and infected with HIV. He is the only one I know from back then who was infected and

1

who is still alive. Michel was not so lucky. His death on page sixty-four of *The Fallen Angels of Karnataka* is my favorite scene of everything I have written, and to this day, I can't get through it without crying. He never really let go of me, and I'm glad I finally got around to telling you more about his life.

The story of Michel is not "just" about HIV and AIDS. It's also the story of an entire generation and a very special time for Christopher's kind. What sort of lives did we lead back then, before the internet, before iPhones? What did we do? What happened to us? We loved, worked, studied, played; we listened to music, watched movies, and yes, we fucked, seeking intimacy in brief physical encounters. Far too often, we would also get hurt by people who knew we couldn't cry for help, people who knew we would find no sympathy if we did. I sometimes find it hard to believe that *I* grew up in those days and survived, albeit with my own set of scars.

My twenty-year-old self "knew" I'd never be able to get married (yet we just celebrated our seventeenth wedding anniversary) or have children (I became a parent at the age of forty-five. Late, but not too late!). My generation has lived through a miraculous change in attitude toward the queer community, at least here in the West. How much of that is due to the HIV pandemic, I don't know. Yet while our new "Western normal" is more inclusive, most of us still live under brutal oppression. For a man to love a man or a woman to love a woman is still punishable by death or imprisonment in many countries in the Middle East and Africa, and in Hungary, Poland, Russia, and countless other countries, queers are scapegoated and painted as villains.

When you read or listen to this book, know that in reality, things were much, much worse for so many of us. Only very few had a Haakon to look after us at the end, someone who loved us unconditionally. Those of us who've survived, we all knew

2

a Michel: many of us have loved a Michel, and we all have lost a Michel, time and time again.

Even so, this is a hopeful novel simply because it's the only thing I am capable of writing. For all the darkness you will find in the coming chapters, rest assured that Her Majesty delivers light, hope, and love, a truly unconventional Happy Ending!

Hans M Hirschi

PS: While there is a connection—obviously—to my novel *The Fallen Angels of Karnataka* (the story that bestowed upon me the honorific of "Queen of Unconventional Happy Endings"), you can enjoy this as a stand-alone story. I have included enough of the backstory for it to make sense. However, I hope you will be enticed enough to give Haakon a shot, too, once you are done here. Bisous!

PRESENT DAY – AN ACCIDENT AND A HURRICANE

IRST THE ACCIDENT, now this! Looking around the empty house, a sensation of loss and loneliness overcame Haakon, quickly overwhelming his senses. Mahender, his husband, had left for the airport on Tortola after breakfast and was currently on a plane heading north to New York, from where he'd fly on to Bangalore. Haakon would follow him soon enough, along with the kids. But not yet.

Nanju, their CEO, had been severely injured in a traffic accident and hospitalized, and it was imperative one of them returned to Bangalore immediately: the children relied on them and the Center for Fallen Angels. However, Haakon had needed to stay on the island to oversee the evacuation of the children recuperating there. A hurricane was forming off the coast of West Africa a few hundred miles south of Cape Verde, and it was forecast to hit the Caribbean Leeward Islands in a few days, potentially as a major storm with all that entailed.

Despite knowing he would soon join Mahender, Haakon was lonely, unaccustomed to being apart from his partner—in life and work—of twenty-four years. Rose had left the house to return to her place on the northern side of the small, private island, undoubtedly passing through the tiny village they had built, where a good fifty children were currently staying while they recovered from their ordeals back in India, having been kidnapped or sold into either servitude, cheap labor for unscrupulous businessmen

5

selling their wares to global corporations who looked the other way, or—worse—into a life of sexual abuse. Every time Haakon looked into the eyes of one of the kids they had saved and saw their gratitude, their innocent smiles, he was instantly transported back in time and reminded of the two small angels he had failed to save, two souls that still weighed heavily on his conscience. Two boys whose deaths he should have prevented.

Avi and Jay.

The two fallen angels who had named their foundation.

By now, they would have been in their early thirties, and they likely would have had families of their own, children around the age they had been back then when Charles...

Haakon dared not finish the thought. The images still haunted him. Always would. Whenever the ghost of that dreadful day came to visit, filling his mind with the horrific scene he had encountered, Haakon felt particularly alone with his guilt. Not even Mahender could make things better, though he had been there, too, and had seen the horror. It had not been Mahender's responsibility to prevent the deed from ever happening. That rested on Haakon's shoulders alone.

Like a caged animal, he paced from room to room, trying to push the image aside. Reaching the section that contained part of their library, a collection of books from Charles's estate along with some of their personal favorites, he slowed his steps but didn't enter. Over the past eleven years, the house had become a regular retreat for them, a way to unwind and recharge batteries that were depleted far too soon by the harsh reality of the poverty and lack of respect for human life that was so prevalent across the Indian subcontinent. They were fighting an uphill battle, losing too many kids for each one they saved, unable to be everywhere at once because there were simply too many of them. That was the most frustrating aspect of their foundation's work.

Still searching for a distraction, Haakon returned to the living room and browsed the bookshelves there, which covered an entire wall, though his thoughts were elsewhere. He traced the spines with his index finger as if the tactile sensation alone could pick the right book to read, to relax and unwind. A flash of bright red amid the muted browns and greens caught his attention, bringing his gaze into focus, and in an instant, Haakon was once again transported back in time, way back to thirty-five years ago and a place far away from India or Mon Bijou: a forest-green, wooden bench in Paris, across the Seine from the Eiffel Tower.

Michel.

Haakon hadn't seen the notebook in years. How had it ended up on the island? Had he brought it here? He couldn't remember but assumed it had been in his luggage when he first arrived. He reached for the red, leather-bound diary of his first love, pulled it from the bookshelf, and caressed the cover.

It was one of a handful of items he had rescued from the small studio apartment after Michel had passed away from complications related to AIDS, right there on that green wooden bench across from the Eiffel Tower. Tears welled in Haakon's eyes as he remembered the particulars of that day—the crisp air, the smells from car exhausts, food, and dog poop, the sounds of cars speeding by and the voices of tourists and locals milling around them despite the time of year. Michel had wanted to enjoy the pale sun, which had barely warmed their faces on that late November day, forever etched into Haakon's memory—another painful one at that.

After Michel's death, Haakon had quickly vacated his boyfriend's place, not by choice. Michel's parents had been en route to claim their son's remains and belongings, so Haakon had taken one or two of Michel's favorite sweaters, still smelling of him, some racy magazines to do away with, and the diary, knowing Michel wouldn't have wanted it to fall into the wrong hands, especially his parents', and then he'd left.

Until now, he hadn't given the diary another thought. He'd read some of it back then and had even re-read the final entries after he had become a part of Michel's life, but he'd never read it all. It had always felt like an invasion of Michel's privacy.

7

But that was so long ago and, thirty-five years later, curiosity got the better of him. Diary in hand, he grabbed a glass of water from the kitchen before heading out to the porch, where he sat in his favorite rocking chair, overlooking the beach. At this time of day, the sun stood high above, and the porch was shaded by the trees surrounding their house.

Haakon took a sip of water and gently opened the cover, marveling at the childlike handwriting in blue ink that met him on the first page. *French, right, I'd forgotten. This might take some time. My French is quite rusty after all these years.*

8

1964 – 1976

THE DIARY

*I*T WAS ON his birthday in 1974 that Michel got his cahier, a vibrant red notebook bought so he could keep a journal, and he absolutely loved it. He immediately jotted down memories of his past, of his early childhood, leaving empty pages to fill later. That done, he began to keep a regular diary, immortalizing the daily events that made up his life, picturing himself as an old man looking back over the entries and musing over memories from decades ago.

11

ST. MALO

THE FIRST ENTRIES in Michel's diary were endearing, at the hand of the sweet, innocent child full of wonder and questions about the world around him. As Haakon read about the memories of a very young Michel, he was reminded of his own youth. They had been written a few years after the actual events had transpired, presumably shortly after being gifted the notebook.

Michel's mom, Emmanuelle, had been in excruciating pain while a nurse at the local hospital in St. Malo had held her hand. She had been in labor for a long time, trying to give birth to Michel.

"Now, now, madame, just a few more pushes and you're done," the midwife had instructed her as yet another jolt of pain traveled from her pelvis upward, along her spine toward her head. Emmanuelle had screamed. "Pull yourself together, madame, the child is crowning now, push, madame, push!"

The orders were barked, and oddly, the cold-hearted and matter-of-fact handling by the midwife had a soothing effect on Emmanuelle, or so she had told Michel on many occasions. Twenty minutes later, it had all been over, and her firstborn was in her arms, cooing. October 4, 1964 had been a sunny fall day in that beautiful town on the coast of Brittany. Emmanuelle had been so proud of Michel, something she would often talk about as he grew up, not that he understood why.

Maybe it was because he would be the only child she would ever have, as the doctors advised her not to have any more, not after her difficult pregnancy—also something she'd never failed to remind Michel of, particularly after he'd gotten himself into trouble over something. Maybe this guilt-induced memory was the reason Michel had felt the need to write it down?

Being the woman she was, obeying and implicitly trusting Church and State, those two pillars of French society, she had convinced Michel's dad, Edmond, to get a vasectomy. It was a difficult decision for her, as she knew the Church didn't condone such things, but just this once, she chose her earthly life and to be there for her child rather than risking him growing up an orphan. Maybe she knew deep within that her husband, as loving as he was, would never be capable of raising Michel on his own, let alone two children were she to die in childbirth after a second painful and complicated pregnancy.

She'd often talk about this, usually to chide Michel or to make Edmond feel miserable about himself—the sacrifice she had made for them, most likely forsaking her heavenly eternity for their short mortal existence. Maybe she knew her husband would be truly lost without her. Emmanuelle St. Jacques had to make a difficult choice, choosing between her duty to God, to bring as many children into the world as he willed, and her obligations as mother and wife, and she vowed it would be the last time she defied the Holy Church. Her guilt was passed on to the next generation.

Michel heard that story often as he grew up, laced with the subliminal message of "it's all your fault!" even though they both realized that none of them were masters of their fate and that it was God who had put this challenge before them, to overcome. Haakon marveled at the strength of faith protruding from those early pages. It was so unlike the Michel he'd later gotten to know.

The family lived in St. Malo until Michel was six years old and moved to Rennes in the spring of 1970, the year after De Gaulle had left the office of the French presidency. There was precious little in the diary about those early days, except for a few stories about the great general and the war efforts to liberate France from the Germans. Both of Michel's grandfathers had fought in

13

the Resistance during the war, and Michel's paternal grandfather had met De Gaulle a few times. The stories must've made a great impression on young Michel since he felt the need to write them down.

Entire neighborhoods were built in modern suburbs outside cities as old as human memory, and when the fishing business slumped, and Michel's dad lost his job on one of the vessels leaving St. Malo every morning, he did what millions of Europeans did in the 1960s and 70s: he left the countryside and moved to a larger city. Rennes, the capital of Brittany and its largest city, became home to the St. Jacques family, and the city where Michel was to grow up.

Michel's father accepted work in a car factory, working long hours every day while his mom remained a homemaker. She looked after their small two-bedroom flat in one of the brand-new apartment buildings sprouting up all over the country, inspired by Swiss-French architect Le Corbusier. They lived in the outskirts of Rennes, near the factory where Edmond worked.

Life wasn't easy. Money was tight. Yet the early entries in the diary, written after the fact, comprised only fond memories of Michel's early childhood. Maybe he didn't remember the negative aspects, or maybe most of those memories consisted of stories told by others, where the hardships had been carefully edited out, forgotten, or suppressed, the blanks filled in by romantic notions of whoever told the story. There were accounts of visits to grandparents on the coast of Brittany, to St. Malo, a beautiful old city with impressive city walls, where he remembered watching the tide come in or go out, with the huge difference in sea levels at this special spot on the English Channel. Michel had often spent his summers at his grandparents' apartment inside the walled old city, to give his parents a chance to rest up a bit.

As he got older, in late July, his father would pack them all into their small car, his pride and joy, a bright-red Citroën 2CV, a "Deux Chevaux" as it was called, and they would head south, or west, to explore other parts of the great country that is France.

There were sketchy but warm memories of the two weeks together with his parents, the old tent Edmond had strapped to the roof of their car, camping out in different parts of the country, the warm summer air, the scents, the food. Those were, Michel wrote, the happiest days of their time together. Michel's dad would help his mom with the food and even the dishes afterward, unlike at home, where he would retreat to watch TV after dinner and leave her to do all the household chores. He'd even help her cook their camping meals. It was, he had always said, "your vacation, too, chérie!"

Haakon found it challenging to reconcile these stories of a happy Monsieur St. Jacques with the man he had only met briefly at Michel's Paris studio about a month before Michel passed away.

1976

MONSEIGNEUR SERRAULT

*M*ICHEL, CAN YOU stay behind for a moment? I need to talk to you."

The monseigneur was not to be ignored. Michel had learned that early on during his stint as an altar boy. "Oui, Monseigneur, how may I be of assistance?"

Monseigneur Serrault was the priest at the Roman Catholic church that the St. Jacques family attended every Sunday and where Michel's mother spent much of her free time. They were gathered in the sacristy after Sunday Mass and had just gotten out of their albs. Michel was looking forward to going home for Sunday lunch when the priest called to talk to him. He watched the other boys leave while he had to stay behind. It was not a pleasant feeling.

"When did you last confess?"

Michel shrugged. He didn't remember. It was not something he did regularly. In fact, he tried to avoid it altogether. He did not enjoy it. Quite the contrary!

"Your mother asked me to take your confession. She is worried about your immortal soul. Why don't you come over to the rectory later today? We can do it there, in a more relaxed environment. It would save both of us the task of having to come back here."

Michel didn't want to do it, but the monseigneur was a kind man and trying to please both parties. Michel's mother was deeply religious and very keen on procedure. She believed that attending Mass every day, going to confession regularly, and observing all the rites and rules of the Holy Mother Church were

19

essential for her salvation, and she'd be remiss if she failed her son in achieving salvation as well.

Michel had been an altar boy for a couple of months now, and he didn't cherish the task. He'd rather spend time with his friends, read a good book, or listen to music in his room. However, since he had to attend Sunday Mass with his parents anyway, he might as well do something rather than sitting quietly in the pews while his overtly religious mother would theatrically go full throttle on every aspect of the liturgy, from dropping to her knees in prayer to loudly repeating the sacred litany after the monseigneur. Their conservative congregation strictly followed the traditional liturgy in Latin. Michel often found the stares from people in the pews around them embarrassing, and he much preferred to be up there by the altar with the monseigneur where he knew people barely noticed him and the other altar boys.

Like most boys his age, Michel had long ago received his First Communion and was on his way to being confirmed. The years between the two rites were spent with Sunday school and scripture reading. While there was no doubt in his mind that Christ was real, that he had lived and died on the cross for the sins of humankind, Michel did not understand why he had to learn about it, what it meant to him and his daily life. He did pray every now and then, primarily when he was in trouble or when he desperately wanted something. His relationship with God was purely transactional, and that was as it should be. He saw no other use for God. Death, salvation, and an eternity in heaven were theoretical concepts to the twelve-year-old.

He felt similarly about the concept of confession. Why would he need to confess anything to a priest? If God really was as almighty as they all claimed, then he would already know every one of his thoughts, and no confession of his would add any essential information. After all, an almighty God could look deep inside his heart at any given time and see past any excuse he might offer to a priest to offset the number of Hail Marys he undoubtedly would be asked to recite. Besides, his life was dull at best, and there wasn't much to confess. He didn't steal, he didn't kill, he had no other gods, he honored his parents, and the idea of coveting his neighbor's wife was a most disgusting thought to Michel. God knew what was in his heart; that was enough. There was no need to bring a priest into it.

Alas, none of that mattered now. He would have to go to the monseigneur's home to confess, and when he asked his mom for permission to slip out after lunch, she readily obliged. Her smile was so beatific that it almost inspired Michel. If his mother was so strong in her faith, why couldn't he at least put in the effort? Who knew, God might just reward him for it. A new cassette tape, perhaps?

When he knocked on the door of Monseigneur Serrault's house, Marie, his housekeeper, opened it instantly.

"Young man, I was just about to leave. Are you here to meet with the monseigneur? He's in his study. Walk right in. He's expecting you." With that, she let Michel into the rectory and walked out, closing the door behind her.

Inside the priestly home, the corridor was very dimly lit. The hallway itself was clad in dark wooden panels, absorbing whatever light came from the candle-like lamps attached to the left side of the hall. Michel cleaned off his shoes and proceeded deeper into the house. He had been here before, for a first interview before becoming an altar boy, then again, a month or so ago, after he and a couple of other boys had completed their first month of service, to celebrate with the monseigneur. He had been a most gracious host and had Marie serve them cake and real Coca-Cola, something Michel had never tasted before. His parents would usually buy local sodas or syrups rather than the more expensive and exclusive foreign brands. Money was tight in the St. Jacques household.

Michel reached the intended door and knocked.

"Come in!" he heard from the other side. He opened it and walked in. The monseigneur was sitting behind a large wooden desk, surrounded by shelves laden with books, lots of books, many of them worn looking. This library, or study as Marie had called it, was impressive, and it made Michel feel very small.

"Ah, Michel! Come in, have a seat over there, on the couch. I shall be right with you. I just need to finish this letter to His Holiness." Monseigneur Serrault smiled and gestured toward an old-fashioned couch with an ancient-looking embroidered floral pattern. It was flanked by a couple of armchairs in the same style with menacingly tall backs like thrones. Between the chairs and the couch was a small, oval coffee table that also had seen better days. A small dish with cookies stood in the middle along with a pot, cups, and saucers to serve tea. Michel sat on the couch and had the strange feeling judgment was about to be passed on him.

Monseigneur Serrault came over after a few minutes and sat next to Michel. He was in his late thirties, or so Michel guessed, an old man from the vantage point of a pre-teen youth. He had a pleasant smile, dark, straight hair covering his ears, and his eyes were of a beautiful green color and very vibrant. He looked kind and curious. He had always had the ability to make Michel feel at ease, regardless, and he seemed to understand how boys his age "ticked," so to speak. It didn't help today.

"Thank you for coming by so quickly, Michel. I appreciate it. Your mother wanted us to have a chat. She insisted on confession, but I don't think we have to be so formal, do we? We'll just have a chat, from man to man, if that is okay with you?"

Michel nodded. *Thank God!*

"Can I get you some tea? Or would you rather have something else? Marie made a pot before she left. It should still be hot."

"I'll have some tea, thank you." Michel felt it would be impolite to refuse it, especially since he had just escaped confession. Better to not tempt fate. Besides, this was an adult beverage, with the beautiful china and all. They didn't have that at their house.

The monseigneur poured them each a cup and placed them on small saucers, added a spoon to Michel's, and placed it in front of him. "Would you like some sugar?"

"Yes, please!" Michel wasn't at all sure he would even have been able to drink it without sugar. He'd had tea once before and did not care for the bitter taste of it.

The priest added two spoons of sugar to Michel's cup, but none to his own, which he picked up and sipped. Michel noticed how delicately he held the small cup in one hand and had to smile. He proceeded to stir the sugar into his tea before mimicking the monseigneur, holding the cup in one hand, saucer in the other, while gingerly stretching his pinkie into the air. He felt very chic, very adult.

After the priest had placed his cup back on the table, he turned and placed his hands between his legs as if to hide them. He was wearing black slacks and a black shirt with a white priestly collar. "So, Michel, tell me, is there a reason why you believe your mother would want me to talk to you, to take your confession?"

His eyes were kind, and Michel began to relax a little. At the same time, the question seemed odd, and he didn't know what to say, so he looked down at the floor and shook his head.

"Is there something bothering you? I know mothers have a sixth sense about these things."

Michel looked up and met the priest's gaze. Again, he shook his head.

"Maybe it's something that you don't think you can talk about with her? Something very personal? Maybe something about you and your body? Something manly? You are growing up, after all."

Michel didn't understand what the priest was referring to, and Monseigneur Serrault understood as much. "Look, Michel, you're nearly twelve years old now, right?"

He nodded in response, wondering where this was going.

"When we grow up, we don't just grow taller. I'm sure you've noticed that men look very different from boys. So will you before long, and you will become interested in girls because they change, too." He smiled knowingly, but Michel had no clue what the priest seemed to be hinting at. To Michel, girls had never held any particular appeal beyond that of playmates in school.

"In a year or so, you will begin to develop into a man. Your body will go through a lot of changes. Your mother, as a woman, cannot understand those changes, but she realizes that you have to go through them. Maybe that is why she felt you might be more comfortable talking to me about it? I am, after all, a priest, and I have taken a vow of secrecy. And I am a man. Or could you talk to your father about this?"

Michel shook his head vehemently. He didn't talk to his father one-to-one. He never had, and most certainly never would about something like this, whatever it was.

Unsure what the priest was talking about, Michel suddenly felt deeply uncomfortable sitting so close to this stranger on a couch, talking about stuff that he didn't understand. What changes was he alluding to? What was going to happen to his body? It scared him to think about it.

"Don't worry, Michel. Everything that happens in here, whatever is said, will stay between you, me, and the Almighty Father. Do you understand? No one else will ever know. No one else must know, is that clear?" There was something in the way the monseigneur looked at him that worried Michel. But then he smiled and continued his explanations.

"Allow me to show you. Please, touch my face." The priest took one of Michel's wrists and guided his small hand to his face. Michel was unsure if he should resist, pull back. The priest noticed. "You don't have to be afraid. I just want to show you something. Here, touch it."

Michel's hand gently patted the priest's cheek. It felt rough to the touch. Stubbly. His father's face felt similar, at least on weekends when he'd only shave after breakfast. He had only touched his father once or twice. His family was not very physical, or emotional, for that matter.

"See, this is a man's face. As we grow into our adult bodies, we begin to grow a beard, and as we shave it, it makes our faces seem rougher to the touch." He let go of Michel's hand, which remained on the priest's face, and with his own caressed Michel's cheek. "See, now your face is still that of a child. Soft, so very soft! And so very innocent! Or is it?" He let the question hang in the air a moment before adding, "But your face is not the only place where you change. Please, could you take off your shirt?"

Michel stared at the monseigneur, trying to discern if he actually meant what he said. He'd changed before him in the sacristy before. It wasn't that big a deal, but why here? Why now? He unbuttoned his shirt and took it off, slowly. It was embarrassing, and he felt the man's gaze on him. He felt ashamed of his pale body.

He was very surprised when the priest removed his white collar and proceeded to unbutton his black shirt. After a few seconds, the two sat next to each other, half-naked. Michel looked at the priest, and something within him began to stir. His mouth felt very dry, a strange sensation pulsated through his body, and even though the room was cool, he felt hot. He couldn't take his eyes off the monseigneur's chest, his naked torso.

As if the priest could read his mind, he said, "You may touch it. This is a man's chest. It is hairy and hard. Muscular! You will also grow hair on your chest, in time, as your body develops into that of a man. Women, however, their development is very different. They won't grow hair. Instead, their breasts will grow, and their bodies will be soft to the touch. Men like the soft touch of breasts and a woman's skin."

As if pulled by a magic string, Michel's hand stretched out for the man's chest. The monseigneur moaned lightly at the touch. "See, this is what it feels like to be a man." He caressed Michel's chest in return, sending shivers down Michel's spine. It was very pleasant, but why was the monseigneur doing this to him? Had he not been a boy himself? Did he not remember what it was like?

"Meanwhile, you still have the beautiful body of a boy. So soft! So soft, and so very beautiful!" Unexpectedly, he leaned forward and placed a kiss on Michel's chest, barely audibly whispering, "Body of Christ," before sitting upright again. Michel felt the man's tongue emerge from his mouth to flick across his left nipple. The sensation rushing through his body made him shiver violently. The monseigneur took that as a sign and leaned in again, gently licking the other nipple before sitting up straight. "Did that feel good?"

Michel nodded, his body shaking.

"But you see, Michel, that is only part of our body. The most important changes happen elsewhere. Here, let me show you. Please, take off your pants." Michel gave him a puzzled look. "Don't worry, I will do the same. Here, see?" The priest stood up and quickly dropped his pants, showcasing a pair of white briefs.

Michel began to fiddle with the button and fly of his pants and took them off.

"Your briefs as well." The monseigneur smiled and took off his underwear. Michel couldn't believe what he saw. He had never seen another naked man before, not even his father, certainly not like this.

He recognized the penis between the man's legs, and his dangling, hairy scrotum, but it was so very different from his own. His penis was huge, and it wasn't hanging. It was bobbing slightly, sticking straight out into the air. Almost imperceptibly, it began to slowly climb upwards, getting bigger and fatter, and it was surrounded by a lot of hair, hair that seemed to grow from the monseigneur's chest down to his penis, all over his scrotum, and farther down, covering his legs as well. The hair was as black as that on his head, and Michel couldn't help but stare.

"Touch it! It's okay. One day soon, you will change, and you may look very much the same."

He smiled at Michel and guided his hand forward, and as Michel touched the priest's now erect penis, something strange happened. Michel's penis began to grow, in a way he had only experienced in the morning sometimes when he woke up.

The monseigneur reached out to caress Michel's private parts as the boy was caressing his. "Does this feel good to you?"

Michel's eyes were squarely focused on the priest's penis, but he nodded, replicating the man's gentle movements up and down the shaft. There was nothing menacing or judging in his voice, but something else, something he couldn't quite decipher.

"I had a hunch you might. Now, women, they look quite different down here. They don't have a penis but a vagina instead, and once you are married, you will place your penis inside the vulva to procreate and please the Lord. Never before! You must be married. Do you understand that?"

Michel nodded even though he had no clue what the man was talking about. His hand was still moving up and down, cupping the priest's scrotum, mimicking the movements of the monseigneur's hand on his.

"I think you and I have a lot in common," the priest said, his voice trembling. "But I think this is enough for one day. I do believe, however, that you should come back soon to continue our conversation and your training. Would you like that, Michel?"

He merely nodded, his hand still firmly attached to the priest's penis, stroking it. The monseigneur scooted backward on the couch, thus forcing Michel to release his hold before he got up and turned around to get dressed.

Seeing the man naked from behind made Michel swallow hard. His head was spinning and his heart was racing, but he couldn't understand why. He did, however, long to touch the monseigneur again. The man's body exuded an undeniable pull on Michel, drawing him closer, daring his hands to reach out and touch his back, his buttocks. But he resisted the urge. Instead, as the monseigneur put his underwear back on, Michel did the same, trying to stay on par with the priest. Within a couple of minutes, they sat on the couch again, sipping tea as if nothing had happened.

"Now, Michel, I need you to promise me something," The monseigneur said in a grave voice, still holding his tea.

"Of course, Monseigneur," Michel responded quickly.

"What happened here today is between you and me. And God! This is a discussion between two men. You are not to tell your mother what we talked about, what we did today, what I showed you. She would not understand. Women have their very own place in God's creation. They do not understand the matters of men, d'accord? In fact, you mustn't speak to anyone about this. It would only bring shame to you, and embarrassment, and you don't want that, do you?"

Michel only nodded. Never, ever, would he tell his mother. There was something within him that automatically understood that what had transpired here was not for the eyes and ears of parents, certainly not his mother. Nor his father, for that matter. Not that he ever talked to him about anything. His father mostly grunted at him or ignored him entirely.

"Good! I'm pleased. When would you like to come back to learn more?"

"Tomorrow?" Michel suggested eagerly. "After school? I'm sure my mother wouldn't mind."

"Excellent!" The monseigneur smiled benevolently. "I look forward to it, very much so. I'll make sure we are alone again."

DISCOVERIES

ICHEL WAS CONFUSED. Lying in bed that night, unable to fall asleep, his mind lingered on Monseigneur's study and what had happened on that couch. It had been scary, and he felt a significant amount of guilt, although he did not understand why. He was conflicted. Had he done something wrong? And why had it felt so good?

There was something else, something he couldn't put his finger on, something that struck him as strange yet invigorating, stimulating, and it kept doing things to his body as he thought back on the encounter. His penis became hard again, and automatically he reached for it, just like the monseigneur had, and began to stroke it.

As he moved his hands along the shaft, images of the priest, his broad chest, his enormous penis, and copious body hair flashed before his eyes. Just as it had earlier in the day, his mouth felt dry, and his heart raced as his entire body began convulsing. What happened next frightened Michel. He had never experienced anything like it and lay rigid under his covers, his hand covered in sticky goo. Scared as he was, he also felt relaxed and satisfied. The feeling that had rushed through his body in the moments before his penis ejected the goo, whatever that was, had been amazing.

Now he was tired, but first, he needed to clean himself up. He found the underwear he had worn that day and dried himself with it to the best of his ability. Goo had also ended up inside his pajama pants, so he changed into a fresh pair and put all the soiled laundry on a pile before climbing back into bed. He fell

29

asleep pondering what it was that had happened, why it felt so good, whether he should ask the monseigneur, and why he felt so conflicted about it all.

He returned to the priest the next day and asked him about the goo. The monseigneur's answer both surprised and shocked him.

"You must never touch yourself, Michel, never again. It's a sin. Your semen is sacred, and it is only meant to be put inside your wife after you get married. Do not risk your salvation by masturbating, son."

They had moved to the priest's bedroom, where they had gotten undressed, and Monseigneur once again allowed Michel to explore his body. "What we do here is training. I am teaching you how to be a good husband to your wife. And I will teach you everything you need to know about the pleasures a husband can bring his wife in the name of the Almighty Father."

The priest caressed the boy's body and brought pleasure to him, while Michel lay still on his back, eyes closed. For every visit to the monseigneur, the lessons became more advanced, and the priest went further and further. One time, Michel ejaculated, quite unexpectedly, and the monseigneur became visibly upset, even though it had already happened to him more than once.

"Shame on you, Michel. You mustn't waste your precious seed."

When the priest proceeded to clean the semen off Michel using his tongue, Michel felt utterly ashamed. *Why is he doing that?*

As if he'd heard the question, Monseigneur simply replied, "Body of Christ!"

Over the coming weeks and months, the priest and Michel embarked on a journey of sexual exploration, and Michel's feelings for the monseigneur became stronger and stronger. He did not understand what it was he felt, simply that it was amazing to be with this man, to touch his body, to smell his manly scent. From Michel's vantage point, his life was better than ever, and his mother and father encouraged him to spend more time with the monseigneur. Little did they know what was going on.

"Monseigneur, why does it feel so good to be touched by another man?" Michel asked one day after they were done with the day's lesson.

"Well, Michel. The good Lord wants us to enjoy being with the woman we marry. He wants us to procreate. He wants us to be intimate. Just remember our lessons when you get married. They will come in useful once you lie with your wife."

"I'm not sure I want to get married. I'd rather be with a man. Like you," Michel said honestly, one of his fingers gingerly twirling the priest's chest hair.

"You mustn't, Michel. You mustn't lie with a man the way you lie with a woman. It's a sin. Do you understand? It is utterly wrong to lust for another man."

Michel didn't understand. But he nodded anyway. It was so confusing. Being with the monseigneur felt so good, completely natural, and he saw that he made the priest feel good, too, or was he just pretending? After all, they both partook in the sin and shared their lust. Was the priest not sinning? Was he merely guiding Michel on his journey to manhood? If so, why did he come? It was all very confusing.

"What we are doing here is part of your education, a rite of passage, from boy to man. You must learn how your body develops and how you are to use it once you get married, to please the Lord. Every boy goes through that process, guided by someone older. How else would you learn about this? But it is the great secret of manhood, and we never talk about it. Never, not to your parents, not to your friends, not to your future bride. Ever!"

Why did the priest spill his semen? Why did he moan, and why did he seem to enjoy Michel's training so much? Was this because Michel secretly desired him? Was this his fault, too? It made Michel feel particularly bad about himself. He genuinely enjoyed being with the monseigneur while the poor man was merely doing his job. The priest did this with a boy, a child, clearly

31

not forbidden, as he was no man yet, guiding him, teaching him. But what about Michel? He lusted for the priest, and he was unable to stop touching himself. He had become obsessed with it, and his guilt grew every time he spilled the sacred semen onto himself, making sure his mother would never, ever find traces thereof, knowing that her judgment would go far beyond the priest's admonishments.

The guilt growing within Michel became more and more difficult to bear, and while he enjoyed the physical aspects of the relationship with Monseigneur, the man always left him burdened with a new coating of shame.

Within a few months, Michel's body showed the first signs of physical change; he began to grow body hair, on his legs at first, and then around his penis. That was when things changed with the monseigneur, as almost overnight, the priest pulled back and considered their training complete.

A few weeks after their final meeting, the priest dismissed Michel from his service as an altar boy and strongly suggested he never mention his training to anyone, under any circumstances. For weeks, Michel barely ate, worrying his parents endlessly. His mother even spoke to the monseigneur, pleading with him to take Michel back, but the priest insisted it was time to give someone else a chance at the altar.

Michel didn't tell his parents the real reason for his dismissal. He couldn't. It was as if there were something in him that prevented him from speaking up, something which told him how utterly wrong it all was. What had happened with the monseigneur—Michel's feelings, the training—was a mortal sin, and he would undoubtedly spend eternity in damnation for it. He convinced himself he had somehow caused this to happen, that it had all been his fault.

Long after he'd stopped seeing the priest, Michel heard rumors in school that Monseigneur Serrault had a history of singling out certain boys in his congregation. It was the first time he'd heard the word pédé—"fag." Nobody knew what happened during those lessons. Those who had been a part of it knew better than to talk about it. But the boys were laughing, and instinctively, Michel realized that whatever "fag" meant, it was a bad thing, a really bad thing, something to be ridiculed for, something to be very ashamed of.

As for the monseigneur—he was transferred to Rome, to the Holy See, where Pope Paul VI, who had bestowed upon him the honorific of Monseigneur, asked him to continue his career within the Curia. Michel never saw him again. It didn't help him though, as the new priest of the congregation often talked about how bad it was to be a homosexual, that to lust after another man was not love but a sin one must repent. Michel retreated within himself and away from a God who did not answer his prayers, a God who, despite Michel's most valiant efforts, hated him for who he was, the emotions he had, and the things he did.

At the St. Jacques' home, things became unbearable. Michel's mother did not understand his reluctance to go to church and the constant weekly struggle to get him to attend Holy Mass. She tried to get him to talk to their new priest, and again, Michel refused. If he was to go to hell for being homosexual, why bother going through the motions of confession and pretending to be something he could never be?

To make matters worse, kids in school had begun to pick on him, as rumors spread that he had been one of Monseigneur Serrault's last boys. Before the end of the school term, Michel had earned himself the cruel nickname of *Saint Cul*—"Holy Ass"— based on his last name. He had no idea what that meant, but the kids on the schoolyard would never call him anything else again.

1978

1978

FAMILY VACATION

ICHEL WAS EXCITED about the family vacation this summer. While he had done well in school, the bullying had taken its toll, and he was glad to be free of it for a few weeks. His father had been busy packing their car for the drive to their old hometown of St. Malo, where Michel's grandparents still lived.

Michel loved visiting his grandparents, even though his maternal grandfather had recently passed away. This didn't change the family's vacation plans, as they usually stayed with his paternal grandparents, whose house had more space, but he especially looked forward to visiting his widowed grandmother in her small apartment in the old part of town and the treats she baked for him and his mom.

St. Malo had always intrigued Michel. Situated on the English Channel, it was particularly exposed to the elements, with average differences of thirty feet between high and low tide, which made for very impressive views, changing the appearance of the town completely every six hours or so, depending on the position of the moon. While he didn't have many childhood memories of living in St. Malo, they flooded back to him once he saw the old walled-in coastal town and all the familiar sights of where he had lived the first years of his life and spent his summers since.

His grandmother lived intra muros—inside the old part of town on the seashore—and Michel loved to roam the narrow cobblestone streets while his mom visited with her mother. His father would usually not join them, preferring to spend his time with his dad, reminiscing and listening to the old man's wartime

37

stories—tall tales of General De Gaulle and the resistance against the Vichy Government and the Germans—or help him around the house, making sure everything was in order.

Since it was a vacation, the St. Jacques took the opportunity to drive along the coast of Brittany and see other towns or visit the beach. Every day included a short excursion somewhere, yet oddly, his parents never took him out to sea. Michel guessed it had to do with his father losing his job as a fisherman. He didn't dare ask because asking the wrong question would leave his father upset for hours, and that was not what he wanted to do, most certainly not while on vacation.

Michel really wanted to visit Jersey or Guernsey, the English Islands off the coast of St. Malo, so different, so exotic, yet so close. The ferry dock was located just outside the old town, the ramps marvels of French engineering that had to withstand the enormous changes in the local tide.

Thus, Michel was somewhat surprised when his father announced they would take a day trip to Mont-Saint-Michel across the border in neighboring Normandy. They would have to get up early because it was quite a journey from St. Malo, and they had to take the tide into account. If they arrived at the wrong time, the high tide would cover the road to the small mountain protruding from the sea not far from the coast, and it would be unreachable.

Michel had always been fascinated by Mont-Saint-Michel, not just because it carried his name but because every visit had been magical. There was a mysterious air to the place, the small village and the abbey it housed inside its walls, the harsh and isolated way of life of the villagers, the beauty of the streets and houses, and the landscape around it.

The family had visited before, though never at high tide, when the mountain turned into a veritable island, albeit one located only a few hundred yards off the coast. Michel had seen pictures of it cut off from the mainland. Mont-Saint-Michel at low tide was the place he recognized, with its maze of streams, sea meadows, and sandbanks that made up the surreal, almost alien landscape surrounding the hill for miles and miles, as well as the narrow road leading out to it.

Michel's father was in an excellent mood today, talking about childhood trips to Mont-Saint-Michel with his parents after the war. Parking on the small beach, he told Michel the story of the English who had once tried to attack the abbey during the Hundred Years' War, but all drowned because the horses were unable to outrun the incoming tide. That image left a deep impression on Michel as he tried to picture the poor horses and the riders being chased by this monster called the tide, unable to escape. Whether the story was true or not, the images it evoked were a fearsome reminder to never underestimate the power of the sea, especially in this spot, where lingering out in the open might prove a fatal mistake.

On their way home, they stopped at a small port to buy oysters, which grew in plentiful supply all along the coast.

"Look at the various sizes, son. See here?" Michel's father seemed to relish the chance to teach him how to choose the best ones. "The biggest are also the most expensive, but they are not necessarily the best ones. We locals much prefer the smaller ones. Here, see, the ones for ten francs." He looked to the shopkeeper and bought a dozen, along with a juicy lemon.

They sat at a table and Michel's father produced a small knife. "This is an oyster knife. I was your age when I learned to shuck my first oysters." There was pride in his father's eyes. "Now watch closely!" He grasped one of the oysters in his big hand, rough from years of working with fishing nets and pulling hemp ropes into the small fishing vessel. "You place the knife, right here, at the back of the oyster, see? And then you push it in, like so. Now, you must be very careful because you could easily cut yourself. Beginners either use a protective glove or a cloth. Once you've inserted the knife, draw it along the edges. Just like this."

Michel watched attentively as his father expertly moved the knife around inside the oyster.

"Finally, once you've cut the muscle on one side, you also need to get in underneath, to cut the other muscle. Like so."

After the oyster was opened, he handed it to Michel, and his mother dripped some lemon juice onto it.

"Go ahead, try it!" his father encouraged. "Brittany has the best oysters in the world. And they are healthy, too!"

Michel wasn't sure he would appreciate eating a live animal, but seeing his father's delight, he didn't want to refuse. He closed his eyes and slurped it into his mouth, swallowing it whole, as he'd seen his parents do before. The combination of the salty liquid from the oyster and the lemon juice made for an interesting taste sensation. He quite liked it.

His father wasn't finished. "Now, I have to show you a few more things. Before you open an oyster, you want to make sure it's still alive. Look at this one for instance. It's a bit open, see? When I press on it, nothing happens. This one's dead! I'll have it exchanged. When you press on an oyster, it should close. That is part of its protective mechanism. If it doesn't, it's bad and you should never eat it. You could get sick otherwise."

Michel nodded, impressed. Meanwhile, his father opened another one. His hand moved so fast that Michel could barely follow it.

"Hold this!" He placed an open oyster in Michel's hand. "Now look. This is how you can tell the oyster is still alive. Look very closely at the edge here—see this dark band?" He touched it with the tip of the knife, and Michel noticed how the oyster retreated from the touch like a hand after a burn.

"Did you see?" His father laughed and did it again. "We have the best oysters anywhere. Fresh, and so delicious! A delicacy!" Even though it was hard to see his smile underneath his walrus mustache, Michel knew how happy and content his father was by the way his whole face transformed. It was a sight Michel was rarely afforded back at the apartment in Rennes.

"Papa, have you ever found a pearl inside an oyster?" Michel wondered, having read somewhere that oysters create pearls by coating grains of sand or other foreign objects that get stuck inside their shells and can't be flushed out.

His father smiled. "Yes, I have, but it wasn't very big. And sadly not something I could've used to turn into a necklace for your mother. Today, people place things into the oysters on purpose to have them produce pearls, and those oysters get to grow very large, so the pearl is inside for a long time."

After his dad had the bad one replaced at the stall and bought a bottle of wine, his mother bought a baguette at another stand, and they enjoyed a simple but delicious meal in the open air. His father and mother were smiling, looking at each other lovingly, holding hands, and for a little while, Michel's world was in order. He cherished this glimpse of his father's true nature, of what had once made him happy, back when they'd still lived in St. Malo and he had been a fisherman.

Noticing Michel's attentiveness, his father smiled sadly. "I miss this part of my life, but the fishing industry is changing. The boats are getting larger and larger, and there is no future for small fishing vessels. It's why I had to go ashore." The longing in his voice was tangible. "I hope you'll find something you are passionate about one day, son. It makes providing for your family a lot easier than if you have to do a job you don't care for. Do you understand?"

Michel didn't, not really. He had no inkling as to what he would like to do when he grew up. Nor did he understand why his dad was unhappy with his new job, but it had to be the reason he was so miserable all the time in Rennes.

"Papa, do you not like working in the factory?"

"It is a job. But fishing? I miss being out on the open water, come rain or shine. To be outside, the fresh sea air, the daily struggle against the elements, to work hard to land our catch, to take it back to port and sell it? That was a real livelihood."

"You forget how scared I was every time you left the house." Michel's mother added her perspective. "Your new job is more comfortable and a lot safer."

"That it is, but there is no challenge to it. Every move I make with my hands is the same, countless times a day, screwing together the same components to make dashboard after dashboard. You can never take a break or you'll stop the entire assembly line. There's always a supervisor looking over your shoulder. There's no freedom, no trust. It was different out at sea. Out there, we had to rely on each other, the skipper and me. Our very lives depended on it." He took a swig from the white wine bottle they'd opened. "That is a big difference. Trust, dependency. That's what makes life meaningful."

Michel was sad that his father was so unhappy in his present job, even if he didn't fully understand the reasons. Whenever he went to the port of St. Malo where the few remaining fishing vessels docked, he hated the stench, the sight of fish guts and blood. It was a life unimaginable to him. On the other hand, when he'd visited the factory in Rennes on a family day, he'd been impressed by its cleanliness. There had been food, drinks, and games for the kids, and a tour of the entire factory floor. Michel had been fascinated by the machines, the countless tools, and all the cars in the making on the assembly line, the bright lights reflecting off the pristine white walls and shining floors. That had been much more appealing to him.

While he couldn't appreciate the fishing trade the way his father did, the memory of that day spent eating oysters stayed with Michel. It had been one of the rare instances when his father had opened up to him.

1979

LE CHAT NOIR

ICHEL HAD COME to realize that there would be no redemption for him. After a particularly fiery oratory from the pulpit during Mass, his parents had discussed over Sunday dinner how disgusting homosexuals were, and Michel had understood that they were talking about him—not that they knew or suspected he was gay. Or did they? Sometimes he thought they cast suspicious looks his way. He'd notice the inflection in things they said, or they'd mention something at a specific time, and it had him wondering if they did already know what a freak he was. A monster destined for eternity in purgatory.

Michel also knew that he could never say anything to them. Ever! It was as if there were a built-in stop, a mechanical device that disabled his vocal cords from ever uttering anything incriminating to his parents. Sometimes he cursed that stop, at the same time instinctively sensing his very survival depended on it.

During one dinner Michel wouldn't be able to forget, his father was particularly incensed.

"Did you know they even have a place downtown? I can't believe the city lets them get away with it. It's appalling. But I guess that's what you get when you put socialists in power. It's what you reap when you let those bastards run the city."

Michel listened attentively. He immediately knew he would have to see the place for himself. He'd heard so many things from his classmates—about old men trying to seduce young boys, about women who looked like men and who would never be

45

married by decent men because of that, about men pretending to be women, putting on makeup, dressing in women's clothes. These pédés, these faggots, were utterly disgusting, a freak show.

Listening to his friends, Michel got the impression that if there were a place where these freaks met, it would have to be like a zoo, a circus of monsters. Yet as much as there was something deep inside his heart that knew he was one of those freaks, he could not reconcile the images with what he saw in the mirror. There, he saw a regular teenage boy with a bad complexion. How could others see what he was incapable of? Was the monstrosity only visible to those who were not monsters themselves? Was his inability to see what everyone else saw part of his freakishness?

Deep within him, there was a struggle between curiosity and fear, and for months, he debated visiting this forbidden place upon which descended all the sinners of Rennes. The way his father talked about it, the disgust on his face, it must've been hell on Earth. Michel couldn't understand why anyone in their right mind would want to go there. Yet he did; he couldn't help it. As soon as he learned about it, it lured him like a siren's call, irresistible. *What's wrong with me?*

Michel remembered well the first time he had "accidentally" walked past it. It was a bar of sorts; at least it looked like that from the outside, the text "Le Chat Noir" printed on the small neon sign sponsored by a large beer company. He noticed the absence of an outside seating area, which was otherwise common for bars, especially during the summer. Patrons would want to drink their beer or their wine in the sun. But Le Chat Noir was not that sort of place. One look at the facade confirmed that. There were windows, but the shutters were all closed. One couldn't look inside. Michel had no idea what to make of that.

He noticed a handsome young man in tight jeans and a white tee walk up to the building. Slim with light-brown, shoulder-length hair, and a slim, trimmed mustache, he appeared to be in his early twenties. Unseen by Michel, the man looked around nervously before opening the black door and quickly disappearing inside.

The image of that young man haunted Michel's daydreams for days. For some inexplicable reason, the mustache turned out to be the young man's most prominent feature, at least in Michel's vivid memory and his masturbation fantasy as he imagined what it would be like to touch it, how it would feel to kiss the lips beneath it. At this stage, he jerked off regularly, daily at least, and the young man became the main character of Michel's two-minute daydreams, quickly replacing the monseigneur's face but not his body, as Michel had never seen another one.

He'd return to Le Chat Noir more often, making the long detour from school on his way home. He couldn't even remember why he'd gone that way in the first place, but suddenly, Le Chat Noir was all he could think about. For months on end, he stalked it, lurking behind a nearby tree, but he never crossed the small square to walk up to the door and walk inside. To just walk past the place, to touch the white plastered walls of the building, had taken weeks of building up courage. He understood that this was a place for the likes of him, this place his father had spoken of with such intense hatred and disgust, and it had only made the allure of it stronger. He sometimes noticed men walking into the bar as couples, or—more frequently—leaving it in twos. None of them looked like monsters or freaks, neither men nor women. Maybe it was his fault for not being able to see that which everyone else saw so clearly.

Michel's curiosity grew day by day, and he tried to build up the courage to walk up to the door, take the handle, push it down, open the door, and confidently walk in. But he couldn't. Within him, the voices of his parents, the monseigneur, of his friends and classmates reverberated with the warnings, the lurking sins, and eternal damnation, and so he stayed clear.

Looking back, Michel realized it was only a matter of time before someone noticed him hanging around.

"Salut! I've seen you hanging around here for a while. Are you waiting for someone?"

Startled by the old man's open approach, Michel vehemently shook his head, pondering if he should run away. But something kept his feet locked to the ground.

"No, I'm just resting for a moment, before I walk home." *Who is this man? What does he want?*

"Sure you are," the man responded knowingly. "Fancy a drink? A soda perhaps? There's a bar just across the street. It's not the safest place to linger out here."

Michel didn't know what to say. He was caught between his flight instinct, the endless warnings from people about "dirty old men," and his curiosity, unable to move.

"Come on. Don't worry. I don't bite. I have a hunch you'll like it." He gestured, and like a puppet on a string, Michel got up and followed the man's lead. Within seconds, he was standing inside Le Chat Noir.

It was almost as dark inside as it was from the outside, and it took his eyes a few seconds to get used to the dim lighting. There was a long bar counter, behind which an older woman stood drying dishes. She was tall, with heavy makeup and flaming-red hair that fell loosely over her shoulders. On the other side, facing him, were six stools, all unoccupied. Across the floor were several small tables with a handful of chairs around each, and in one corner there was a dance floor with a sad disco ball turning slowly above it, meekly reflecting what little light was illuminating the room. *Maybe they have more light in the evenings?* Michel liked to dance, and Joe Dassin could be heard singing "Et si tu n'existais pas" from the speakers in the corners of the dance floor, but there were no other patrons to be seen.

A couple of doors led into the back of the establishment. The one on the left had a sign above it: "Toilettes"; the other was covered by dark drapery, but no sign announced what might be found behind it.

The man who had spoken to Michel outside steered him toward the bar and sat on one of the stools, gesturing for Michel to do the same.

Wiping her hands on her black apron, the woman behind the bar barely looked at them as she asked, "Bonjour, messieurs. What can I get you?" When she noticed the man sitting beside Michel, she smiled and added, "Apologies, Antoine. I didn't see it was you. How are you today?" She gave Michel a brief once-over. "Are you rescuing strays again?"

"Salut, Giselle. You know me. I can't help it. I believe it's better that he's safe in here than at risk of being abused out there. I'll have the usual." Looking at Michel, he asked, "What would you like, young man?"

"A Diabolo Menthe, please!" Michel answered, still cautious yet reassured by the short exchange between Giselle and Antoine.

"Good choice." Giselle smiled. "How old are you, anyway?"

"Fifteen!" That wasn't entirely true: he wouldn't turn fifteen until October, but he seemed to get away with it.

"Well, at least you're honest. They usually claim to be eighteen." She laughed and turned away, and Michel watched in fascination as she prepared the drinks, returning a moment later with his green concoction and a pint of beer for Antoine.

"Santé!" Antoine picked up his glass and toasted toward Michel. "Now, young man, what's your name?"

"Santé, monsieur!"

His response had Antoine laugh. "I may be an old man, but we're all family in here. I'm Antoine, d'accord?"

Michel nodded, overwhelmed. "My name is Michel," he replied, still not sure why he'd followed Antoine into the bar. Yes, he'd been curious, but who knew what might happen to him in here? Who knew what people did in here? His parents had repeatedly warned him about these homosexuals, old men who only desired to molest young boys. Was Antoine a homosexual? And what about Giselle? Was she one, too? But she was a woman, and they both seemed nice enough. And what did Antoine mean by *family*? Michel could hardly keep up with all the thoughts running through his head.

"Just ask." Antoine smiled encouragingly and took a gulp from his drink. Giselle watched from the other side of the counter, glass in hand, drying it with a towel. "Like I said. I don't bite, and I promise I'm not here to take advantage of you. Unlike others out there." There was a sad undertone to his voice that didn't escape Michel.

"Is this really a bar for homosexuals?" he asked, barely able to say the word out loud.

Antoine laughed and nodded, taking another swig from his beer.

Michel almost pointed at him but quickly lowered his hand, stuttering, "So, uh, you're a homosexual?"

This had Antoine in stitches. "You're very perceptive, kid. And yes, I am, although I prefer the term gay. And I'm not into young boys like you, contrary to popular belief. So you needn't be afraid."

Michel's mouth hung open as he looked at Giselle, who cut in before he could say a word.

"No, dear, I'm not. I have plenty of gay friends though, not that it matters. I've always had a soft spot for you lot, and so I opened this place, as a safe haven."

"Giselle is known as *Maman* in town," Antoine explained. "Every gay and lesbian in and around Rennes knows her." He made a sweeping gesture with his right arm and bowed his head.

Giselle blushed. "You silly old coot!" She made a dismissive gesture with her hands and turned her attention to Michel. "Tell me, Michel, what's your story?"

He wasn't sure he understood, and his facial expression probably said as much, as Giselle quickly added, "Are you in trouble, love? Do your parents know you're here? Did you run away from home?"

"Oh! No, I'm not in trouble. Not that I know of anyway, and no, they don't know I'm here. They wouldn't approve. My dad hates this place. They'd probably kill me if they knew I was in here."

Giselle sighed. "Yes, I've heard that story before. Although I'm sure you exaggerate. It's not very French to kill our children. We drag them off to church and let the clergy deal with them instead. We kill their souls, not their bodies. It's much more efficient, and a lot less messy. We let the Church drive out everything good and beautiful about our capacity for love and compassion, and if you're not careful, they'll also take advantage of you in the process. Far too many priests who can't keep their hands to themselves, sexually abuse boys and girls instead. So beware of the Church, Michel. People like you and I will find no understanding from the pulpit or the sacristy."

The words cut right through Michel, as he thought back to his encounters with Monseigneur Serrault. Was that what Giselle was talking about? Had his mother sent him there because she somehow knew something was off—knew that her son was gay? Was she hoping the priest would cure him of that? Or had it been the priest who had recognized that Michel was different? Had he been a homosexual, too?

Antoine leaned on the bar, addressing Giselle. "I think it's safe to say our young friend here isn't out to his parents." To Michel, he said, "And you shouldn't tell them. Not yet anyway. This is a conversation you need to be prepared for, or the consequences could be dire. For now, if you ever need to talk, if you have questions, about anything, feel free to ask me, or ask Giselle. D'accord?"

There, it was out. They, too, deduced he was gay. How did they know? Yet their reaction was different. There was no condemnation, no judgment, nothing at all. No warnings of eternal damnation, no talk of mortal sin, no attempt to drive the demons from him. There was something else entirely: acceptance. Antoine and Giselle spoke to him as if he were a regular youth, despite knowing *what* he was.

51

"Listen, Michel," Giselle said. "You are always welcome to come here. I'm always here, and I promise to look after you. But be careful when you meet other people. Many of the younger boys are just like you. They come here to have a safe space, but there are a few patrons who might take advantage of you, some who might even hurt you. You know of sex, I presume?" She looked intently at him. Michel nodded and began to blush.

"Okay. Look. It's okay. You mustn't worry about sex at your age, but before long, you'll want to experiment, meet other boys, and be intimate. That's okay, most of us do. I just want you to be careful—promise me?"

Michel nodded, unsure as to what she meant.

"Especially that room over there." She pointed to the opening on the right side of the room, the one with the dark drapery. "That's where I don't want you yet. Okay?" She laughed, looking at Antoine. "Not that my admonishments ever stopped anyone. You're all such a horny lot." Shaking her head, she added, "I should never have let Claude talk me into a darkroom."

"Darkroom?" Michel asked.

Giselle walked away and disappeared into a room behind the bar, but not before telling Antoine, "I'll leave it to you to explain that particular aspect of gay life..."

Bemused, Michel turned to Antoine, who held his glass tightly, and for a second, Michel thought the man was praying.

"Well, you said that you already know what sex is all about?" he finally said, letting out a deep sigh.

"Yes." Michel recited the monseigneur. "It's when a man sticks his penis into the vulva of his wife, but only after marriage." He remembered the words and the repeated admonishments of the priest well. For some reason, it made Antoine laugh.

"Yes, that is one tiny aspect of sex, but it's not all. Do you know how *we* have sex?"

Michel gave him a puzzled look.

"Well, you're a guy, and you have no vulva, do you? So how do you think two men have sex? Or two women for that matter?"

Michel didn't know, but his thoughts went back to the time he'd spent with Monseigneur.

"Here we go." Antoine sighed exasperatedly. He took another swig from his glass, then put it down and turned around on his stool to face Michel. "Sex, or making love, is all about being intimate with someone else. Normally, you would be in a bed, naked. You touch each other in ways that are pleasurable for one another. Are you with me so far?"

Michel nodded, his head filled with images of himself with the monseigneur. *Sex? Did we have sex?*

"Now, gay sex isn't that different from heterosexual sex. You can touch each other's penis, stroke it, and if you're a top, you can penetrate your partner. If you're a bottom, you will enjoy having a penis up your rear end."

"Rear end?"

"Your rectum, your ass. That is how gay men have penetrative sex. But trust me, far from all men do. I, for one, never cared for it. But some do, and some both give and take."

St. Cul. Suddenly, Michel understood the joke of his classmates.

"Isn't that pretty gross?" he asked, not fully able to wrap his head around the concept.

Antoine laughed. "It can be. But don't worry about that now. You're too young for that anyway. The thing is, it's pleasurable for many, and that's why we keep doing it."

"Is that what's going on behind that curtain?"

"Yes, I guess that happens. But I think mostly it's just hand jobs or maybe blow jobs."

"Blow jobs?" Michel had never heard that phrase, but once Antoine had explained it to him, he remembered how the monseigneur had taken his penis in his mouth and then licked up the goo, the spilled semen. *Sex! We did have sex.*

"Oh, I've done that already!" he said absentmindedly.

Antoine looked shocked. "What? At your age? May I ask with whom? A friend from school?"

Michel didn't know if he should say anything and decided against it. The monseigneur's admonishment to keep quiet still worked. "No, it was someone else."

"Well, whatever you do, please be careful. Giselle and I want you to be safe here, but we can't keep you from going behind the curtain. Just be careful if you ever do, and never, ever do anything you don't want to or anything you aren't ready for. Most importantly, never do anything with anyone you don't want to be with. Do you understand? There are too many who would take advantage of you. If you feel unsafe, leave, and tell us. Okay?" Antoine had placed both his hands on Michel's shoulders to emphasize his point.

Michel looked around, staring at the curtain-clad doorway, drawn by its mysterious allure as he thought back to the pleasures he'd experienced at the hands and tongue of Monseigneur Serrault.

Perhaps to distract him from the darkroom, Antoine bought Michel another drink and told him about how, nearly every day, on his way to the club, he had noticed a youth loitering nearby, always trying to hide either behind a tree in the tiny park adjacent to Le Chat Noir or sitting on a park bench and facing the opposite way. Antoine chuckled as he described the way Michel had turned almost acrobatically just to catch a glimpse of patrons coming or going.

Horrified as Michel was that someone had seen him, he liked Antoine and felt safe in his company. There was one question still on Michel's mind: why had the priest not told him they were having sex? Why had he kept it a secret, masquerading it as marital training? It made no sense to Michel, but he dared not ask Antoine.

BERNARD

*M*AMAN?"

"In the kitchen," came his mother's response as Michel entered the apartment and took off his shoes in the hallway. He'd called for her the same way some people say hello, a way of inquiring whether anyone was home. In his case, his mother would always be home, so it had become his way of greeting her.

Michel took off his jacket, hung it up on the coatrack in the hallway, and proceeded to the kitchen where his mother was busy making dinner.

"Salut, chérie! How was school?"

Michel shrugged. "Fine, I guess. School is school."

"You're late. It's almost six o'clock. Your dad will be here soon. Do you have any homework?"

"No, no homework. I did that already."

"Good! Now please go wash up and get ready for dinner. We'll eat as soon as your father gets home."

Michel was glad she hadn't asked him where he'd been. It would've been difficult to explain. Then again, he'd been coming home late a lot since he'd begun to frequent Le Chat Noir. It had become a sort of second home to him, a safe environment where he could meet others like him, mostly boys his age whom Antoine had magically picked up on the streets of Rennes. He'd asked Antoine about this but didn't grasp how he was somehow able to recognize these so-called "friends of Dorothy." Michel was hopeless in that regard. He would often see young men enter Le Chat Noir and be completely oblivious to the fact that they

55

were frequenting the establishment for the very same reasons he did: to be among others just like them.

Still, he'd learned a lot in the last weeks—about sex, different practices, how to stay clear of certain people—and he'd come to understand that he had not been the only one to have *met* Monseigneur Serrault. The man had quite the reputation, and it had been the rumors of him being gay that led to his transfer to Rome. More than that, Michel learned what the monseigneur had done to and with him was illegal, as he was still a child. Etienne, a boy a couple of years older, who'd also been an altar boy under Monseigneur Serrault, was adamant.

"He took advantage of you, of me, and a lot of other boys, too. He's not gay. He's a disgusting pedophile. But it makes no difference to the Church. They love to lump us all together. Not to mention that they only ever act when it becomes embarrassing to Rome."

Michel had no idea what being a pedophile meant, so Etienne had gone on to explain. It was an illuminating conversation, after which Michel wasn't sure if he felt better or worse. What he did know was that he felt conflicted. Part of him cherished the memories, the intimacy with the priest, and was still hurt by his sudden dismissal, but at least now he understood the reason. What the monseigneur had done to him had never been about marital training, but the priest's lust. Michel had been taken advantage of, and that hurt him deeply, but he couldn't talk to anyone about it. Not to Antoine, not to Etienne, who, despite having been through the same experience, had very different memories and hated the monseigneur. Michel felt guilty for having enjoyed their time together, but he dared not admit that, afraid he'd be judged for it. Maybe he was one of those vile pedophiles, too?

After washing his hands, he returned to the kitchen to offer his help, which his mother accepted with a grateful smile. Michel set the table, but in his mind, he was far away, replaying an encounter he'd had at Le Chat Noir earlier that day, with a mysterious man named Bernard.

Michel had been sitting by the bar, as usual, talking to Giselle. She was the steady lighthouse in the stormy sea of his foraging into gay life, looking after him and all the kids whom she encountered. She knew, of course, that she would get into heaps of trouble with the authorities if they ever found out about the adolescents frequenting her establishment with its darkroom and all, but at least she could make sure the boys were safe from the physical abuse of the fists and boots of homophobes in the streets, safe from sexual predators, safe to be themselves and to explore their sexuality on their terms, at their own pace.

Michel felt safe at the bar, yet every time the door opened and someone walked through, he instinctively turned around to see who it was. So did everybody else, albeit for their own individual reasons. For Michel, it was the fear of finding his parents standing there, or the police or a teacher. The fear of being exposed. Often, he'd watch the new arrival walk straight past the bar into the darkroom and hear Giselle say, "He never drinks anything," or, "Just wait until you see the smug look on his face after he's had his cock sucked dry." She could be crass and at times came across as slightly envious, but she never turned anyone away, although she had her favorites.

However, when the door had opened today, it hadn't been anything scary, or not to Michel. The guy who walked in was mysterious looking at first, but then Michel recognized the tight jeans, white T-shirt, and short brown leather jacket. It was the same guy he'd seen on his first walk past Le Chat Noir, the young guy with the mustache, but this time he was close enough for Michel to see his face. It was a handsome face, chiseled, of timeless beauty with a Dorian Gray–like quality. This was the man who had fueled so many of Michel's bedtime fantasies for weeks on end, and he walked confidently up to the bar and sat down right next to Michel.

"Bonjour, Giselle! A Stella, please." Looking sideways at Michel, he said, "Aren't you a little young to be in here?"

"Leave him alone, Bernard. He's one of Antoine's rescues. He's welcome here. You weren't much older when you first showed up. Just keep your paws off him."

"Oui, maman!" Bernard laughed and put his arm around Michel's shoulders. "I wouldn't do anything the pup here doesn't want me to."

Giselle rolled her eyes and served him his beer. "I mean it, Bernard."

"All right, all right! So, what's your name, kid?"

"Michel."

Bernard stretched out his hand. "Nice to meet you, Michel. I'm Bernard. You come here a lot?"

Michel nodded. Bernard was so handsome and so confident.

"Same here. Isn't that right, Giselle?"

She made a grunting noise and walked out back, disappearing into her office.

"Have you been in the back room yet?" Bernard asked without looking at Michel, taking a big gulp from his beer.

"Back room?"

"Yeah, the darkroom. Where all the fun happens? Why else come here? I take it you haven't?"

"No."

"You should check it out. Just make sure maman doesn't see you. She doesn't like it when the young ones go back there." He laughed out loud. "Antoine brought me in here, too, about six or seven years ago. It was three years before I finally got the courage to go back there. Best day of my life. I fucked my brains out. So if you want a piece of advice from ole Bernard? Don't wait too long. If you want to have sex, that's the best place in town. Beats having to go into the parks or the toilets at the station and risk being picked up by the police or beaten to a pulp by some fucking idiot."

Giselle came back from the office. "You're still here?"

"Yes, maman! We're having a civilized conversation. I hope you don't mind. Besides, I still have half my drink left. I don't like to come back to a warm beer." He took another swig from the glass and put it back on the counter, empty. "Happy?"

Michel had the impression that there was no love lost between the two. Bernard got up from his stool and turned away, but before heading into the darkroom, he put money for the beer on the counter, grabbed Michel's chin with his strong hand, and kissed him on the mouth.

"See you around, Michel. And remember what I said." He blinked at him and disappeared into the darkroom.

Michel was stunned. Bernard had kissed him. *On the lips! Why did he do that?*

"You be careful, Michel. This guy is only going to get you into trouble." Giselle woke him from his daydream. "You hear me?"

"What?"

"Bernard. He's a slut, basically. He'll spread his ass cheeks for just about any willing cock. I think he's been with pretty much everyone who's walked through these doors, so please be careful, okay? Don't do anything stupid. You're still very young, and I'd hate it if you got yourself into trouble."

Michel had very little knowledge of sex, especially in real life, and the idea of anal sex was utterly unappealing. The monseigneur had never even mentioned that. Why would people put their penises in other people's asses? He found the image very distasteful and couldn't fathom how it might be pleasurable. But it must be, or else people wouldn't be doing it. He wasn't sure he wanted to try it, though. Jerking off, yes. Holding someone else's penis, yes. Even putting his in someone's mouth had been nice. The monseigneur had been very good at that. But he didn't like taking it into his mouth. It had been so big, and it hurt his jaw. The priest had pushed too hard, making him gag, holding his head. Only when Michel cried had the monseigneur stopped.

Some aspects of sex with the monseigneur had been very pleasurable, though. While it was the image of Bernard in Michel's mind when he touched himself, it was the things he had already experienced with the monseigneur that fueled his fantasy, never anything like what Giselle was talking about.

These thoughts still occupied his mind when he'd finally come home that day and continued to do so for the entire evening until he excused himself to go to bed early. He put on his pajamas and climbed into bed, quickly taking his stiff penis in his hand, and he thought of Bernard's kiss, of his chiseled, stubbly chin, his beautiful long hair, his brown eyes and the way they looked at him as their lips touched, the feel of his hard body.

Michel followed Bernard into the darkroom, followed him as he navigated the maze, passing other patrons in the near-pitch-black, idly sweeping his index fingertip across chests and backs, finally settling in a corner, unzipping his jeans, pushing them down to his ankles, standing with his hairy ass on display, waiting. Michel approached, from behind and put his hands on Bernard's ass, caressing the cheeks, kneading them, spreading them, exposing more, and suddenly, he exploded all over his chest.

Quickly, he cleaned himself up and got dressed again. Never before had he experienced such an orgasm, and he vowed to himself to check out the darkroom sooner rather than later.

THE DARKROOM

A FEW WEEKS LATER, Michel was back at Le Chat Noir. He'd been in a few times since the evening he'd fantasized about following Bernard into the darkroom, but he hadn't seen Bernard. Giselle explained that he was a trucker and would sometimes be gone for a few weeks, assuring Michel, "He'll be back!"

Today was the day. The door opened, and Bernard walked in, as usual wearing tight, washed-out blue jeans that highlighted his semi-erect penis, Michel noted, and a white T-shirt through which his pecs were visible, nipples straining against the thin, cotton cloth.

Bernard made a beeline to the bar. "Salut, Michel!" He grabbed his chin and kissed him on the lips. Michel blushed. "Bonjour, Giselle! A Stella, please."

"How come you never kiss me like that?" she complained. "Am I not pretty enough for you?"

"Oh, come here then!" Bernard stood and stretched over the bar counter. Giselle giggled as he grabbed her and planted his lips on hers. "Happy?"

Michel watched the exchange, trying to make sense of it. So the kiss didn't mean anything? It was just Bernard's way? Would he have kissed Antoine the same way? Would he kiss everyone like this? Michel was disappointed, and Bernard must have picked up on it, as he leaned in, his right hand resting high on Michel's thigh, and whispered into his ear, "Don't worry, I will do things to you I would never, ever do with her, chéri!" He kissed

Michel's right cheek, lingering longer than expected, his tongue gently licking at the skin.

"Here's your beer, and remember what I said last time." Giselle's tone was different from before. "It's been quiet, and you two are the only people here right now. I think I'll go order some supplies. Bernard, I'm trusting you to look after Michel. You behave, all right?" With that, she disappeared into her office behind the bar.

For a while, the two sat quietly next to each other. Michel fiddled absentmindedly with his Diabolo Menthe, while Bernard nursed his beer. After a couple of minutes, Bernard seemed to tire of the pretense, as he said, "Wanna see the darkroom?" Not waiting for a response, he took Michel by the hand and pulled him from his stool and through the doorway that Michel had never dared to cross. Not until today. Giselle had said they were alone.

"Just be quiet," Bernard said. "We don't want her to find out."

It was a frightening space but enticing at the same time. As he'd imagined, it was pitch-dark, and he instinctively put up his free hand to make sure he didn't walk into a wall, following Bernard deeper into the maze. Finally, Bernard stopped and pulled Michel to him, closing the distance between them. He took his head into his hands and kissed him passionately. With their lips locked into their dance, Bernard's tongue was free to explore Michel's mouth cavity. Michel put his arms around him, holding him, enjoying the moment, while Bernard's hand moved south to unzip his pants.

For the first time, Michel had real gay sex. They didn't have anal sex, but Bernard promised him they would, in time. He would show Michel just how sensitive and pleasurable that part of his body could be. "Trust me, little one, you'll love it. It'll drive you insane, that scent of man, just seconds before you plunge your cock into my ass."

They returned to the bar to find Giselle standing there again, and they both blushed and didn't say a word as they sat down in front of their lukewarm drinks. Neither did she, simply letting out a deep sigh and continuing to dry glasses. After a few minutes, Bernard paid up, kissed Michel again, and left. "See you soon, chéri."

Michel felt empty. His heart ached with longing for Bernard. He wanted to be with Bernard and already missed him.

"Are you okay? Did he hurt you?" Giselle asked.

Michel shook his head. "No."

"You didn't do anything you regret, did you? I'll ban him from the premises if he did."

"No!" Michel said, his emotions in turmoil. "Giselle, what is love?"

She didn't answer but put down the glass she was drying, stepped around the bar, and hugged him. "Oh, kiddo, whatever love may be, what you just experienced most certainly is not! That was carnal lust. Sex. Don't confuse the two. Sex is fine and for most people an important part of the human experience, and very pleasurable, but don't you ever mistake it for love." She stepped away from the embrace and moved her hand through Michel's hair gently. "Love, Michel, is when you want to spend the rest of your life with somebody. When being apart makes your body ache."

"But my body aches to be with him."

Giselle laughed, tousling his hair. "Oh, Michel! Yes, it does, but that's just lust. That's because you want to have sex again. Right? If you were with Bernard right now, would you want to be intimate or would you rather cook a meal together or go see a movie?" Michel avoided her gaze. "That's what I thought. Love is different. Having sex is oftentimes an integral part of loving someone, but love is also imagining yourself getting old and gray with that person. Can you see yourself in a retirement home, sitting next to Bernard in matching rocking chairs?"

Michel shook his head and laughed. "I can't even imagine myself being old."

Giselle walked back to her chores behind the bar. "Well, dear, you will. When you meet the right guy, you'll be able to see yourself growing old with them, and that thought will fill your heart with joy, immense joy, and peace. In time, you'll also find out that having sex and making love are mechanically similar yet totally different experiences. Trust me."

For a while they stayed silent, Giselle working behind the bar, Michel toying with his lukewarm Diabolo Menthe.

Finally, she said, "Look, I understand that you wanted to take this step, and it could've been someone who hurt you. At least Bernard is gentle, and deep down he's a good guy. But he's still a slut. And before too long, he'll move on to someone else. Once he's had you up his ass, he'll drop you like a hot potato. So the sooner you move past him, the better for you. Bernard is not a relationship guy. He's the guy for casual hookups. Keep that in mind."

That night, before going to bed, Michel confessed to being gay to his diary: *pédé, je suis pédé!* It felt good, and he jerked off to images of future encounters with Bernard.

In time, Michel experienced a few of those encounters for real, and they did eventually go all the way, but Bernard would not return the favor. Being exclusively a bottom, he left Michel curious and unfulfilled, and over the coming months, Michel would venture into the darkroom by himself, looking for love, finding nothing but sex, and plenty of it.

Bernard eventually moved on, and away. By then, Michel had taken his place, numbing his need for affection with casual sexual encounters, his ass taking a roll call of gay Rennes. He never heeded Giselle's warning, increasingly using sex as a means to quench his growing thirst for love and intimacy.

CLAUDE

As so many times before, Michel had gone straight to Le Chat Noir after school. His mother had stopped asking questions, as he regularly came home a couple of hours late. She probably assumed he was with friends.

The bar was a place where he could be himself rather than pretending to be something he was not. For every week, for every visit to Le Chat Noir, for every man he met, the more he knew that he'd eventually have to confront his parents. But coming out at his age was not an easy thing, and he'd met many at the bar who had warned him of doing so too soon, especially before turning eighteen.

Parents who were still in control of their children's fate would turn to psychiatrists, priests, and other quacks who promised to cure their children of their deviant thoughts because no one believed what they were feeling was genuine and worth taking seriously. Love was never love but erroneous behavior, a phase at best, a mortal sin at worst, and while it was perfectly fine for a man to love a woman, "Christopher's kind" were met with pity if in luck but usually with disgust. Some souls never got to see another day.

Michel had heard too many awful, heartbreaking stories, and they scared him more than anything else ever could. His parents were devout. Well, his mom was. His father was primarily concerned with his standing in society, now more than ever as a manager at the car plant. Part of that was to be able to show off his perfect family every Sunday at ten o'clock. You attended Sunday Mass, you partook of the body of Christ, you drank the blood of

Christ, and then mingled with others in the very same position as yourself outside in the parking lot. Few cared; most were simply there to keep up appearances, perhaps except for Michel's mother and some of her friends.

Listening to Michel Sardou singing "En chantant," which had taken the French charts by storm the previous summer, Michel was lost in thought and didn't see the man approach until he heard the barstool scratch as it was pulled back so the man could sit next to him. He was not unattractive, probably in his forties, with an unkempt mousy mop of hair that made him look like a clochard.

Giselle approached the man with one of her more neutral expressions. Michel had spent months trying to figure out how to read her behavior, but he wasn't always right. If a patron was a friend, she'd usually smile, sometimes leaving the bar for a quick hug or leaning over the counter for the traditional cheek-to-cheek kisses. There were also some guests she didn't like as much, but being the professional she was and relying on their business to sustain her, she'd always put on her best face, never showing her disdain, much as she might have felt inclined to do so.

"Salut, Claude! What can I get you?" As she asked the question, she continued wiping down the counter with a cloth, barely looking at him.

"I'll have a beer. Thanks, Giselle." Looking at Michel, he added, "As you've heard, I'm Claude. And you are?" He smiled, revealing a set of yellowed, crooked teeth. Michel felt his stomach churn and adjusted his previous thoughts. *Attractive?*

Claude took out a pack of Gauloises, pulled out a cigarette, and lit it. "Ashtray?" he said to no one in particular as if he expected someone to just bring one to him, giving Michel a sense of why Giselle might not like him. She was partial to cordiality and politeness, and this Claude was positively rude. Nevertheless, Michel reached to his right for an ashtray he'd noticed there and pushed it to Claude. "Here you go." He smiled back.

On the other side of the bar, he heard Giselle take a deep breath as she topped up a glass with beer for Claude.

"So, you're new here? I don't think I've seen you before..." He paused like he was going to answer his question, but he didn't continue. "And I still don't know your name."

"I'm Michel, and I'm not new here. I've been coming to Le Chat Noir for months now, usually after school."

"You're *the* Michel? I've heard about you, all right. Giselle raves about you. One could think you were hers." Claude laughed heartily, then breathed in through his cigarette, holding the smoke deep within his lungs before blowing it out again while turning toward Michel, who got the brunt of the smoke straight in his face and coughed.

"Please don't do that again," he managed to say before he had to cough again. Claude kept laughing.

"Leave the kid alone." Giselle put the beer on a cardboard coaster in front of him.

"I'll let the kid be the judge of that." He took a big swig from the beer, put it down, and looked at Michel. "So, do you want me to leave you alone?"

Michel shrugged. "It's not my bar."

"No, but it is mine. At least you know your place. That's good! So you're in high school? How old are you?" He gave him a solid pat on the back. Michel tried to look over his shoulder to make sure no cigarette ash had fallen on his jacket. His mother would never forgive him for that.

"I'm sixteen," he lied defiantly.

Claude laughed again. "Sure you are."

Michel tried to change the subject. "What do you do for work?"

This had Claude laughing some more. "You haven't heard of me yet?" He looked at Giselle and shook his head. "I thought you told every lamb chop who walked through these doors about me?" He found this all very amusing.

"Claude, leave him alone!" Her voice was low, and the way she'd said it sent shivers down Michel's spine. He was a little afraid of this man, yet the self-confidence he oozed was intriguing. It was utterly confusing. Despite his ugly teeth, Claude acted as if he owned the world, the Sun King reincarnated, right here in Rennes. Sure, Bernard had been cocky, but this was different. Claude had an aura that said he'd been born arrogant, and as much as Michel wanted to look away from that foul mouth with the cigarette hanging from one corner, he was mesmerized.

Smiling, never even looking at Giselle, Claude fixed his eyes on Michel. "Let the boy speak for himself. If he's old enough to be here, he's old enough to meet your husband."

Michel's jaw dropped. "You're Giselle's husband? I thought Giselle—"

"Technically, her ex-husband, but…"

"But…?"

"It's a long story. Maybe I'll tell you someday." He made a mock cross over his chest, looking up at the ceiling. "All you need to know is that all of this—" he pointed to the room around them "—happened because I wanted it to. It was my money, my connections that made this possible."

Michel was impressed. "You're so lucky." His parents had never been rich. His father had made a good career, and Michel was on his way through high school and on track to go to university— the first in the family—but his classmates were almost exclusively from upper-class families who owned German cars much nicer than Michel's father's Citroën, summer homes on the Côte d'Azur, and lofty apartments in Paris. Michel had always silently envied his friends, who'd be whisked off to skiing vacations in the Alps or to the French departments in the Caribbean for surfing. His parents had never had the means for that, and even if they'd recently begun to drive to the Atlantic coast or the Mediterranean for their summer vacation, it was a far cry from what many of Michel's peers were used to.

Claude finished his beer, left a large banknote on the counter, and got up. "Keep the change." He laughed, winked at Giselle, and left without looking at Michel again.

Giselle cleaned up and put away the money in her cash register before she came back to Michel. "You be careful with that one. Claude's a bit of a player, okay?" She laid her hand over his to emphasize her point but never really explained what she meant by "a player."

Michel thought of Monseigneur Serrault. He'd never told his parents why he'd stopped serving as an altar boy. There were protests and tears, and his father was most displeased, but Michel knew they wouldn't understand the real reasons and wouldn't believe him, so he stuck to the official story that others also needed a chance to serve the Lord. He bottled up the secret and wrapped it in the guilt of leaving behind all those other boys to be preyed upon, and he hid it deep within him. He hadn't thought of it for a while, until today.

I wonder why? Is Claude like the monseigneur? Is that what Giselle meant? Or is it something else? Is he like Bernard? Or like the faceless men who fuck me in the darkroom?

SEX EDUCATION

A FEW DAYS LATER, Claude was already at the bar when Michel walked through the door.

"Ah, if it isn't young St. Cul!" He laughed, enjoying this joke at Michel's expense.

"Quit it, Claude. I don't like you using that name, most certainly not in Michel's presence." Giselle slapped him on his hand for good measure.

"Yes, my wife, your wish is my command." He laughed some more.

Giselle didn't respond but simply rolled her eyes and turned her attention to Michel, who had sat a couple of stools along the bar from Claude. "Salut, Michel. How are you today? The usual?"

"I'm good, thank you, Giselle. And yes, the usual, please." He returned her smile.

"You can put it on my tab, Giselle." Claude had gotten up and moved over to sit on the stool next to Michel's. "I owe you an apology."

Michel was puzzled. "For?"

"For being so mean to you the other day. It wasn't fair. I tend to forget how young you boys are. I'm sorry. I didn't mean anything by it. But I'm a straight shooter. I speak my mind, and you, my young friend, already have a bit of a reputation in here."

"I do?" Michel looked to Giselle for help, but she didn't seem to notice.

"Look, I understand your curiosity," Claude continued, "I wish we'd had places like this when I was younger. Alas, we didn't. Which is just one of the reasons why I insisted we put a darkroom in here when we remodeled this space. What I didn't imagine was that our friend Antoine would shlep his rescues here and let them loose like mice in a dairy. The temptation is great, and once you're in there, you're as gray as that proverbial mouse. People can't tell how old you are. Does that make sense?"

Michel nodded, although he was unsure what Claude was saying.

"Look. I'm not into kids. But back there, if I came across your bubbly little ass, I might just want to fuck you…and live to regret it. The whole point of the darkroom is anonymous sex. Being in there is the equivalent of consent, and you can't expect people to ask to see your ID. If you go in there, you're fine with whatever happens. Well, most of what happens anyway. You can always walk away." He took a swig from his beer, then put his arm around Michel's shoulder. "You're not even sixteen. You need to take it slow, be careful. I'm sure maman's already given you the speech?" He turned to Giselle, who placed Michel's drink in front of him and smiled at Claude.

"Yes, she has indeed, but it is a speech that doesn't hurt to be repeated."

"Aye," Claude agreed pensively. "I guess it's a bit too late for this one." He patted Michel on his shoulders affectionately. "Just promise me you'll be careful, all right?"

They went on to chat about this and that—school, his parents, what his father did for work, his past in St. Malo. The time went by far too fast, and when Michel realized it had become dark outside, Claude offered him a ride home. "I'll get you there in time for dinner. We wouldn't want you to get in trouble with your folks, now, would we?

They left the bar, Claude and Giselle parting with traditional cheek kisses, and Michel noted how she was smiling at him. He must've misread her the other day, or maybe she'd been in a bad mood. Had they really been married? He found it hard to believe.

Michel met Claude more and more often at Le Chat Noir, and as time passed, they became friends of sorts, with the older

71

man often answering Michel's questions, driving him home, or helping him with his homework, something Michel often ended up doing at the bar counter. He never found out why Giselle had been so weird that first time. Maybe she and Claude had fought or something? And why had she called him a player? Was it because of his wicked sense of humor or his sharp tongue? People who didn't know him often mistook him as mean or cruel, but it was all good-hearted banter. There wasn't an evil bone in Claude Montand's body, just a set of really bad teeth.

1980

A HOUSE FOR
THE ST. JACQUES FAMILY

ONE EVENING AS Claude was driving Michel home during a particularly nasty winter storm, he asked about Michel's family. "You told me you grew up in St. Malo, right? Why did your parents move here?"

"My dad got work at the car factory here, and he's recently been promoted to foreman. It's good money, he says, but our apartment sucks. It's tiny and noisy. My parents are looking to move elsewhere."

"Yeah, I can see that. This isn't the best of neighborhoods either. Are your parents looking for a house or an apartment?"

"They've been looking for a house, but they haven't found anything yet that fits the profile of what they want and that they can afford. It's either not right for them or too expensive."

"I see. Do you want me to help? As you know, I own a lot of real estate in town, and there's always something on the market."

"Would you do that for me?"

"Sure! Why don't you come by my house someday after school, and we can see what you're looking for and what I have available?"

Michel beamed. "Wow, Claude, that's amazing. Thank you. Of course I'll come to see you." Then it dawned on Michel that he was facing a challenge. "How do I tell my parents without outing myself to them? I shouldn't know you."

Claude laughed. "Don't worry about that, kiddo. We'll figure something out. All right?"

75

Michel was so happy he leaned over and hugged Claude. "Thank you so much!"

Claude blushed as he returned the hug. "Don't mention it. We'll talk tomorrow, okay?" He pulled out a card from his jacket. "Here's my home address. It's in the old town, not too far from Le Chat Noir. Do you think you'll find it?" Michel took the card, looked at the address, and nodded. "Sure, no problem! I'll see you in a couple of days then. Thanks again for the ride, Claude."

"See you soon, kid!"

After a weekend that seemed to last forever, Michel's final lesson on Monday was canceled, and since Le Chat Noir was closed on Mondays, he decided to see if Claude was home. The offer of potentially helping his family find a new house was too tempting for him to pass on. Coming from a family where money had always been tight, he was enormously impressed by Claude's wealth, even though you couldn't see it on him. While he drove a very nice car, it wasn't the latest model, and then there was his appearance. He didn't own fashionable clothing and never wore suits; the outfits didn't look expensive either. His mousy dark-blond hair otherwise defied description, both straight and disheveled, sticking up and out everywhere, was more of a mop than a style. As for his teeth—if he was so rich, why didn't he go see a dentist? Claude seemed completely unconcerned by his appearance, which at best could be described as Bohemian. In any case, he did not meet Michel's idea of a rich man: he'd seen them in the papers and on TV, with their three-piece tailored suits, coiffed hairstyles, and Porsches or Ferraris.

When he reached the address in the old town of Rennes where the card had indicated Claude lived, he realized how wrong his views of Claude had been. The building was old, large, and very stately. There were a couple of doorbells next to the front door, but only one had a name tag on it. It was Claude's.

He rang it, and after a minute, the door opened, and Claude welcomed him with a broad smile of his brownish-yellow, crooked teeth. *Yeah, that's another reason why he doesn't look rich. This house on the other hand... Mon Dieu!*

"Welcome, Michel. Come on in. I was just opening a bottle of wine. Can I get you something? A soda perhaps?"

"Do you have a Diabolo Menthe?" It was Michel's go-to drink in the absence of alternatives.

"Sorry, I can't stand that stuff. I have Orangina or Coke. And if we're lucky, the milk's not gone sour yet."

"I'll have a Coke then. Thank you." The thought of Claude's fridge with bad milk was appalling yet fit with the image Michel had painted in his mind.

"Coke it is. Why don't you go on ahead upstairs? Two flights up and then down the corridor to the right. You can't miss it. My living room is the largest room on that floor. I'll be up in a minute."

"Sure," Michel answered enthusiastically, curious to see more of the house. He climbed the old wooden staircase, which creaked underneath his feet. At the top of the first flight, there was a corridor off to the right, leading to several rooms on either side, most likely bedrooms and bathrooms, Michel thought but didn't want to appear nosy, although curiosity very nearly got the better of him.

Instead, he climbed the stairs to the next floor, where he found the living room, as instructed. It was a large room and not unlike the monseigneur's study, as it was clad in wooden panels, although these were not quite as dark. In one corner of the room was a bar with a large mirror behind it, and the entire wall—from the bar counter and up—was filled with bottles of various liquors and glasses in different shapes on slick glass shelves.

In front of the bar was a modern seating group in white leather with steel frames and a glass coffee table also framed in steel, all sitting on a beautiful red rug laid on top of the hardwood floor. Where Michel stood, closest to the door, was a large TV set against the opposite wall with a VCR, a comfy couch, and a couple of reclining chairs. There was another rug that matched the dark-gray color of the couch. Along the walls were several paintings, and various exotic plants stood on the windowsills. Expensive-looking curtains hung to the side of every window.

Michel entered the room carefully, as if he might accidentally break it somehow, and walked up to the windows overlooking the street below. Claude's house was on one of the most exclusive streets in the old town of Rennes, on rue Saint-Georges, not too far from the magnificent Palais du Parlement de Bretagne, which housed the local court. Michel couldn't help but be impressed by it all. He was enthralled looking down onto the street a couple of floors below him and didn't hear Claude walk into the room.

"Not too shabby, eh?" He laughed. "Let's sit over by the bar, shall we?"

Michel followed him over to the white seating group where Claude gestured for him to sit down and placed a glass and a bottle of Coke on the table. "I'll just go grab my wine. One more second." He shuffled off in his socks. *Ahh, that's why I didn't hear him come in.*

"So, Michel, tell me," Claude began when he returned, "what kind of house is your family looking for?"

Michel had to think about that before he could respond. "Well, we need at least three bedrooms—one for my parents, one for me, and one for guests, for instance when my grandparents come to visit. Ideally at least two bathrooms, and I know my mom would love a yard out back, and my father wants a garage for the car."

"Okay, that sounds reasonable. Dining room? What about the kitchen? Would you want to be able to eat in the kitchen or perhaps both? And what about the living room? Should it be big or small?"

Michel shook his head. "I'm sorry. I don't know. I haven't talked to my parents about this. When they mentioned buying a house, all I cared about was having my own bathroom."

"I hear you. Grown-ups can be a bit peculiar when it comes to that sort of stuff, though, and I guess they don't tend to involve their offspring. How old are you again?"

78

"I'm fifteen."

"Ahh, you're practically a man. You'll need some privacy, eh? A room on your own floor, so you can jerk off with other guys without your mom hearing anything." Claude's laughter was loud and infectious, even though Michel reddened at the comment. This was so typical of Claude, straight to the point, a tad crass, yet masking it behind his laughter.

Michel had never had friends over at his house, let alone jerked off with anyone else, certainly not at their apartment, and his lack of response gave Claude the opening to continue.

"It's okay. I know sex is a touchy subject for kids your age. But it's natural, completely normal. Heck, I still jerk off every day unless I get to fuck with someone. Which is, of course, always preferable, trust me! Another man's hand on your dick is so much better than your own." He laughed again. Michel cringed. This was not where he wanted the conversation to go.

"Okay, I can see this is making you uncomfortable. Sorry! Let's talk business, shall we? I think I may have a property that will become available soon. It's not too far from here, to the north-west, on rue Anatole le Braz, a two-story stone building with a yard and a nice big garage. It has trees to shield it from the surrounding homes, and there is an extra room, right on top of the garage, which I think would be perfect for a young man like you. You and your parents will just have to go and see it for yourselves, to see if it's a match for what you're looking for."

"Sounds perfect...but also very expensive. Could my parents afford it?"

"I don't know about that, since I don't know what budget your parents have, but I'm sure we can work something out. I need you to understand that money isn't the issue here. The challenge is how we can bring this information to your parents without raising any suspicion. You said so yourself the other day. We need to be smart about this."

Michel shrugged. This had been on his mind, too, and he didn't have an answer.

79

"Well, how could we know each other in a way that doesn't get us into trouble? I mean, you can't exactly tell your folks that we met at Le Chat Noir because I presume they still don't know?"

Michel shook his head.

"I thought as much. Probably the smart thing to do at this point in your life. Could we have met through your school? A tutor perhaps?"

Michel shook his head again. "I doubt my folks would buy that. I have really good grades. I've never needed a tutor. Quite the opposite! I've been asked to help others."

"All right, let's see. Do you know what realtor your father uses? Does he have any help looking for properties?"

"I don't know about any realtors. I know he reads the paper every day, and he and Mom have been to some viewings after they've seen an ad that sounded appealing. Do you maybe have a flyer I can drop off in the mailbox? Or something else I could sneak home?"

"I'm afraid not," Claude said. "Do you remember the last house your parents went to look at?"

Michel nodded and mentioned the address in the southern part of the city, not too far from the plant where his father worked.

"Are they only interested in buying or could they imagine renting a house?"

Michel shrugged, as he didn't know.

"Let me figure out what that house was. The address sounds familiar. I think I own something in that part of town, too. I'll talk to my accountant. What's your phone number?"

Claude must have picked up on Michel's panic, as he quickly put up his hands to assuage him. "No, no, don't worry. I wouldn't do anything foolish. If I call, it's for a good reason, and I won't say a word about knowing you."

Reassured, Michel gave Claude their home phone number.

Enjoying their drinks, they chatted a while longer, about school, life in Rennes, Claude's family, and how he came to own Le Chat Noir. "We've always owned the building, but it used to be a grocery store way back in the sixties and early seventies. It had stood empty for a while, but there was a large warehouse in the back, which was perfect to convert into a darkroom."

He laughed and continued, "When my dad passed away, the building had been empty for a year or two, and we didn't have a good place for the community to come together in, so I changed it into Le Chat Noir. Giselle and I were married at the time, and I knew she had been working in a bar. The rest is history. But now it's all Giselle's. It was part of our divorce settlement. She owns the building, and it's her name on the license. I just help out if she has any trouble from the authorities."

"She's amazing. She makes everyone feel so comfortable."

"Yeah, she sure is. She's one of the most amazing people I've ever met and a really good friend."

Soon after, Michel had to catch his bus to get home. For the next two days, he was anxiously looking at the phone every night while they ate dinner and watched TV, afraid that Claude might call and somehow give away that they knew each other, leading to questions and certain doom for him. But the phone never rang, and after a week of sitting on tenterhooks, Michel began to relax and mostly forgot about it all.

CELEBRATING

IT WAS A Friday a couple of weeks after his visit to Claude when Michel went to Le Chat Noir after school and was surprised that Claude wasn't there. Michel had a drink with some of his friends and chatted to Giselle; he didn't mention his conversation with Claude. He was trying not to build up his hopes and didn't want to jinx anything. Had Claude forgotten? Or had he not found the right place yet? Michel was curious and impatient, but there would be no answers, not tonight.

When he arrived home, his parents were chatting in the kitchen, and they seemed to be in high spirits.

"Hello, Michel. How was school?"

"Good, thanks. What's for dinner?"

"I thought we'd go out tonight. To celebrate," Michel's father replied, smiling broadly under his large mustache. "You won't believe what happened today."

Michel was puzzled.

His father continued, "We received a phone call, out of the blue really, from a monsieur Montand. He'd heard we had been looking at this house a few weeks ago and said he had a property he wanted us to see. Seems he knows the family who was selling that place we looked at. They had spoken well about us and told him what we needed. He thinks his property might fit us perfectly. We can go have a look tomorrow. Best of all, we can either buy or rent." Michel's father looked to the ceiling and marked the cross on his chest. "It seems the good Lord is looking out for us." With a smile at Michel's mother, he added, "And it's almost downtown.

Imagine what the boys at work will say. They'll be so envious." He positively beamed with excitement.

Michel's mother filled in. "We have an appointment tomorrow morning to look at the house. Will you want to tag along?"

Michel nodded solemnly and hurried to his room to wash up and change. Claude had come through for him without revealing anything about his identity. A huge weight fell off his shoulders, leaving him free to thoroughly enjoy their dinner at a restaurant nearby and their Friday night together watching a family show on TV.

The next day, they left their apartment and drove to the address Claude had previously described to Michel. When they arrived, Michel was more than impressed. The property was beautiful— a three-story, Tudor-style house with an attached garage. Above the garage there were a couple of windows. Was that the room Claude had mentioned? Where he'd be able to have some privacy?

At that moment, Claude emerged from the house. Michel had to be careful not to react; his parents didn't know what Claude looked like. His father parked the car on the street, and they all got out as Claude approached them head-on. *Easy for him, he knows me.*

"Good morning! Are you the St. Jacques family?" he greeted without giving anything away.

Michel's dad stepped forward, hand outstretched. "Monsieur Montand? Thank you so much for doing this. We can't believe our luck. Is this the house?"

"Yes, it is. The current tenants will be moving out at the end of next month, but I figured you'd want to take a look as quickly as possible. I know what a nightmare it is to find a good home. It's such an energy drain, isn't it? My family has owned real estate for several generations. Trust me, I know what you're going through. If I can be of assistance, all the better.

"Besides, we'd be helping each other because I wouldn't have to look for tenants publicly and vet all those strangers. You have no idea what an ad for a house like this attracts in terms of weird

83

responses." Claude laughed knowingly, although the St. Jacques had no clue why. "I've spoken to my friend Emile, who owns the house you looked at a while ago. He mentioned what an amazing family you are and that your income is stable. That's exactly the kind of tenant I look for. Or buyer, right? You're considering both options?"

Michel's dad's smile was moronic as, like a butterfly drinking nectar from a flower, he swallowed every word Claude said. Michel had to hand it to him: his friend was smooth, the perfect salesman. They all shook hands, and when Claude shook Michel's hand, he winked at him, grinning broadly, at a moment when his parents were looking at the facade of the house. Michel was struck by the urge to scream, *"You can thank me for this opportunity— thank your faggot son!"* But he didn't, knowing full well what the consequences would be.

"Let's go in," Claude suggested. "The tenants aren't currently at home, so we're not disturbing anyone."

They entered the house, and Michel hung back to let his parents explore. Claude was an excellent guide, pointing out everything Michel had told him his parents were looking for in a house. It was the perfect setup, and they had no clue this house had been selected specifically to meet their dreams.

They all loved the bedrooms, especially the fact that there were two large bathrooms, the dining room with its alcove overlooking the street, and the living room with large windows and a door leading into the garden. They spent quite a while in the garden, where Claude drew their attention to the calm atmosphere, the trees, the vegetable garden with a small greenhouse, shaded and sunny areas.

Michel's mother seemed to be in heaven. Her reaction to the kitchen was similar. It was large enough to fit a table with four chairs, and a new stove and oven, with lots of storage space for china, pots, pans, etc. There was also a small pantry. Michel's dad was barely able to leave the garage. It wasn't as luxurious a home as Claude's, but for Michel, who'd spent his entire life in a two-bedroom apartment, this was a dream come true.

"There's one more thing I need to show you. I think this is something your son is going to love..." Claude didn't finish the sentence, and he didn't mention Michel by name. He led them back up to the second floor and along a narrow corridor, which opened into a large room used for storage by the current tenants: the room above the garage.

"A perfect space for a teenager," Claude said. "Or so I'd think if I were your son's age. It's part of the house yet separate. The guest bathroom in the main house is easily accessible from here, but the room itself is set apart, making it an amazing bonus for parents when your son listens to loud music or has friends over and it all gets a bit too noisy. It's like a studio, with enough space for work, play, and sleep. He could even stay here if he decides to continue his studies at a local university." He gestured them inside.

"Let me give you some space. Have a look around at your leisure! I'll be outside waiting. But please, take your time. D'accord?" With that, he left the room.

Michel's parents instantly looked at their son, grinning like Cheshire Cats.

"Well, what do you think?" his mom finally asked.

"It's okay," Michel replied, shrugging casually even though he loved it. This would be the perfect bedroom, but he was scared to let on in case his parents didn't want him to be separated from the rest of the house. He also liked the house itself but didn't want to be too enthusiastic. He was afraid they might suspect something as if they could magically put two and two together and infer his gayness—and the fact that he knew Claude—from a facial expression or a casual word. He couldn't shake the feeling that anyone looking at him would know whatever he did.

"Okay?" His father was puzzled. "This house is perfect. It's as if someone read our minds and knew exactly what we were looking for. Look at this room. This is three times bigger than the room you have now. You always complain about the noise from the other apartments and how crowded you feel. Here you could have friends over and listen to music without disturbing anyone. Wouldn't that be amazing?" His father had parroted every word Claude had said back to him and seemed utterly perplexed that Michel wasn't more thrilled. They had fallen for Claude's story, hook, line, and sinker.

"I guess." Michel agreed with his father but didn't dare say so. He could only hope they'd buy the house so he would finally get a real space for himself.

"You're very ungrateful, son," his mother scolded him. "I love this house! The kitchen is beautiful, the laundry room is perfect, the garden quiet and lush—I adore this place! But can we afford it?"

"Let's go and find out," Michel's dad suggested and turned on his heel, leaving the studio.

Outside, they found Claude smoking in the driveway. "Ah, the St. Jacques, what do you think? Do you like the house?"

"We do indeed," Michel's father said, "but I'm afraid we can't afford it. To buy or even rent a place like this would be very expensive."

With a smile, Claude approached Michel's dad, pulled him a few feet aside, and whispered something into his ear, adding for everyone to hear, "Let's discuss this between us men, shall we?"

Michel could see how his dad's jaw dropped as he struggled to find words. "But, uh, are you sure?"

Claude merely nodded, still smiling.

"And you say it becomes available at the end of next month?"

"Yes, that is what I said. Why don't you take your family home and think about it to make sure this is what you really want? Here's my business card. Let me know what you decide. I hope you find my offer appealing enough to seriously consider it."

Michel's father reached out to shake Claude's hand, taking it in both of his large hands, shaking enthusiastically, much longer than decorum dictated. "Thank you, monsieur Montand.

Thank you so much. We will. We will indeed, and I will call you before the end of the day with our response. Thank you. Thank you ever so much. You are most kind and most generous. Merci, monsieur." He bowed to Claude repeatedly, and Michel stifled a laugh, wondering if he'd behave so subserviently if he knew the truth.

They took their leave and drove back to their apartment in the south of the city, and it became clear on the ride that the decision had already been made. Michel's father was highlighting how much better the car would fare if it spent nights in a protected garage. His mom commented several times just how unsafe she felt where they currently lived and how much better it would be to live downtown, and his parents kept exchanging meaningful glances. Had he been able to, Michel would have smiled and shaken his head. No more bus rides to get to and from school and Le Chat Noir. His life was finally within walking distance. Another thing he couldn't tell his parents.

After lunch, he asked if it was okay if he met up with some friends, and without asking about it, his parents let him go. They were in a good mood. He took the bus downtown and headed straight to Claude's apartment, but he wasn't there. Instead, he found him at Le Chat Noir.

"Well, did you and your parents like the place?"

"They loved it, and to be honest, so do I. Especially since my father already sees me in the studio above the garage." Michel smiled at the mental image. "But how much are you going to charge us?"

Claude lifted his hand as if to silence the question. "That is between your father and me. Don't concern yourself with such things."

"But aren't you going to lose money that way?"

"Look, Michel. This is the last time I'm going to have this conversation with you, d'accord? How I choose to spend my money is none of your business. I have no family and no children. When I die, everything I have left goes straight to the government. I'll do what I can to make sure they get as little as possible. Understand? Now, let's celebrate, shall we?"

Michel shrugged again and sat down next to Claude at the bar. The man had a point. If he wanted to waste his money, and if Michel and his family stood to profit a bit, who was he to argue?

***

It would be the first time Claude helped Michel in a major way, but far from the last. Over the coming years, Claude became a sort of surrogate father to Michel, and since he was officially their landlord, his parents weren't surprised when he'd show up at their door or ask if Michel could assist him with something—an excuse to get him out of the house. The St. Jacques were so grateful, and it gave Michel a lot of freedom to spend more time outside the house, either at Claude's or at Le Chat Noir. Michel had no reason to complain.

88

YO, WAIT UP!

RIDAY AFTERNOON, GETTING out of school at last, Michel was dying to go to Le Chat Noir for a drink and a chat with his friends there before heading home. By now, his parents had come to expect that he wouldn't be home until after six p.m., so he had that freedom. If they ever asked, he'd make up a friend here or there he'd visit after school to hang out with, but they rarely did ask. Given that Michel brought home straight A's from school, they had no reason to second-guess him. Now that they had moved, he could stay longer at the bar since their house was within walking distance. Another welcome perk of having moved into the city center.

It was late in the fall, and by the time he left Le Chat Noir, it was already dark out, and fog blanketed the city. It had been like this for days, driving everyone insane. To reach home, Michel had to cross the park in the square, and he hadn't realized that a small group of people was hanging out in the park. Nor did he see them as they followed him into the alleyway that connected the square with the main boulevard that Michel would take to walk home.

"Yo, wait up!"

Instinctively, Michel stopped to look around at the person addressing him. A group of three young men, he wasn't sure how old they were, were quickly approaching him. The shortest one, walking in the middle, was talking.

"Can I help you?" Michel tried to be polite, but there was something that scared him about the whole situation, and he took an involuntary step backward.

89

"Maybe you can," the young man said as they caught up with him. "You're a faggot, right? You love to take it up the rear end? A fruitcake?"

There was laughter, and Michel realized he'd made a mistake. He tried to turn around and run off, but the two taller guys grabbed him and pushed him up against one of the buildings.

"Not so fast! Why the rush? You haven't answered my questions yet." The guy talking had ashen hair, straight with a cheap cut, and his face was plump. He was breathing heavily and grinning all the while.

Looking at the other two, Michel noticed they were not much older than he, maybe eighteen or nineteen, and he hadn't seen any of them before. Judging from their dialect, they were from up north, near the coast. *What are they doing here in the city?*

He tried to gather his wits, say something that was both funny and appropriate, maybe disarming; the last thing he wanted was to get hurt. He'd heard enough stories, but for some reason, he had never imagined anything like that could happen to him.

"Well?" the leader of the group said, again. "Are you deaf? Mute perhaps?" He laughed at his supposedly funny remark. His friends certainly seemed to appreciate the joke.

"Let me go. I just want to get home before my parents worry about me."

"Look at that, the faggot can speak. I think we should keep him here for a bit, have some fun. What do you say, boys?"

Michel knew he was in trouble, but he didn't figure out what it was they wanted until it was too late. He steeled himself for the first fist to land somewhere on his body or face and was completely unprepared for what happened next. In front of him, the plump-faced boy opened his pants and pulled out his erect penis, directing his two friends to turn Michel around. He tried to fight, but they were stronger, much stronger.

"Please, don't do this. Let me go!" he cried, but the alley was empty and dark, the nearest streetlight too far away to shine any light on the scene. When they pulled down his pants and he was forcefully taken, the intensity of the pain mercifully allowed Michel to black out.

When he came to, the three had already left, and he was lying in the alley, pushed up against the wall. He looked at his watch and was surprised to discover it had only been a few minutes. He was wet from the moisture on the ground and shivering from the cold. As he tried to get up and pull up his pants, the pain came rushing back, bringing new tears to his face. Barely able to walk, Michel hobbled back to Le Chat Noir.

"Oh, my God!" Giselle cried when she saw him come through the door. "What happened to you, boy?" She dropped the cloth she was holding and rushed toward him. Other patrons turned around, their faces concerned, shocked. Michel collapsed straight into Giselle's arms, and she had no choice but to go down with him, breaking his fall to the floor, holding him.

"Michel, talk to me, child. What happened? Did someone hurt you?"

The questions were too much, and Michel began to sob, the pain unbearable.

"Someone call Doctor Dupont. Tell him to come over immediately." Giselle barked her orders at her customers, then lowered her voice to a comforting murmur as she caressed Michel's face and stroked his hair. "Everything will be fine. The doctor is on his way."

CONSEQUENCES

*A*N HOUR AFTER Michel's battered return, the atmosphere at Le Chat Noir was subdued. Most of the patrons had left, some using the back door, afraid to face whatever threat lingered out there in the streets. Others were encouraged to leave in pairs or groups. Michel had been able to give a statement, albeit not to the police. Giselle knew that would be pointless. The flics secretly endorsed gay-bashing as a way to keep the nascent gay and lesbian community at bay, on the down-low so to speak. Her establishment was barely tolerated, mainly because Claude secretly paid off several of the senior members of the police in Rennes. While she didn't approve of that, she was grateful for the limited protection it provided.

Michel's attackers had probably heard about Le Chat Noir, and they had stalked the establishment, waiting for a suitable victim to emerge from it. Michel was perfect for their plan: young, slender, non-threatening, and leaving on his own. One look at this face and you knew he couldn't hurt a fly.

Doctor Dupont had examined Michel and given him some ointment to treat his anus and a small supply of strong painkillers. He'd been lucky and nothing had torn, which was not unheard of in these cases. "You'll be in a lot of pain for the next few days. Take these as you see fit, but not more than four a day, you hear me? Here's my number. Call me if things get worse, and at the latest on Sunday. I want to make sure you're okay." The doctor patted Michel on the back, walked over to Giselle, and whispered something in her ear before leaving.

92

"How are you? Are you feeling any better? I'll take you home now, okay?" Giselle put her arm on his shoulder, gently squeezing it. Michel barely nodded. "Don't worry, I'll tell your parents you saved me from a robber. Unfortunately, I've had to do this before. You just tell them that the robber landed a couple of punches to your gut, and you fell to the ground. It'll explain the stains on your clothes. Okay? They'll never suspect anything—unless you decide to be honest."

Michel stared at her blankly. The painkiller hadn't kicked in yet, nor had the shock left his system.

"Do they know about you? Trust me when I say this. Even parents who know their kids are gay do not necessarily cope well with their sons being raped. It's not a can of worms you want to open. There are too many variables out of your control. They could force you to see an unsympathetic doctor who probes you, causing you more pain, not to mention the endless rounds of questioning you'll have to endure. People generally don't understand your kind, and even if they love you and mean well, the results can be quite disastrous."

Michel shook his head. "No, they don't know." His voice faltered, and he began to cry anew. The pain, the betrayal, the sudden loss of his sense of security and safety in public had barely sunk in. Why would anyone do this to him? What had he done to deserve this?

Giselle interrupted his destructive thoughts. "Let's stick to the robbery story. You're the hero who saved me. That story I know how to sell, and it gets you out of trouble for coming home late." She smiled kindly, tousled his hair, and kissed him on his forehead, and for the first time since he left Le Chat Noir earlier that evening, Michel felt a warmth spread within him. Giselle was such an amazing woman. So strong, he almost wished she were his mother.

As they left her office and returned to the bar, Claude stood behind the bar and gave Michel a nod. "Are you okay, kiddo? Anything I can do to help?"

"I'll take him home now," Giselle said. "I'll be back in less than an hour. Mind keeping an eye on things until then?" There was a pleading tone to her voice, but Claude merely nodded.

The drive home was quick, although reaching the front door was another story. Michel didn't want Giselle to tag along, but she insisted, so they compromised, and she stayed a few feet behind. He opened the door to the house and walked in. His parents came rushing from the kitchen. He could tell how worried they were.

"Where have you been?" his father demanded.

"Michel?" his mother asked more gently. "Are you okay? What happened to your clothes? They're all dirty!"

Giselle walked up behind Michel but didn't enter the house. "Your son may just have saved my life. I was attacked by a couple of thugs, and this young man here..." Her voice cracked, and she pulled out a handkerchief, dabbing the corner of her eyes before continuing. "Your son saw what was transpiring, and without a second thought, he yelled at them and came rushing to my rescue. Unfortunately, as they fled, they hit him, and he fell to the ground. I insisted on taking him to my personal physician first. He's fine, there are no internal injuries, but he might be in pain for a day or two. Your son is so brave. You have raised a hero!" She blew her nose for good measure, and Michel smiled, despite the pain. He couldn't help but be impressed by her acting talent.

His mother virtually flew to him and threw her arms around him. "Oh my God! Michel, I am so proud of you. Was this near your school? Were there no witnesses?"

Michel nodded, and Giselle answered. "I'm afraid not. It all happened so quickly, and they ran off. I have spoken to the police, and they are aware of it, but you know what it's like these days. They don't care."

Michel's father stretched out his hand to Giselle. "Thank you, Madame, for taking the time to bring our son home. We were worried sick. And we are very proud of him, of course. I'm glad he was able to help you."

"Is there anything else I can do for you?" Giselle put her hand on Michel's shoulder. "Tell me. Anything?"

Michel looked up at her, tears in his eyes, but he shook his head.

***

The next day, Michel visited Claude. He needed to talk about the incident. After he'd relayed the story, Claude gave him a long hug.

"Giselle told me about it after she returned. Why didn't you say anything last night? I could've taken you home."

Michel shook his head. "And say what to my parents? Giselle's story worked out just fine. My parents bought everything she said."

"I guess. But more importantly, are you okay? I mean physically and emotionally?" Claude was still holding him.

"I don't know. I'm in a lot of pain. The pills from Doctor Dupont work for a while, but I don't have that many left."

"Ah, don't you worry about that. I can get you as many pills as you need. We just need to make sure you don't get hooked on that shit. Besides, your ass will feel better in a day or two, trust me. Been there..." Claude rolled his eyes but didn't elaborate. "I'm much more worried about your emotional well-being. Your body will heal, but what about your soul, your heart? If you need to talk about this, let me know, and I'll help you, okay? If you need a professional, I'm happy to pay for one. D'accord?"

Michel had half expected Claude to make a pass at him after they had moved into their new house, as a way of extracting some sort of payment in gratitude, but nothing happened. Michel had often thought about it, and he would've willingly obliged. His parents were so much happier now they had moved up the social ladder and were living in a house in the inner city rather than in one of those huge housing complexes near the car factory.

Michel felt a warm and fuzzy feeling in his chest. Claude was a good man, always worried about others, often helping

95

others. There had been so many instances where he could have been pressured into doing something untoward with Claude, something that he didn't want to, but not once did Claude try to take advantage of him.

And here he was, in Claude's arms, being comforted after what had amounted to a brutal rape less than a day ago.

"I'm fine," he finally managed to say. "There's not much to talk about. And I can't go to the police, can I?"

Claude broke their embrace, took a step back. and held Michel by the shoulders. "Look, I won't lie to you. We can't go to any police station and report this, no. The police are so homophobic that it wouldn't do us any good. However, that doesn't mean there's nothing we *can* do. I know one of the officers at headquarters. He's a good guy, and he's gay, too. I'll talk to him, see if he can find those guys and book them for something else—theft, assault, or whatever. No promises, but we have to try because this isn't just about you. These guys could do it again. We can't undo what happened to you, but if we can stop it from happening again, maybe it will help you in your healing process.

"Now, can I get you something to drink? Oh, and I have something to show you! I've gotten a new toy to play with."

Michel gave him an odd look, wondering where this was going.

Claude laughed. "No, you pervert, not another dildo. Besides, those are not the kind of toys I'd share with you. It's a brand-new computer, and it has some games with it. Want to try it out? Take your mind off things for a while?"

They shared a couple of beers and played around with Claude's new Atari computer. Michel was happy to have his mind taken off the whole episode, at least for a while. He was never bothered by the gang again: there were rumors of them having been run out of town, and there had been no further incidents. He never asked Claude about the discussion with the police. He was too busy dealing with his own shit to care that much about other people's.

96

1981

1981

MICHEL SAINT CUL

FOR WEEKS AFTER his rape, Michel stayed away from Le Chat Noir. He felt miserable, inside and out, and even though his physical wounds had healed, and the pain in his rectum had ceased, he was far from fine.

Inside of him raged a war. He was torn between the abuse by the monseigneur, the rape, and all the negativity surrounding him, and the love and acceptance he had found at Le Chat Noir with his friends, Claude, Giselle, Antoine, and all the other patrons. There was this tight-knit group of people who accepted him for who he was and treated him with respect. But then there was the hatred he felt toward his kind every Sunday, from the pulpit, or at dinner at home.

To Michel, none of it made sense. He couldn't reconcile the two worlds except to accept that he was a freak. And if he was a freak, he might as well prove them all right. If they thought he was a lost cause, why not live up to their expectations?

Michel's first visit back to Le Chat Noir was short. Giselle was worried and hovered over him, asking him how he was, how he had been, if he was okay. He didn't feel like talking about it and took the opportunity to sneak into the darkroom the second Giselle walked back into her office.

In the darkness, Michel found a corner, pulled down his pants, and stroked his cock. It wasn't long before a figure appeared in the dark, touching him, and upon feeling his freed cock, going down on it. The whole encounter lasted only seconds, and Michel emptied himself into an eager mouth, pulled up his pants,

99

and walked out again. He had hoped the release would make him feel better. It did not.

He returned to the bar, finished his drink, and left.

He returned the next day, and the day after, and the day after that, repeating what he'd done. Ordering a drink, walking into the darkroom. And for every visit, for every time he left dissatisfied, he'd go a step further.

In time, the emptiness inside drove him to spread his cheeks again for men prowling for ass. Despite his fear of the pain he'd undoubtedly feel afterward, there was also a part of him that longed for it, like a flagellant chastising himself, where the pain transformed into a warped aphrodisiac of sorts. For Michel, it also served as a reminder of what a freak he was and how much he deserved it. Time and again, he returned to the bar to sit and drink his Diabolo Menthe, pretending he was still the same boy even though he could barely sit still because of the pain, far too often being manhandled by men thinking less with their brains than their balls. He never said a word to Giselle, though he suspected she'd noticed the dried tears on his cheeks, and she never mentioned it.

Regardless of the pain, regardless of the amount of sex he had, no matter the number of men he allowed to use him as a cum dump, the void inside Michel didn't go away. The empty feeling the rape had left inside him spread like a cancer, numbing his ability to feel anything real.

Michel lived two lives: the boy nursing his Diabolo Menthe at the bar and the eager slut in the darkroom. He never tried to reconcile the two personas, and when other patrons in the bar joked to each other about having met "St. Cul," this nickname that followed him like a shadow wherever he went, he shrugged and gave them a dirty look, edging them on to dare him again. Many took him up on the offer. Once, Michel had been searching for intimacy and love, yet the more time he spent in the darkroom, the less he felt anything, only ever finding the quickest of physical encounters. Michel would part the curtains and walk into the darkness; St. Cul would part his ass cheeks, forcing Michel to retreat further into submission.

Sex became his addiction, every push inside his ass a hit, every pair of lips around his cock a moment of clarity. Sex was the only thing that allowed Michel to function and reconcile the two worlds that battled for domination inside his mind, at least for a few seconds or minutes at a time. He had transformed into the monster his parents had always talked about. It concealed the dark hole that had swallowed his heart, and he felt vindicated by being able to keep it from them.

At home, he was the good son, the boy with excellent grades, making his parents proud, eating his mom's cooking with gusto, all the while barely able to sit still from the damage the latest stud had inflicted on his ass. The smile his mother and father saw on his face was not one of joy but of satisfaction that he was so expertly able to dupe them.

1982

HAPPY BIRTHDAY!

CLAUDE THREW MICHEL a huge birthday party at Le Chat Noir. Eighteen years old! He was finally an adult, with all that entailed. At long last, he would be able to drink his wine legally and not have to chew a bunch of gum before going home to his parents. He would be able to go out without having to ask them for permission and simply enjoy all the elusive perks of being a grown-up.

"Happy Birthday, kiddo!" Claude kissed him on both cheeks as he walked into the bar that day. He was followed by Antoine, Giselle, and all the other regular patrons that Michel had gotten to know in the past few years. He could barely believe he'd been a regular here since before he had turned fifteen, still a child, yet he dared not imagine what his life without his second family here at Le Chat Noir would have been. Giselle and Antoine had been the understanding foster parents, providing emotional support in accepting who he truly was in ways his actual parents would never have been able to, and Claude was his best friend or maybe older brother. Michel was grateful to have them in his life.

He felt empowered by his adulthood. If his parents found out now, he'd be able to move in with Claude, and he wasn't particularly worried about money either. Claude had made it abundantly clear he'd support Michel financially if the need arose.

Claude was such an odd fellow. The man had been there for him at every turn of his recent life, always helping, never asking for anything in return.

The party was amazing. Le Chat Noir was packed, with an open bar tab, compliments of Claude. People drank way too much, and everyone was having a great time. Michel got drunk for the first time in his life, and by the time the bar was closing, he was barely able to walk.

Claude laughed and suggested wisely, "You know what, you stay at my place tonight. We'll call your parents in the morning. I'm sure they won't be too worried. You are, after all, a grown-up now. Time to make adult mistakes. Come on, let's get you into bed."

When Michel came to again, he was in a bed he didn't recognize, although there was a familiarity to the place. He turned onto his back and noticed he was almost naked, only wearing his underwear. As he adjusted his eyes to the semi-darkness of the room, he realized he was in Claude's bed.

"Well, well, look who finally woke up!" Wearing a shabby blue terry-cloth robe and a pair of fluffy slippers with wisps of fur, Claude walked into the room sipping a cup of coffee.

"How did I get here?" Michel sat up in bed and stretched his arms out, yawning.

"You pretty much passed out the second you crossed the threshold. I had to carry you upstairs, and since it was late and I hadn't made any of the guest beds, you had the distinct pleasure of sleeping in my bed. You're most welcome, by the way." He made a mock bowing gesture.

"And you? Where did you sleep?" Michel was worried that he'd forced Claude to sleep elsewhere.

"In my bed, of course. It is a double bed, so plenty of space. Although you do snore, or maybe that was just the alcohol." Laughing, Claude climbed back into bed and picked up the newspaper. "Want some coffee?"

"Yeah, thanks. That would be good." Michel tried to reach over Claude to grab the cup which he had placed on his nightstand. He failed and fell over his friend.

"Ouch, get off me." Claude half-laughed. Michel propped himself up against one of Claude's legs and accidentally rubbed against his crotch. "Hey, what are you doing?"

"Nothing! I swear. It was an accident. Sorry!" Michel managed to retreat to the side of the bed where he had slept, without the coffee, but the encounter had the undesired effect that he now had an erection himself, and a big one at that, given his natural endowment. Of course, Claude noticed.

"Really? You're sporting morning wood? In my bed? What a cliché!" Then he laughed. But rather than going back to what he'd been doing—as he'd usually do—he put his hand on Michel's crotch, very gently. "Dear Lord, that is quite the tool you have..." His voice had become hoarse.

Michel was confused. He was also horny and didn't understand why, but the next thing he knew, he'd moved over and was kissing Claude.

"I'm sorry. Have I ruined things?" Michel said afterward, searching Claude's face for reassurance that he hadn't destroyed their friendship.

"Don't worry, kiddo. We're friends. We've had sex. Big deal. I don't mind doing it again sometime. Your cock felt amazing!"

"Giselle is going to freak out and accuse you of taking advantage of me."

"Giselle? What are you talking about?"

"Nothing. She just warned me about you once, that's all. But I'm a grown-up now, so I guess it doesn't count."

"Look. That woman needs to keep to herself. She can play mother hen to all the gay boys in this town, but she shouldn't judge. Besides, I'm not going to tell her. Are you?" Angry, Claude got up and left the room.

Michel hung back a moment before he dressed and joined Claude in the kitchen. "I think I'd better head home. While I may be legally an adult, my parents are going to freak out if I don't make an appearance soon."

Claude didn't respond, and Michel left.

OUTED

MICHEL'S PARENTS WERE about to head out to Mass when Michel appeared in the doorway. He immediately picked up on the tension in the house.

"Where have you been?" his father demanded.

"I've been worried sick all night!" his mother added for good measure.

"I was at a party for my birthday, all right? I need to get to bed. I drank too much last night." Michel squeezed past his parents into the hallway and headed for the stairs.

"So you're not coming with us to Holy Mass?" his mother called after him.

"I'm sorry. I'm too tired. I need to get some sleep." For the time being, that seemed to satisfy his parents, who left without another word.

When they returned less than two hours later, Michel was fast asleep in his bed. His father came to check in on him and woke him up.

"We need to talk. Your mother and I will be in the living room. Make it quick." There was a tone to his voice that scared Michel. He was in trouble, serious trouble, but he had no idea why or what he had done. He couldn't imagine that his late night had inspired such a strong reaction. He was, after all, eighteen now and entitled to a bit more freedom, even though he still lived under his parents' roof. *Well, Claude's actually,* he mused. He quickly put on a T-shirt and a pair of sweats and headed downstairs, but not before taking a couple of pills for his headache.

Walking into the living room was like walking into a funeral parlor. His parents sat side by side on the couch, his mother crying silently while his father stared absently out the window, his arm draped around her shoulders. A creak from the hardwood floor gave Michel away, and his father turn to face him.

"Sit down, Michel!"

He sat in the armchair next to the couch. "Did something happen? Is Grandma okay?"

"What were you doing at that god-awful place—what's it called again? Le Chat Noir?" His father's question was like a punch to the gut, and Michel didn't know what to say.

"Someone saw you there last night. There's no denying it. You do realize what sort of a place that is, right?" His father's voice was elevated, laced with disgust and condemnation.

"Yes, I know what sort of place it is. It's a place for the likes of me," Michel said flatly. He didn't see it coming, the slap across his face, but the burning sensation his father's hand left on his left cheek lingered.

"You will not speak to your parents in this manner. You are breaking your mother's heart. I will ask you again. What were you doing at that place?"

Michel was unsure what his father expected him to answer. That he had walked in there by accident and left as soon as he discovered it was a place for *those* people, homosexuals?

He repeated his first answer. "I was there because it's where I feel comfortable, and—" Another slap across his face, harder this time.

His father stood up, towering menacingly in front of him. On the couch, his mother's crying had turned to a desperate wailing as if someone had just died, but since the secret was out of the bag, Michel decided to continue, unprepared as he was. This was not how the conversation was supposed to be. He was supposed to talk to his parents when he was ready. He wasn't.

"I am gay. I am a homosexual, papa. I always have been. I celebrated my birthday there last night, and it was great.

I've been going to Le Chat Noir for years. All my friends are there. It's my second home."

His father hadn't expected Michel to be so forthcoming and sat down again, silently. Likewise, his mother's crying changed, taking on a quieter quality. To Michel, it seemed as if both his parents were aging before his eyes.

They sat like this for minutes, in silence, until his mother's tears had dried up and her demeanor changed, a strange, accusatory gleam in her eyes as she lifted her head to look at him.

"Is it something I did? Are you doing this to punish me?" Her tone was more than judgmental. It was full of loathing and disgust.

Michel reached out to her with his hand, but she instantly recoiled. "Don't touch me!"

"No, maman, it's not you. It's me. I was born this way, and there is nothing you can do to change this."

"We'll see about that. Nobody is born a homosexual!" his father cut in harshly.

"It's a sin, an abomination," his mother implored. "Unless you change your ways, you will end up in eternal damnation. You know that." She began to cry anew, and Michel wondered if it was for his soul or her standing in the congregation.

"As long as you live in this house, you will abide by our rules, do you understand? Those include not being a homosexual and never setting foot inside that place again. Is that understood?" His father tried his best to lay out the rules, but Michel detected a faint sense of insecurity. There was not a whole lot of conviction behind his words.

Michel had played through this particular scenario in his mind countless times, and he was at least prepared for this outcome.

"Okay. I guess I'll just have to leave, then, because no matter what you say, I can't stop being gay. It's who I am. If you can't accept me for who I am, so be it."

He stood up and left for his room, where he packed a bag with the most important necessities, his schoolbooks, and clothes for a few days. He could always send a friend to pick up the rest. As he came downstairs again, his father was standing in the hallway.

"Where are you going?"

"You said you didn't want me to be here as long as I'm gay. That means I can't stay, so I'm leaving." He squeezed past his father and left the house. He didn't look back but imagined his father standing there like an abandoned statue in a warehouse, following him with an empty gaze as Michel quickly walked down the street, turned a corner, and headed straight back to Claude.

EXILE

LAUDE WAS MORE than happy to let Michel stay with him for a few days. Michel attended school, did his homework, and spent an hour or two at Le Chat Noir every day. For the first time in months, he stayed away from the darkroom. He was too preoccupied with real life to care about sex, and it had been comical to see some of his regular hookups walk past him into the space, giving him meaningful glances, only to return minutes later when he hadn't joined them. He was at Le Chat Noir more out of spite than feeling a need to be there. To frequent Le Chat Noir daily had become a sort of rebellious act against his parents, whom Michel had assumed knew nothing about it, and he had no idea who had outed him or if they were still present and reporting back to them. It could also simply have been a freak encounter. In a smallish city like Rennes, it was not beyond the reasonable.

Giselle was very supportive but also tried to excuse his parents' reaction, claiming they were afraid and uneducated.

"Look, Michel, here's the deal. Your parents belong to a very different generation, and they don't know how to deal with this piece of news, okay? You told me more than once how religious your mother is, and the Catholic Church is not very gay friendly, except when she recruits her priests. Imagine how scared your parents must be, to lose you to the devil. I mean, if you truly believe that stuff, wouldn't you be devastated to learn your child is going to hell? Give them time. They'll come around. You might regret it otherwise."

"I'm not so sure about that."

"Well, there's only one way to find out, and that's not by avoiding them. You know what it's like to be gay, they don't. To them, being gay is an alien concept they've only heard about from the pulpit. It's not something they can relate to. You need to show them that you're still the same person you were before they found out, and to do that, you need to talk to them. Maybe call them? Go home for a visit?"

Michel still wasn't convinced.

Giselle tried another approach. "Consider this then. How long have you known you're gay? When did you truly accept it?"

He shrugged. "A year ago? Maybe two? I mean, I've known I was different for a long time, but how and what that meant? I don't really know."

"But it's been on your mind for some time, and as you said, you struggled with the concept, what it means to be gay, how hard it's been. I'm sure there were times when you wished you were not?"

"I guess? I don't know. I've never really seen myself married to a woman."

"That's kind of my point, isn't it? You've always known, deep inside. For your parents, this all came as a surprise. Boom! One day their son was straight, a good student, on his path to get on with life and to get married, provide them with grandkids. The next, they know their son is going to hell, no marriage, no grandkids, and he'll never see any happiness in life, at least not in the way they would define happiness. And all of this happened in the blink of an eye. Can you see just what a shocking revelation that is? Even the most liberal, the most understanding parents might have their entire world shaken by this."

"Maybe?"

"Your parents love you, of that, I am sure. Being gay is still not easy. We've made some progress in recent years, and it's easier to be open about it, but will you ever be able to get married or have kids? Given the way the world looks, most likely not. When your entire existence revolves around that concept of family, and for one generation to follow the generation before it, to suddenly

113

have a wrench thrown into the machinery, that's a lot to take in. Trust me, I have been down that road. For parents, that's a lot to digest and process. Just give them time. You also mustn't forget that they will have to come out, too, to friends and relations, just as you did."

"I guess." Michel saw merit in her argument.

When he returned to Claude's house and told him over dinner what Giselle had said, Claude agreed.

"As much as I like having you here, kiddo, I think Giselle makes a very good point. I'm sure your parents are worried sick. You know where the phone is. Call them. Worst case, you'll still be here afterward, but at least you'll know. You'll have closure."

Michel had to laugh, and he shook his head in disbelief. "Did you two strategize this conversation and stage an intervention?" Claude didn't respond.

They ate the rest of their meal in silence, and even afterward, as they did the dishes, no words were spoken. Michel needed to think things through, and Claude gave him the space he needed. Later, Claude retreated to his study, dealing with some paperwork, and Michel went into the living room to play some computer games. As simple as they were, they provided a distraction from the hurricane of conflicting thoughts in his mind—should he call them, should he not, why, why not? around and around—but he couldn't focus and so he turned off the TV and went back to his bedroom.

Claude had moved him into a guest room when he had unexpectedly shown up again the day after his birthday. That was fine with Michel. Not that he regretted the sex they'd had, but he didn't have the sort of feelings for Claude that meant he wanted to repeat their carnal encounter. They were friends, and the sloppy sex they'd had was proof of that. *Hangover sex, done that, we can strike that from the list.*

As he passed the phone in the hallway, he stopped. What did he have to lose?

Nothing.

My parents, my family!

He lifted the receiver and dialed the number. It rang. Once, twice. On the third ring, someone picked up.

"Hello?"

"Dad? It's me."

His father didn't respond immediately, and the uncomfortable silence expanded around Michel. He held the receiver in both hands as if in prayer. *Say something, please?*

"How are you, son?"

"I'm good. I'm staying with a friend. How is maman?"

"Not good. She worries about you. Would you please come home? So we can talk?"

Michel let the question hang in the air. It had come a bit unexpectedly, although he'd hoped to hear something like it. His father's voice was even, cool and distant, perhaps, but that might just be the connection. He hadn't spoken to his dad like this before.

"Okay, does tonight work for you guys? I could be there in half an hour?"

"Tonight is good. See you in a little while then." His father hung up. Michel had been dismissed by the click of a disconnected phone line, the fast and regular beeps reminding him of cutting an umbilical cord. His relationship with his parents had changed for good, no longer the tether of parent and child, forever defined by his gayness. He was on his own now. There was no going back.

He loved his parents, there was no doubt about that. Did they still love him? For a moment, he was unsure if he should go home, afraid to find out where the future would lead their relationship. He put down the receiver on the hook, took a deep breath, and went to tell Claude.

"That's great news, kiddo. You really should go. They've matched your first step. Now you must take the next one. Don't make the same mistake Giselle made."

"Giselle? What about her? She's not gay, is she?"

"I know, I know, but she hasn't spoken to her parents in thirty years, ever since..." Claude made a dismissive gesture with his arms. "No, I won't say. Ask her. This really is her story to tell. But you get your ass home to your parents, okay? Talk to them, and remember that they still love you, somewhere deep underneath all the shock, the disappointment, and all that religious doctrine, and the pretense that follows along with that. Right now, they're probably just as scared as you are."

Michel wasn't sure this was a good idea, but he was also afraid that Claude might run out of patience with him. They were, after all, not family, but friends; Claude might just throw him out on the street—and his parents, too, for good measure. Michel had, after all, a responsibility for their safety. At least his parents were blood, and while there were strings attached, they hadn't technically thrown him out. He had chosen to leave. Even though, in reality, he'd had no choice.

DÉTENTE

*H*ALF AN HOUR later, Michel rounded the corner into his street. The final steps to the house were difficult, and he considered several times just turning around and running back to Claude's. He didn't know what to expect. He arrived at the house a couple of minutes after he'd said and rang the doorbell. *What are you doing? This is your home, too!*

"Son, come on in. Why are you ringing the bell? You're not a stranger. You live here!" his father scolded him. "Your mother is in the kitchen. Let's go there."

Michel followed his father into the kitchen where his mother was putting away the last dishes from dinner. His father sat at the kitchen table and gestured for Michel to take his seat. The atmosphere was laden and stale, even though there were faint notes of rosemary and sage in the air, probably from a roast his mother had prepared for dinner.

"Are you hungry? Have you eaten?" his mother asked. Her voice was thin, and Michel could tell she had been crying a lot.

"No, thanks. We ate earlier."

His mother sat down, a broken woman. She seemed to have aged years in the five days he'd been gone.

"Where have you been?" his father demanded harshly, but quickly added, "Sorry, that came out wrong. We were worried sick when you disappeared. You may be eighteen and legally an adult, but we still worry about you. And your mother and I still love you. You are our only child."

Opposite Michel, his mother began to cry. "I'm sorry. It's just so hard. I missed you, Michel, and I've been trying to wrap my

117

mind around this whole thing, but I can't. The Church is very clear on this." She looked up at her son, tears streaming down her cheeks, "I've spoken to our abbé, and he confirms that there is hope for you yet—if you repent, if you come back into the embrace of the Holy Church. Michel, I beg you, please come back."

"Mom, this is who I am. I am gay, and nothing you or anyone else wants, prays for, or does is going to change that."

"How can you be so sure? You are always so stubborn. You always know best, and everyone else has to bow to your will." She was very upset.

"The Church has been around for almost two thousand years," his father said angrily. "Don't you think they know more about the human condition than you?" His big mustache quivered with every word he said.

"They sure know how to take advantage of children when it suits them." Michel was defiant, remembering Monseigneur Serrault and how his parents had effectively driven their son into the arms of a pedophile. The statement did not have the desired effect, though, and it angered his father even more.

"What *are* you talking about?"

Michel wasn't sure it was a good idea to mention the monseigneur at this point. They wouldn't believe him anyway. So he simply said, "Nothing," and let it slide.

"Maybe you could see a doctor instead? Monsieur l'abbé said it's an illness? Maybe there is a treatment for this." His mother did not give up easily.

Michel had to chuckle and thought about Doctor Dupont, one of his regular hookups. Maybe he should invite him to give his parents a lecture on modern medicine's view on homosexuality. But somehow, he doubted they'd take his word for it. So he said nothing, again.

Silence fell around the kitchen table, interrupted only by Michel's father's heavy breathing and his mother blowing her nose every few seconds. After what felt like an eternity but probably only lasted a minute or two, his father finally asked, "Are you moving back home again?"

"I don't know. Am I welcome?" Michel let the question linger before he said, "I'm not going to change, you know? I am who |I am."

The answer came after a few moments. "You are our son. And we will keep on praying for your soul, for your salvation. But you are always welcome in this house."

"Always?" Michel wasn't convinced.

"Well, your mother and I aren't happy that you choose this life for yourself, but as you said before, you are a grown-up, and there's not much we can do about your choices in life. But we ask you to keep this to yourself, to not flaunt it openly, and obviously never to bring any such people into this house."

"Such people?" Michel repeated. He couldn't help but picture the day when Claude had walked out of *this* house to greet them. *Such people* had frequented *this* house before his parents had even moved in. *Such people* owned *this* house.

"You know exactly what I mean. Homosexuals. I don't want any homosexuals in my house," his father added sharply.

Silence fell again, and Michel briefly considered mentioning that their landlord was gay, but he figured it was better to not let that particular cat out of the bag. He needn't make things worse.

So it was agreed that Michel would move home again. To assert his independence, he left the house to spend one last night at Claude's and to pick up his things, but before he went there, he dropped by Le Chat Noir. Not as a stretched-out middle finger to his parents, although that was certainly an appealing thought, but because he was curious about the story Claude had alluded to, about Giselle not speaking to her parents for such a long time.

GISELLE

ISELLE WAS BEHIND the bar, as always, drying large beer glasses as he walked in. "Michel, it's late, what brings you here?"

"I went to see my parents, just as you wanted me to."

"And? I take it things didn't go well or you wouldn't be here." She put down the glass in her hand and the towel and walked out from behind the bar to hug him.

"No, no. It went better than I expected," he said as she embraced him.

She took a step back and looked at him questioningly.

"They want me to move back. They just don't want me to be gay, or act gay, and I'm not allowed to bring anyone to the house, at least not unless they are certifiably straight." He laughed and made air quotes around the last two words.

"Well, that is good, isn't it? It's a start, you know? They love you, clearly, and given time, they will come around. Besides, in less than a year, you'll graduate from school and move on with your life. And you'll be able to put some distance between yourself and their less palatable views. You know what they say—absence makes the heart grow fonder. At least you still have a relationship with your parents. That is more than some people." Michel could feel the hurt in those words.

"I was going to ask you about that," he began carefully. "Claude mentioned something but deferred to you to tell the story."

"Did he? How nice of him!" She turned on her heel and walked back behind the bar.

"I'm sorry. I guess it's not my place to ask."

"It's okay. It's not a big secret. I should have told you a long time ago. All my friends know. I got an abortion when I was about your age. My parents never forgave me and cut me off completely. I wasn't ready to have kids, didn't want any, at least not back then." She paused to dry another glass. "I made a mistake and got knocked up. Served me right. But my parents, like yours, were very conservative, and they couldn't look a murderer, as they put it, in the eyes, ever again. I haven't spoken to them in going on for thirty years. I don't even know if they're still alive. I was completely cut off from my entire family."

"You never had children?"

Giselle shook her head. "No, you have to understand that abortions were illegal back then. To find someone to perform one was very difficult, and it involved unsanitary rooms, quacks, and a lot of money to keep things hushed. There were complications, which is also how my family found out. I needed surgery, and they had to remove my uterus. You don't want to know all the gory details."

"I'm so sorry to hear that." Michel stretched out his hand across the bar.

Giselle shrugged. "C'est la vie! I can't undo what happened. I only wish I still had a relationship with my parents. But they disowned me right there and then, in my hospital room, after they found out that my injuries were the result of an abortion. I was sentenced to time in prison, too, for good measure. Had it not been for Claude, I'd have probably ended up homeless and in a heap of other trouble."

"He said he'd seen you working as a waitress?"

"Well, that's not the entire truth. He's being kind and sugarcoating things. I *had* worked as a waitress in Brest before I met Claude. You see, before Le Chat Noir, there were no gay clubs in Rennes, so most gay men went to the cruising areas in the parks or public toilets to meet each other. He and I met in the park one night just after I was released from prison. I served my time right here in Rennes, at the Centre pénitentiaire. I didn't

121

have anywhere else to go and was roaming the streets, and I ended up sleeping on one of the benches in the park. I had no idea it was a cruising area." She smiled at the memory.

"I was inadvertently cock-blocking him, and he was quite upset with me." She was laughing now. "That prick. He walked up to me and told me to take a hike. He had no idea why I was there, and I sort of lost my shit, began bawling my eyes out, and, well, the rest is history. We were even married for a while. This—" she indicated the room they were in "—was my divorce settlement."

"Married, right. Claude mentioned something once." Michel hadn't believed it because Claude was so open about his sexuality.

"Those were different times. We were able to help each other out. I was a fallen woman, and he was surrounded by rumors of being gay. His father was still alive at the time, and Claude was afraid that if those rumors reached his dad, he'd be stricken from his will. He's an only child, and had his father found out, I think he'd have given away everything rather than Claude seeing a penny. So we got married at City Hall in a private ceremony. I moved in with him, which was perfect for me, and we lived as a couple until his dad passed away and the estate had been settled. A year later, we quietly divorced, I got Le Chat Noir and enough money to get me started, and Claude's reputation was untarnished."

She shook her head and picked up drying glasses where she'd left off. "Can I get you anything or is your curiosity satisfied?"

"I think I'm good for today. It's getting late, and I don't want Claude to worry about me. I'll spend the night there and then move back tomorrow, after school."

"Good for you. Well, please say hi to the old bastard when you see him." She didn't look at Michel as he left, but he knew that she meant no harm.

***

The coming weeks were tense in the St. Jacques household. Michel's mom stayed mostly to herself, keeping busy in the kitchen or her garden, picking up leaves from the ground, getting everything ready for the winter, even though she had insisted on Michel doing that in previous years. Facing him all the time was still too painful, so she withdrew. Michel's dad began to work longer hours, and he spent less and less time at the house. Oddly, as Michel moved back in, it seemed his parents were gradually moving out.

His father started going to soccer matches of the local club, Stade Rennais, and he never invited Michel to join him. Previously, he'd often sit in front of the TV at home on Sunday afternoons to watch whatever game French TV was broadcasting, and Michel would join him. Michel had never been a huge soccer fan, but it was a fun game to watch, and he did have a crush on a couple of the players from his favorite team, Olympique Marseille, goalkeeper Gerald Di Georgio and forward Hervé Florès. His father had always been a supporter of the local team— an endeavor of love, as they mostly sucked, at least in Michel's eyes. Alas, Sundays now meant he was alone in his room, his father away after dropping his wife off after Mass. She would then disappear and busy herself with housework.

There was no reason for Michel to stay in the house either, and so he, too, began to spend most weekends with Claude, his friends, or at Le Chat Noir, where he would drink until someone of interest showed up and then follow that person into the darkroom.

He quickly fell back into the routine he'd acquired over the past year, numbing his emotions with sex, lots of it. It was so much easier than having to deal with them. Michel was handsome and young. It was easy for him to get laid, and he did have a lot of sex, always had. *Michel St. Cul at your service!*

He sometimes wondered if he would ever be able to get rid of that reputation, of being easy, a slut. Part of him didn't care. As long as he got to get his rocks off, he couldn't care less. Another part of him, though, felt very differently about it and was quite aware of the void that was growing inside, leaving him dissatisfied, often cranky or in a dull mood. His friends all noticed and would ask him about it. He could snap at Giselle or Claude—he even once told Antoine to go fuck himself and rushed out the door—but he had no idea why he felt the way he did.

Instead, he buried himself in his schoolwork as it was the one thing he knew would eventually buy him his freedom—a fresh start where there was only one Michel St. Jacques. He dared not jeopardize that freedom, his ticket out of Rennes. Get excellent grades, go to a good school, and leave this forsaken city for Paris. *Paris.*

The sheer thought sent shivers down his spine. There was nothing he dreamed of more than a future in the national capital. To live in Paris, to be free—it seemed like bliss, and it was the only thing that could calm him down and keep him focused on his goal.

1983

PROBABLY JUST THE FLU

*M*ICHEL HAD BEEN sick as a child, like most people—chickenpox, rubella, the mumps—but this felt different from a run-of-the-mill virus. The fever was high, he felt miserable, he was extremely tired, and his throat ached. His mother was worried sick, and the family doctor came by and prescribed chicken soup, paracetamol, and lots of rest. He'd be fine. He had probably just caught the flu; everything would be okay.

Michel was too sick to argue. He slept through most of the day for more than a week, and the fever didn't break until after six nights. Meanwhile, his mother hovered over him like a brooding hen, checking in on him regularly, helping him change soaked pajamas, changing his bedding once or twice a day, and spoon-feeding him soup and tea.

When the fevers finally subsided, Michel had lost a lot of weight, and he felt completely drained of energy. Missing important days of school this late in the scholastic year wasn't popular with his teachers, but his mother had arranged for a friend to drop off his schoolwork every day, and when he finally felt up to it, Michel began to slowly catch up. It was another two weeks before he felt strong enough to return to school, just in time for the final month before graduation. The flu had drained him more than any illness before, and his body didn't feel the same after it.

The day before school was out for Pentecost, he dropped by Le Chat Noir for the first time in weeks, and there was a big smile of relief on Giselle's face when she saw him walk in.

"Here you are. We were so worried about you. What happened? Where have you been? Claude wanted to come to see you several times, and Antoine was 'this' close," she gestured with her hand, thumb and index finger less than an inch apart, "to contacting social services. We were worried that your parents and you had a fight or something. Are you okay?" She emerged from behind the bar and quickly approached Michel to hug him.

"I'm fine. Just tired. I had a bad flu, and I've been in bed for a couple of weeks."

"The flu? At this time of year? Is there a new strain making the rounds?"

Michel shrugged. "I don't know, but it knocked me out completely. I don't think I've ever felt this sick."

"Well, I'm glad you're back. Can I get you something?"

"I'll have the usual, please. Where is everybody?"

"Oh, you know. It's too early in the day. Not to mention the holiday this weekend. I think most of the guys have either traveled back to their families in the country to celebrate with them or gone away for a long weekend. But I'm sure Antoine and Claude will be in later. We usually spend the time together. I keep the place closed on Pentecost, and Mondays are closed anyway, but those of us without any better plans will come together and share a meal at Claude's Sunday night. We've done it for years, as you know. Will you be celebrating with your parents?"

"Yeah, I guess." He smiled at the question. "Not that I look forward to all the services my mother will try to drag me off to. And they always get cranky when I refuse. But I get that it is a big day for her. Her God has finally settled in heaven and the moving cards have arrived. It's a big thing…" He laughed at the mental images it evoked. Michel had lost all faith in recent years and found his mother's religiosity annoying, given what it had cost him. Alas, she didn't know, probably couldn't even fathom it.

"We're open again on Tuesday if you want to pop in?" Giselle suggested. With the topic exhausted, she broke the hug and returned to the bar to fix Michel his Diabolo Menthe. Even though he could drink a beer or a glass of wine legally when on his own, he still preferred the sweet minty concoction.

After the holidays were over, Michel decided to visit Claude at home. He hadn't seen him in a while either, given how sick he had been, and since his parents didn't know how close he was to their landlord, he couldn't just pick up the phone and call.

"Hello, stranger!" Claude answered the door and bade him inside. They kissed on the cheeks, as tradition dictated. "You look thin. Giselle just called. She says you've been sick?"

"Yeah, I had the flu. I was sick as a dog."

Claude looked at him. "Did you also grow, or do you just seem taller because you've lost so much weight? Or maybe both?" He laughed and put his arm around Michel. "Yes, you've definitely grown."

"Yeah. I hope this is the last time. I'm one-seventy-seven now. My mom wasn't happy that I grew again. We'd just been shopping for my graduation outfit before I got sick, and now not only is it too big around the waist, but the pants are too short. She can't just take them in. She'll have to go back and exchange it all. I feel sorry for her."

"Looks good on you, although you'll have to gain a bit of weight, too. And you're sure it's just the flu?"

"I guess. I've had all the other infections you get as a kid already. Whatever else could it have been?"

"I don't know. Just something I read in a paper recently. But as you say, it was probably a bad flu. Come on, let's have a drink. Beer? Or a glass of wine? I've got some new games for my computer. Boring as fuck, but it beats the shows on TV this time of year."

They walked upstairs to Claude's huge living room, where they sat on the large, white couch by the bar, drank a couple of glasses of red wine, and talked. It made Michel feel alive and vigorous.

"So, tell me, anyone special in your life?" Claude asked. "You spend so much free time at Le Chat Noir, even more so now since you moved into town. I'm sure you must've met someone?"

Michel blushed. "No, not really. I've had a few...brief encounters, but nothing serious." He was embarrassed to talk about it with Claude, even though he was probably, no, definitely, his best friend.

"Good for you. Still making the most of that darkroom, I hear?" Claude was never one for secrets, and he was obviously aware of Michel's reputation. "That's why I had it built. I want us to feel liberated. We should make the most of our lives. Be happy and carefree, you know? Fuck the government, fuck society. I just need you to be careful, do you understand? There's this new thing going around, they call it SIDA. It's killing gay men all over the place and there have been a couple of cases here in France, too." There was genuine concern in Claude's voice.

"SIDA?" Michel had never heard of it.

"That's what we call it here in France. The Americans call it AIDS. It's an immune deficiency syndrome, but they still don't know what causes it. I read an article in the *Gai Pied* the other week. You should check that out. You need to be informed, Michel. This is serious stuff."

"Okay, okay, I will. Jeez, you're scaring me." Michel chuckled, not taking Claude seriously. "Why would I get this SIDA in the first place? And how?"

"They suspect it could be sexually transmitted, but nobody knows for sure. Don't worry too much, Michel. I'm sure you're fine. Besides, you're way too young anyway. And most of the cases have been found in America." Claude made a dismissive gesture with his hand and got up to pour himself another drink.

After a couple more drinks each, they headed over to Le Chat Noir together, and Claude quickly disappeared into the darkroom. Michel had the impression that all this talk of sickness and sex had made Claude horny, and to be honest, he felt the need, too. It had been a few weeks, given his recent illness. But he didn't want to accidentally bump into Claude back there. That might be awkward. They were friends, after all, not lovers. That one time didn't count, and they had both agreed it would be better not to make that mistake again.

Instead, he went home, as he realized he was much more tired than he was horny. He still felt weak after his illness. Besides, he also had a few school weeks ahead of him yet, with final tests before he would graduate.

GRADUATION

THANKS TO HIS excellent grades, Michel had a choice of schools and had opted for the Sorbonne, where he was already accepted, provided he graduated. His parents were too proud of the first member in their immediate family to ever graduate from high school, and the first to ever attend university, to fight him on the idea of Paris. Yes, there were universities and colleges in Rennes, but how could they stop their son after he had been accepted into one of the most prestigious universities on Earth?

They worried, of course, how they would be able to support him through college, but they had saved up, in secret, for this day. In the spring, in the weeks leading up to his graduation, the anticipation of the event, his amazing grades, and spring bringing life back to the garden had greatly improved his parents' emotional well-being. Things were a lot less tense at the St. Jacques' house. Not that they had returned to normal. His parents still went to Mass on Sundays but no longer asked him to join them; they would return to Michel having made lunch; they'd eat together and chat about politics or the lives and misfortunes of celebrities. All three had mastered the art of circumnavigating the shoals of uncomfortable topics that might arise. On the weekend before his graduation, Michel realized that he might even miss his parents after moving to Paris.

He graduated top of his class, and while his classmates were going to celebrate the achievement together, Michel decided he'd rather spend the evening with his friends. He had mentioned this to Giselle, who had asked him to leave it to her.

After the official ceremony at the school, the St. Jacques returned to the house where they had lunch together. Spirits were high. His father opened an expensive bottle of Bourgogne, and his mother had outdone herself in the kitchen. The meal was spectacular. There was a genuine sense of pride and joy, even though Michel knew the feeling was skin-deep at best.

"What are you doing tonight? Are you going out with your classmates? Will you join them for the Mont-Saint-Michel trip tomorrow? I'm sure that'll be a lot of fun?" his mother asked after lunch.

"No, I don't think so. It's just about getting drunk. Besides, it's not my scene. I'm going to see my friends later. We'll celebrate here in town."

"Your friends?" There was a sense of foreboding in that question, and Michel picked up on it but didn't see any reason to be dishonest. He was happy with his accomplishment and wanted to share it with his parents without subterfuge.

"Yeah, my friends at Le Chat Noir. You should come, meet them. They're good people." He felt a strange sense of hope after the way things had evolved these past weeks, even more so after the meal today, and how happy and proud his parents seemed. Maybe, just maybe, they were coming around to seeing things from his point of view?

"But they..." His father struggled with the word needed to express his thoughts. "Aren't they all...homosexuals?"

"So?" Michel answered in a mixture of defiance and childish hopefulness. "Plus, that's not entirely true. Giselle is straight, and Claude—well, you could probably call him bisexual. Those two were married for a while."

It was too late. The name had been dropped, and Michel instantly realized he'd made a mistake, but even long after, he was unsure whether, subconsciously, he had done it on purpose, or if it had been a slip of the tongue, a momentary lapse of thought.

"Claude? Claude as in Claude Montand, our landlord?" His father was incensed.

"The very same, yes. I've known him for years." Michel didn't like his father's attitude, that smug look of condescension as if he'd just found out their landlord was somehow a lesser being, despite everything he had done for them and the adulation he'd shown him earlier. As if he suddenly and no longer had to hold the man in high regard for his help in securing their home. As if monsieur St. Jacques was instantly worth more because he was not a faggot.

"But *how* do you know him?" his father demanded, screeching with indignation.

"How do you think we got this house in the first place, huh?" Michel shouted, which was unusual, especially at home, as his father would frequently use the palm of his hand to make sure his son stayed in line. But not this time. Of course, Michel had realized the potential fallout the second the words crossed his lips, but he hadn't expected this response. It was as if all the air had left his father's lungs. Next to him, Michel's mother fainted and fell to the floor as she undoubtedly had successfully visualized the meaning of Michel's statement.

He and his father both pressed the pause button on their quarrel to attend to his mother. His father picked her up and carried her into the living room, where he laid her down gently on the couch. "Quickly, get me some water."

Michel dashed to the kitchen to fetch a glass of cold water. When he returned, his mother looked at him through hazy eyes, as if he were a stranger.

His father took the glass and then said quietly, "Please leave."

Michel didn't fight him. Despite it having been close to nine months since his coming out, his parents had not changed their views. To them, Christopher's kind were still as loathsome and vile as they had always been—aliens, perverts of the most disgusting variety. Their Catholic upbringing was so deeply rooted that they no longer saw their son but the devil himself, a demon living right under their roof. Had it not been for the laicism of French governance, Michel was fairly sure he'd have been tossed out on the streets long ago. But his father was afraid of the impression it would have, and for his standing in society.

Liberté, Egalité, Fraternité

Those were the three cornerstones of French society. For once, Michel was glad that they protected the likes of him, at least to a degree.

He left the house and wandered the streets of downtown Rennes, with no particular goal in sight. It was late in June, and it would be three more weeks before he would finally be able to get out of here, if only for his National Service.

The promise of freedom, albeit within the confines of the armed services, increased his spirits, and he subconsciously directed his steps toward Le Chat Noir, his true home. He found the front door open and music coming from the inside. Giselle often left the door open in the summer, as the lack of air conditioning meant temperatures inside could get rather balmy. He walked in and instantly relaxed as he saw all his friends gathered around the bar or sitting at the tables.

Claude spotted him and walked over to welcome him. "Congratulations, kiddo. We're so proud of you. Wish we could've been there. Did everything go well?"

Michel accepted the congratulatory hug but instantly began to sob.

"What's the matter? Did something happen?"

After the initial turmoil had subsided and Michel had calmed down and been congratulated by his friends, they had been able to relax for a while and celebrate his accomplishment. A couple of hours later, people began to leave, and things turned pretty quiet at Le Chat Noir with only Giselle, Claude, and Michel left at the bar.

"I'm glad you came here." Giselle was doing dishes again. "I cannot fathom how parents can be so cruel. You'd think the past months would've demonstrated to them that you are still the same person you have always been. Can't they see that?"

The party had been fun, but everyone was saddened by the way Michel's parents had reacted, their lack of progress in accepting their son for who he was.

"Let's get out of here," Claude suggested. Most of the guests had left to spend the summer night outside in a park or get ready for work again. This was, after all, not a weekend night. "I'll buy you dinner."

"Before you go," Giselle interjected, "haven't you forgotten something?" She gave Claude a meaningful glance.

"Oh, yeah, right." Claude fumbled around in his pockets and produced an envelope. "We didn't know what you wanted as a graduation present, so we all got together and collected some money for you. We figured you may need to buy some things for uni or maybe just head out for a while, go see the world. It's not much, but it's a start." He handed the envelope to Michel, who stood there frozen, utterly surprised by the gesture from his friends.

"Congratulations again, Michel! We are so proud of you," Giselle added from behind the counter, wiping a wet strand of her red hair from her face.

Michel took the envelope and opened it to find a wad of notes of different denominations.

Claude laughed. "No need to count it, it's all there. Come on, let's go. I've made reservations at the Galaupin. You'll like it."

They reached the restaurant a few minutes later after Claude had found parking for his old Mercedes. The maître d' knew Claude and seated them in a quiet corner of the restaurant.

Not sure how to broach the subject because he was afraid he'd anger his friend, Michel said tentatively, "I think I may have accidentally outed you to my parents."

"You think?"

"I, uh, somehow may have mentioned that you would be at my graduation party. I stupidly thought they might come and join me there if they already knew some of the other attendees. And mentioning someone they respected was how I thought I could convince them. Let's just say that backfired."

Claude became pensive, his hands folded in front of him. "Look, the fact that I'm gay is not a secret. It hasn't been for years. Did you speak to Giselle? She mentioned something along those lines." Michel nodded. "I never really cared if people knew, you know? But on the other hand, why would I forsake my father's fortune just because of that? I don't mind principles, but that didn't mean I had to be stupid about it. Giselle needed help, I needed help. It was a win-win situation for both of us.

"I'm using my fortune to help people, people like you and your family. And while I don't have kids of my own, and could just give it all away, my fortune allows me to live my life fully. This, my friend, is my real challenge for the future. I'm only forty-nine years old. I have a few decades still left in me, but what is going to happen with my estate when I die? I hope that once you are done with school and you start your career, we will have the opportunity to sit down at some point and talk. Maybe we can find a way to use my money for good. I don't trust the government. To them, it's peanuts, and it'll just go to defense programs or some stupid monument in Paris."

Listening to his friend, Michel saw yet another version of Claude, a more serious human being, worried about his legacy, caring for others, not just having fun and helping people as a form of entertainment.

"What do you say?" Claude prompted. "I know you have a ton of other things on your mind, but promise me we'll stay in touch even after you dash off to university? That we'll stay friends? I don't have that many." There was a profound sadness in Claude's voice.

"Of course we'll stay friends, old man. How could we not? I owe you so much…"

"You don't owe me anything."

This was the moment they were saved by their server, who came by with menus and to tell them about chef's specials for the evening. They listened, bantered about the wine selection, flirted with the handsome guy, and ordered. The mood at the table changed, lightened, and conversation flowed smoothly throughout dinner. At some point, Michel picked up the envelope and counted the money. His friends had collected almost five thousand francs for him, undoubtedly most of it from Claude.

"Look, kiddo, if you need more, if you need *anything*, you let me know, okay?"

"Thank you, Claude. Merci! I don't know what to say. You guys are all amazing."

"Any idea what you're going to do with this?"

"Well, first I have my National Service to get through. Not sure how I feel about that. But once that's behind me, I'd love to go to London. I've always dreamed of visiting that city. Put what little English I've learned to some use, maybe pick up one of those redheaded English lads?" He laughed out loud at that. "Have some fun before university starts next fall."

"You do that. Sounds like a good plan. But don't spend all the money on London. You'll need to buy books, too."

"Yeah, I know, Daddy." He stuck out his tongue. "You're just jealous that I'm still getting some."

Claude laughed and shook his head. "Maybe, maybe not. You just promise me you'll be careful, okay? This AIDS thing is beginning to spread here in France, too, and I'd hate for you to get sick. I for one am done with sex. It's just too big a risk, you know? I want to live, grow old."

The mood at the table changed again, and Claude took the opportunity to finish a thought he'd had earlier in the evening. "Look, don't worry about your parents. If your father starts to spread rumors, I don't care. You'd be surprised what a willing ass or tongue can accomplish in this town. Heck, I've been fucked by half the zoning commission in my heyday. I know more dirty secrets about politicians in this city than you could ever imagine. If they try to take me down, which I doubt, I could take quite a few people with me. So don't worry. Besides, I don't think your father will do anything. He's just in shock, and he'll come around. Once he thinks through how little he's paid to me in rent, and why, and all the money they've saved over these past few years, I doubt he'll make a fuss. He'll realize that people would start asking questions he wouldn't want to answer."

"I'm not sure I follow."

"The rent your parents pay for the house is about forty percent below market level. How would he explain that? Your father knows that his rent is *very* low, and if people also knew about us being friends, don't you think they'd start connecting the dots? And would it be so far-fetched to add another line to him, to your parents peddling their son to get to their dream home?"

"But nothing untoward ever happened between us!" Michel wasn't sure he was following Claude's line of reasoning. "Well, at least not back then."

"True, we know that, but gossip doesn't. And judging from your parents' reaction, they don't know that either. Don't forget, my friend, misconceptions can be dangerous, but they can also be an ally."

Michel thought about Claude's words. He wasn't sure how much power his friend really wielded in Rennes or if what he said was merely posturing, but he seemed to be sincere in not being angry at him for outing him to his parents. They finished their meal with a delicious dessert and a glass of aged Armagnac before Claude drove Michel home.

"Are you okay here? You can stay at my place if you like?"

"Nah! I'm good. They'll be asleep by now anyway. I'll let you know if anything out of the ordinary happens." He leaned over and kissed Claude on the cheek. "Merci, my friend! For everything!"

"Don't mention it, kiddo." Claude blushed and looked away. *Somehow, this feels like goodbye, but why?*

Michel had been right. His parents were asleep when he went inside, and when he got up the next morning, his father had already left for work. Michel was now an adult, graduated from high school, and caught in this weird limbo time until his next life chapter began: the military.

He wasn't leaving for another couple of weeks. Like most young French, Michel had to complete his yearlong military service and had been selected to serve in the French Infantry. Once that was behind him, he'd finally be able to start his university studies in Paris. He wasn't looking forward to the year in the army, but he couldn't wait to get out of this house.

PRESENT DAY –
MON BIJOU, BRITISH VIRGIN ISLANDS

AAKON PUT DOWN the diary, frowning. He'd been sitting and reading for hours. He had to get up and stretch. Walking back into the house, he recalled Michel mentioning Claude, his friend back in Rennes. He'd also talked about Le Chat Noir, and Giselle, and how they had been like parents to him, his chosen family if ever the term carried any meaning. But it had all been in passing, bits and pieces here and there, morsels during a conversation about something else.

Reading this latest post about Claude and the man's fear of dying alone, of not having an heir, made Haakon think. He would have to be about ninety years old by now, but he could still be alive, and so could Giselle. *What if they are?* Haakon hadn't understood how close they'd been, not back then, or how important they had been in Michel's youth, or else he likely would've gone to Rennes way back when, after Michel's passing. Suddenly he felt guilty about having dropped that particular ball, about never having read the diary in full. He had been so completely engulfed by his grief that he never even considered how Michel's passing might affect other people who had known and loved him. *Is it too late now?*

He sat down in front of his laptop to email his assistant back in Bangalore. It was the middle of the night in India, and they were hopefully all fast asleep.

141

Dear Nidhi!

I need you to do me a favor. I am looking for someone in France, in a city called Rennes. His name is Claude Montand, and from what I can gather, he'd be about eighty-eight or eighty-nine. He was into real estate and seemed fairly wealthy. I also have a lead to a place called Le Chat Noir, a gay bar in the same city. It used to be owned by a woman called Giselle. No last name. She had once been married to this Claude, so maybe she's still going by his name?

Let me know what you find out.

Thanks,

H

He fired off the email, curious as to what Nidhi might find out in her research. He went to the bathroom first, and then to the kitchen to refill his water. Back on the porch, he looked out over the ocean's surface, quiet and mirror-like. He could barely hear the tiny waves lapping ashore.

The proverbial calm before the storm, he thought, as he'd looked at the latest forecast. The hurricane was approaching out there, intensifying rapidly from the east, hundreds of miles away still but barreling toward the Caribbean, on a trajectory to likely strike the Leeward Islands head-on.

I'll deal with that later. He had a great crew who had already begun to prepare for evacuating the kids, and they had the plywood all ready to board up the buildings in the morning, if and when the hurricane's path was confirmed. The European and American forecast models were still not entirely synchronized about the trajectory. There was a fifteen percent chance the storm would take a northern path toward the continental US, toward Northern Florida and Georgia, but even if the storm passed them to the north, the effects could be significant.

The red notebook was still in his hand, and he was too curious to stop reading now. He let his mind be transported back in time to France and the next step in Michel's life. He'd already mentioned his desire to travel to London, where they had eventually met. But first, he had his military service to contend with, which brought forth memories of Haakon's own.

1984

PASCAL

FOR THE LONGEST time, Michel had contemplated ways of getting out of conscription to avoid his military service. In the end, when he stood there and they asked him if there was any reason not to do his duty for the fatherland, he didn't say a thing. He couldn't. Being gay might have gotten him out, but he didn't feel like coming out to the burly officer sitting in front of him, eerily reminding him of his father with his big walrus mustache. Instead, he reported to his infantry regiment for duty, hundreds of miles away from Rennes.

During those first difficult days and weeks of stringent officers barking orders, trying to instill a sense of duty and order into the young men in front of them—most of whom had grown up sheltered during the economic boom of the sixties and seventies— Michel often longed to be elsewhere. Then he remembered how tense things had been back home after his graduation, how his parents had been disgusted with him choosing to celebrate with his deviant friends rather than his classmates. They couldn't even fathom that he had nothing in common with them apart from their graduating class.

After receiving his baccalaureate, living with his parents had become unbearable, and in the end, being able to get away, albeit to the rigid life that the military provided, was a liberation of sorts. It wasn't all bad. The officers mostly treated the recruits with respect, and there was generally good camaraderie among the young men.

147

A few weeks into his service, Michel noticed a pair of eyes on him in the communal shower. Pascal, a boy from the southwest of the country, had been watching him, trying to keep it a secret, but Michel noticed. He had long ago become accustomed to the eyes of others on him, and he wasn't put off by it. Pascal was not unattractive, and Michel hadn't had any sex since leaving Rennes, so he decided to play the game. He looked back confidently and casually ran his hand over his cock, flicking out the tip of his tongue as he did so.

Pascal seemed utterly surprised by this and looked away, which made Michel laugh as he continued to lather up his body with the soap provided by the army. It wasn't long before Pascal's gaze was back on Michel, as if he couldn't help himself. It was enough of a signal that Michel decided he would act upon it.

Later in the evening, after dinner, the young recruits had an hour of free time, and Michel approached Pascal, guided him away from the others, and went down on the young man in an abandoned shed. No questions asked, no explicit consent sought, he lapped up every last drop the young man expelled in his mouth after just a precious few seconds. Afterward, they talked, and Michel learned that Pascal was deeply closeted.

They began to spend a lot of time with each other, and Michel gradually fell for Pascal. He was a gentle soul, kind and helpful, but also naïve and unaccustomed to the world of gay men. However, even as they regularly had sex, Michel got the impression that Pascal wasn't entirely comfortable being with him, as if he was struggling with something. He couldn't bring himself to let go completely, and it seemed as if he were always holding back somehow.

One night, Michel confronted him about his misgivings. "What's the matter with you? Every time we're together, it feels like pulling teeth. Is it me? Do you not find me attractive? Don't you like me?"

Pascal blushed and looked away. "No, it's not you. I do like you! You're so confident and knowledgeable, so sure about who you are, what you are. I, on the other hand... I'm nothing like you."

"What do you mean? You're gay, are you not? Your cock certainly seems to think so." Michel made to grab Pascal by the crotch, teasing him, but Pascal backed away a couple of steps.

"No, I'm not. Or at least I don't want to be. I can't be gay. Look, Michel, once I'm out of the service, I'll have to go home again, to work on my parents' vineyard. They will expect me to get married, to have children, to make sure the business survives and is being passed on to another generation. My family has been in the wine business for centuries. Our château is one of the most prominent in the entire Bordeaux region. I just *can't be* gay. I wouldn't have the time to."

"Time to do what exactly? Is being gay more time-consuming than not being gay?" Michel found Pascal's line of reasoning illogical. He had no idea what he was talking about.

"You know what I mean."

"No, actually, I don't. Enlighten me, please!" Michel was getting angry, but he had no clue what Pascal meant.

"You know, all those clandestine meetings, driving to places, meeting guys, fucking. I would never have the time for that once I take over the vineyard." He threw his hands in the air. "Heck, I don't even have time to find a girl. I'll be lucky if my mother finds one for me to marry."

"But would you be happy?"

"Why do you care if I would be happy?"

"Oh, come on. You know that I like you. I like you a lot! That's why I care about your happiness. Why I care about you. Even if I didn't, why wouldn't you want to be happy? Isn't the pursuit of happiness an important part of the meaning of life? I mean, if not, why live in the first place?"

"You don't understand, do you? This—" Pascal pointed at Michel and himself "—has no future." And he abruptly walked away, leaving Michel standing with his thoughts and bruised emotions.

MARC

A COUPLE OF WEEKS later, another one of the recruits, a good-looking fellow named Marc, approached Michel after the shower. "Hey, look, I've seen you with Maupin. Think you and I could? I mean, I'm not gay or anything. No offense, I just need to get my rocks off, and you look like you know how to handle dick."

Michel laughed, looking Marc over as he considered his reply. "Do I now?" Then he remembered his nickname from Le Chat Noir, earned after plenty of darkroom sessions. "Michel St. Cul at your service! Why don't you meet me in the shed behind the armory after dinner, and we'll see if and how I can be of assistance to you?"

Marc and Michel met up that night, and they quickly got down to business. It was only later that Michel realized Pascal had overheard their conversation and followed them to the shed, clandestinely watching what transpired. Halfway through the act, Michel heard a noise, turned around, and saw Pascal peeking through the doorway. Still hurt by the way he'd been dismissed by him, Michel simply grinned and shrugged before turning away again, moaning as Marc climaxed inside him.

When they left the shed, Pascal was nowhere to be seen. He didn't say anything either when he saw him at breakfast the next day, simply looking away as Michel approached. Pascal was found in the far corner of the base's enclosure three days later, hanging from a tree.

Michel was devastated. Maybe the young man had felt more for him than he'd let on? Maybe seeing him with Marc had pushed him over the edge? Michel placed the blame for Pascal's suicide squarely on his shoulders, although it seemed no one else had any inkling why the young soldier had ended his life so prematurely.

It wasn't until several weeks later that Marc, who had been privy to the event, told Michel about it. Michel had allowed Marc to fuck him in a bathroom, and afterward, Marc had casually remarked, "I only wish Maupin had been as willing as you."

"What are you talking about?"

"Don't you know? I thought you two were close. He had sex with a bunch of guys the night before he died. Probably didn't enjoy it the way you do."

"No, I didn't know." Michel pulled up his uniform, disgusted. "What do you mean by 'had sex'? I doubt he'd have done so voluntarily. He was hardly the type for a gang bang."

Marc laughed. "You can say that again. He didn't really have an option." He shrugged. "I didn't fuck him, though. I couldn't! I don't like to force myself onto people, especially not a guy. It's just wrong, you know? It's annoying enough when a girl whimpers and begs you to stop, but a guy? I don't think I could keep it up. Although I have to say, it was hot as hell to see him being fucked by five guys. I came just from watching. But nobody thought he'd go and hang himself because of it. We kind of assumed he'd like it. He was a faggot after all. I mean, he could've taken it like a man, you know, *the way you do*? Stupid idiot! To go and kill himself over it. There're all kinds of investigations into this now."

Michel was numbed. His vision blurred, and he pushed himself past Marc out of the toilet stall.

"You're not going to be a snitch, are you?" Marc called after him.

Michel ran outside to get some air. Luckily, Marc didn't follow him.

What was he going to do? Should he report it? Could he even? Because what could he possibly say to his superiors? *I was fucked in the ass by this guy who told me a bunch of them raped Pascal Maupin, which is probably why he hung himself.* No, that would not be a successful strategy. Instead, Michel walled himself in and stayed away from Marc and his friends, even though Marc tried to approach him regularly, wanting to get his rocks off.

After a few weeks had passed, Michel felt horny, and he hooked up with Marc again. At the same time, he felt emotionally drained and didn't enjoy any of it. Michel assured Marc that he wouldn't talk about the events with Pascal. He was no snitch. This seemed to relax Marc, who began to spread the word, and within a few days, his old honorary title, Michel St. Cul, had spread like a wildfire through the barracks. Michel obliged every guy who called upon him, not because he wanted to but because he could take it. Because he wouldn't hang himself for it. Because he felt the need to atone for Pascal's death. Michel also knew that if he said no, they'd likely take it from him anyway, and he already knew that pain intimately. So he silently numbed his bad conscience about having failed Pascal with the only coping mechanism he knew: sex.

Quite a few of the guys in his regiment used him as a cum dump, undoubtedly some of whom had also raped Pascal. Michel tried to justify his actions as a sort of prevention and rescue for yet another potential victim, someone who was not as used to it as he had become over the years. But every time he bent over, he turned off more and more of his emotions, his heart shrinking, withering further with every final thrust inside his rectum.

While he had once thoroughly enjoyed sex, giving and receiving, even just the raw act of it at some point in his life, he couldn't shake the image of Pascal hanging from the old oak, gently dangling in the wind, the sound of the rope grinding against the bark of the supporting branch. Before his inner eye, he saw the young man being forced to do something he hadn't wanted to, being raped, again and again, all the while being watched and laughed at. He could literally hear the guys roar, edging themselves on and on until they had all exhausted themselves into their innocent victim. *If only I had been there!*

Michel sometimes daydreamed that he could've saved Pascal, that he would've taken the young man's place and talked Pascal off the ledge. Alas, he also remembered their fight and Pascal leaving, and how closeted Pascal had been, how depressed, resigned to a life that was never going to be happy. Maybe it had just been that last straw?

Michel would never know, but the image of Pascal hanging from that tree stayed with him for the rest of his service and beyond. The investigation into Pascal's suicide had ended quickly and quietly, and there were no other rumors on base about what might have happened that led Pascal to kill himself. He'd been hauled off secretly and sent south to Bordeaux where a centuries-old wine dynasty ended in tragedy.

Michel St. Jacques had entered the military service to get away from the situation at home with his parents; Michel St. Cul left it twelve months later, disillusioned, an emotional shipwreck, his heart rendered incapable of any real emotion.

He returned to Rennes and his parents to pass what time was left before he began his studies in Paris. He didn't care. To him, life had been reduced to a sequence of days, one lined up neatly after another, and while they were each identifiable by a specific numeral or a name, to Michel they had become indistinguishable. It didn't matter to him if he was fucked by an army buddy on a Monday or slept in a barrack on a Thursday or was given a blow job by a stranger at Le Chat Noir on a Friday or slept above his father's garage on a Wednesday. Same, same, nothing made any difference. Nothing really mattered.

1985

FACING THE PAST

MICHEL HAD RETURNED home from his stint in the military a few days ago, and he'd spent most of the time asleep in his bed. The time of Michel St. Cul reporting for duty was officially over. From now on, the decision of who he would be with, or even if, was his again, as it had been before. He could go to Le Chat Noir and make a choice: walk into the darkroom or just stay put at the bar and talk to Giselle and his friends. He wondered what Marc and the others would have done, had he not volunteered. Would they have left him alone? Or would they have simply taken that which they thought was theirs, the way they had with Pascal? Would they have found another victim instead?

He went downstairs but couldn't find his mother. He made himself some breakfast, showered, and decided to head over to the club. There wasn't much else he could do. He'd called Claude's house, but there had been no answer.

He would have a long summer to pass before university started, and he'd saved up some money from his time in national service, so he didn't need to look for a summer job. He just wanted to unwind and relax after the military. Although, spending that time at the house wasn't holding much of an allure either. It was all very confusing, and Michel began to mindlessly wander the streets.

At some point, he passed a travel agency, stopped, and marveled at the many pictures of cruise ships, beaches, and model airplanes in the window display. *Travel!* He'd always said he would get away. Now was the time! He decided to walk in and inquire about a trip to London.

157

"Bonjour, monsieur!" The woman behind the desk greeted him with a broad smile. "How may I be of assistance?"

"I would like to go to London. How much would that cost me?"

The young woman giggled. "Well, that depends entirely on how you wish to travel, sir. You can fly from here to Paris and then on to London, or you could take a train to Calais and then the ferry to Dover, followed by another train to London. Then there's the question of the hotel. You can spend as much as you like, but I assume you are on a budget?"

They talked about the different options, and Michel quickly realized that flying was out of the question, not unless he wanted to waste all his savings on one short weekend. They booked a second-class ticket on the trains and the ferry, and the travel agent found a cheap hotel for him, right near the Waterloo railway station in London, so that he would easily find it. He hadn't brought along the money, but the travel agent put his reservation on hold, provided he came back later in the day.

Suddenly feeling better and with a spring in his step, he continued straight to Le Chat Noir. Giselle was already there, mopping the floors. The place was lit up brightly, and for a moment, Michel barely recognized himself in the mirror behind the bar.

"Oh my God, Michel. You're back!" Giselle rushed over to hug him. "When did you get in?"

"A few days ago."

"Welcome home. We missed you around here." She couldn't help herself and reached up to tousle his hair, even though he had grown taller than she was years ago. "But just so you know, I don't open until noon."

"I know, no worries, but there's nothing else for me to do right now. Claude isn't home, and my parents and I aren't really on speaking terms. They weren't even home this morning. And I don't have that many other friends."

"That's not the impression I got at your graduation." She gave him a questioning look. "There were a lot of people here to celebrate your achievement."

"Were there, though? I mean, yes, there were plenty of bodies crammed into the bar, but were they here for me or to commiserate the loss of easy access to my ass?"

"Don't be crass, Michel. And even if that were true, don't you bear at least some responsibility? Ask yourself—do you let people into your mind and heart easily, or is your ass, as you put it, the only place you'll allow just about anybody into? And let me remind you that your ass never walked itself into that darkroom."

"I can't believe I'm having this conversation with you!" Michel chuckled and rolled his eyes.

Giselle stretched her back and adjusted her bosom before replying. "You started it. Also, this is my darkroom, as much as I never wanted it. But that's a different story! If I charged ten francs for every guy walking through that doorway grinning like an idiot, I could've retired long ago. Instead, I charge less for beer and wine than any other bar in town, and now I have the government breathing down my neck about this AIDS thing. They want me to provide you guys with condoms, and there's even talk of closing down every darkroom in France. A lot has happened in the year you were gone.

"But enough about me! Tell me, how have you been? How was the national service? Did they treat you all right?"

There was genuine concern written across Giselle's face as Michel told her about Pascal and Marc and his ultimate transformation back into Michel St. Cul—"Since we're apparently having this conversation." By the time he was finished, he was crying.

She hugged him. "Oh, honey! That is just terrible, and you had no one to talk to? You must be devastated. You do realize this behavior is not healthy, especially not in this day and age? Maybe you should take a sabbatical from sex? At least for a while?"

159

Michel took a deep breath, sobbing in Giselle's embrace as he made his confession. "It was horrible. He hung himself, and I could've saved him if only he'd come to me, you know? I thought we had a connection, a real bond. It wasn't love, but it was a kinship of sorts. I really liked him. He was such a gentle soul, so tormented. Why didn't he talk to me?"

Giselle held him close and caressed his head as Michel let go of all the bottled-up grief. "I don't know, dear, I really don't. But if he was as closeted as you say, maybe the shame was too much for him? To be forced into something like that? I can't even begin to imagine what that must have been like. Remember when that happened to you a few years ago? What would you have done without us?"

Michel shrugged and extricated himself from her embrace. He didn't want to talk about this anymore, and he didn't feel like reminiscing or remembering Pascal either when the only image he was capable of conjuring of his lover, if he was even allowed to call him that, was his limp body hanging from that old oak tree.

Finally pulling himself together, he took in Giselle and her mop and asked, "Do you need any help? I mean, there's nothing else for me to do this summer anyway, and things back home haven't improved since I left. They avoid me like the plague. I think I'm better off if I stay away as much as I can."

Giselle leaned heavily on the wooden shaft of the mop, looking at Michel as if sizing him up. "Well," she replied after contemplating something in her mind, "I could use some help, although I can't pay you much, but I would love to take some time off. Come to think of it, I haven't been on a vacation in years. This place has kept me so busy. Even on Mondays, when we're closed, I'm usually here cleaning, doing books, or ordering supplies."

"I could run the place for you," Michel offered. "Just for a few weeks so you could get away. I mean, I've practically lived here since I was fourteen. I know my way around."

"True, but do you know how to order? How to restock? Have you ever tapped up a beer or balanced a cash register, boy?"

"Show me. It can't be that hard for me to learn. And if you prepare, I'll be fine for a couple of weeks. I can always ask Claude to help me. Or Antoine."

Giselle fell silent, and Michel could tell that she was seriously considering the idea. After a few seconds, a big smile spread across her face. "You know what I'll do first? I'll go see my parents. I've been doing a lot of soul searching after our discussion last year, and I think I deserve some closure. Who knows, the past thirty years might just have mollified them a little."

She laughed, but Michel could tell she was frightened by the prospect of seeing them again. Thirty years was a long time. How much would they have aged? Would she recognize them? And would they have changed? Changed to the point of reconsidering a decision made long ago to disown their daughter? Forgiveness she didn't need, as she had done nothing wrong, but the words "I love you" were something every child needed to hear from their parents, frequently. Michel knew firsthand how important that was, or would have been, and he acutely felt the pussing wound left behind when those words had suddenly and entirely disappeared from his parents' vocabulary.

In the coming days, Giselle made plans for a vacation, or rather a journey to seek answers in her native Brest on the Atlantic coast, while instructing Michel in the less visible machinations of running the bar.

Antoine, still trying to rescue stray boys and girls off the streets and introducing them to Giselle and Le Chat Noir, thought it a brilliant idea. He'd recently suffered a mild stroke, and he was proud that he had once "rescued" Michel. Looking at the old man, who had just celebrated his eightieth birthday, sitting at his usual table by the window, Michel knew he could not expect much help from him. He was glad for his moral support, nonetheless. Other regular patrons were also willing to pitch in, as was Claude, whom Michel had come to see as a sort of mayor of gay Rennes. He knew everybody and everything, and if he put his weight behind something, things tended to happen.

On the last Monday in July, Michel and Claude drove Giselle to the station where she'd take a train to Brest. She'd booked a hotel in the city, not too far from where she had grown up. She'd only reserved for a night, not knowing if she'd stay or move on elsewhere. It all depended on what happened with her parents.

"Who knows, if it all goes south, I'll be back here before the end of the week," she joked, but her voice was anything but upbeat. Michel acutely felt her insecurity and the courage it took to undertake this journey.

"Listen, if they don't want you, the loss is all theirs," Claude remarked forcefully. "And rather than coming back here and moping, why don't you go south? Head to the Côte d'Azur, or why not check out La Rochelle or Nantes? Bordeaux? Rent a car, go and get to know this beautiful country of ours. You most certainly deserve a vacation, and I don't want to see you until the end of the month, d'accord?" He crossed the short distance to her as she stood on the platform and hugged her. "Now go, ex-wife, and have the time of your life. Send us postcards! I love you!"

Michel hugged her as well and helped her carry the luggage aboard the train, noticing Claude wipe a tear from the corner of his eye. The coot really did have feelings for Giselle.

After dropping her off, they returned to Le Chat Noir. It was weird opening the front door with a key and walking into this familiar place, empty, darkened. No Giselle.

"It feels strange without her."

"Yeah, I know what you mean." Claude shook his head. "I've never actually been here without her. We first walked through these doors twenty-four years ago. This place was a mess, and it looked very different. My dad had just passed away, I was a young pup, and Giselle and I had been married, quote, unquote, for four years. After his death, we wanted to get a divorce and live our true lives This was my gift to her, albeit with a slightly egotistical twist, I'll admit."

"The darkroom?" Michel chuckled. "She's told me all about that."

A POSTCARD

*A*FTER A WEEK, a postcard arrived at Le Chat Noir. Michel was curious to read what Giselle had to say. The fact that the card had come from Brest seemed a good omen. He turned it over and read:

Hello boys! Greetings from Brest. All is well here.
I will tell you more when I'm back. I'm staying with
my parents, playing catch-up. Be good, stay healthy.

Bisous, Giselle

Michel smiled. This was good news indeed. It seemed as if time could indeed heal all wounds. Hopefully, it was something he could look forward to himself at some point in his future. Maybe his parents would finally see reason, or at least acknowledge that they still loved him, after he'd been off to Paris for a few years. If not, he did not doubt that he would make it, have a career and a good life in the best city on earth, the City of Lights, gay Paris.

He quite enjoyed working at Le Chat Noir, even though it turned out to be very hard work. He had to get up early to be on site when the various trucks arrived from suppliers, delivering beer, sodas, liquors, or wine. He had to clean the bar, and especially the darkroom, which he hated. Going in there, lights on, was not a pleasant experience, and he suddenly felt disgusted by the things going on in there, things he had been a part of quite willingly just a year ago. He found it difficult to sweep the floors clean of all the condoms people had begun using, most of them

163

filled, the wrappers and lube packets strewn everywhere as men, driven only by carnal lust, quickly mounted the thin rubbers to get off inside whoever stood in front of them, legs spread, hairy asses wiggling in eager anticipation.

Is this what love is for gay men? Is this all I can expect from life? Is there nothing else? The only thing in my future? Was Pascal right? Is it all just a big waste of time and energy?

He contemplated the incident the year before when he'd woken up with Claude after his birthday party. That weird sensation of waking up next to someone he cared about, that almost domestic feeling, seeing Claude in a morning robe, coffee and paper in hand. Was this not to be for him? Would he never have what his parents and countless other straight couples took for granted?

At the same time, the thought seemed so utterly ridiculous. *Play house. Two men. Hah!* He shook his head and focused his attention on cleaning up the bar and getting it ready for opening hour and another long day. Today was a Friday, and he'd be up and serving customers until the wee hours of Saturday, then walk home in the middle of the night, long after any bus had stopped running, and sneak quietly into the house to avoid waking his parents, sleep for a few hours, only to return here to start all over again for the equally busy Saturday shift.

How does Giselle do it? Yes, she lived above the bar in a nice little apartment, and maybe he should've asked her if he could crash there on weekends, but still. Weekends meant long days, excruciatingly long ones. *Probably why she closes the place on Mondays.*

Back at the St. Jacques' residence, things were still as uncomfortable as they had been after his graduation. Since he worked so late every day except Monday, he barely saw his parents. On Mondays, Michel would rather be out for a jog or meet with Claude than sit at home in his room. He'd already packed up most of his belongings and had those ready to be shipped to Paris. There was no interaction with his parents except a fleeting greeting if they happened to cross paths in a hallway or the kitchen, and given his work, he never ate at home anymore, except for breakfast. By then, his father had already left, and his mother also seemed to often find reasons to be elsewhere in or out of the house.

One day, he came home to a note from the parish priest, asking him for a conversation, and unlike that time when he had been eleven years old, he was determined not to fall for that trick again. Ever! While the priest, in his note, talked about the risk of eternal damnation and being determined to save his soul, Michel couldn't shake the image of Monseigneur Serrault fondling him. Of course, he now understood that this was not how things were supposed to happen and that the monseigneur had never cared about him, especially considering how quickly he had been discarded once he showed the first signs of puberty. Still, after all these years, he felt deeply conflicted. While it had opened up a world of sex and pleasure to him, and even though the priest had not used any physical force to get his way, the psychological manipulation, the thinly veiled threats, the secrecy, and the so-called training had all been subterfuge to puppeteer a young, innocent mind into submission. The combination of enjoyment and the fear of its consequences were still fighting their battle for domination inside him.

No, he was done with God, the Church, and their clerics! At the same time, he realized the Church was far from done with young boys and girls, or even him for that matter. The Church was the real demon, and it sickened him because he was utterly powerless to do anything about it. Who would ever believe the word of a faggot over that of a priest? But the irony of the Church's insistence on saving the souls of the young while it happily kept corrupting the same wasn't lost on him.

LONDON

MICHEL HAD ALWAYS wanted to visit London, ever since he had first seen images of the soldiers in their red uniforms guarding Buckingham Palace. He was fascinated by the bearskin caps hiding the young soldiers' handsome, chiseled faces. As he grew older, Michel realized that he was equal parts intrigued by the uniforms as he was by the young men they hid inside.

But London, and England by extension, held a much wider appeal to him. It symbolized an elusive freedom, a hip culture with modern music, a language that largely escaped him yet fascinated him, nonetheless. Be it the Beatles or the Rolling Stones, the Sex Pistols, David Bowie or Elton John, Michel listened to them all, and they were a welcome distraction to having to listen to his mother sing along to her favorites Johnny Hallyday or Charles Aznavour. Not that there was anything wrong with French music. For Michel, it wasn't about either-or, but rather both-and. He quite enjoyed listening to the likes of Joe Dassin, Sylvie Vartan, or Serge Gainsbourg, but he spoke their language and there was little mystery to their lyrics. While he had English lessons in school, it had never been his forte, and the French were immensely proud of their language, so the emphasis on learning other, "lesser" languages was symbolic rather than earnest.

Then there was the allure of the boys. Michel had always had an affinity for the rusty, strawberry-blond hair, and the palish-freckled complexion of so many of the English, and he was quite sure he'd meet more than one of them in London. He had also learned about some of the big gay clubs and couldn't wait to see what they had in store. Club Heaven sure sounded like it had been named appropriately.

Michel only had a couple of days to spend in London. He had arrived the day before, having booked a bed in a cheap hotel south of the River Thames in a rough neighborhood right by Waterloo station. The only window overlooked several railway tracks, and it was quite noisy at all times of the day, but the bed was clean, and that was all he cared about. He didn't intend to spend a lot of time in his room.

He'd explored Soho, Greenwich, and the Tower and spent the night dancing away to the latest tunes at Club Heaven. This morning, he'd finally been to Buckingham Palace to admire the Queen's Guard. He was a bit disappointed to see that they were tucked away behind a tall iron fence at a distance where he could barely make out their facial features.

From the royal palace, he walked along the Mall and through St. James's Park to Trafalgar Square and on to Westminster to see the famous Houses of Parliament, where he was now relaxing on the lawn behind this famous bastion of modern democracy. He was not alone, and looking around, he could make out people from all over the world who had come to admire Big Ben and Westminster Abbey. Hordes of English, Americans, Germans, Spaniards, Italians, and, of course, a lot of French tourists were all around him, admiring the sights, taking pictures, smiling, enjoying their time in this historic place.

He overheard a bald, rather large man with a broad American accent explain to his wife and two young daughters that this was where Princess Diana had married her Prince Charming, pointing toward Westminster Abbey. Michel had to put a hand over his mouth not to laugh out loud at the man's ignorance, even though it was a forgivable offense. It had been a dream wedding, and he remembered watching it with his parents on TV. She had been so beautiful that day, Diana, and she still was immensely popular in France.

Secretly, he'd hoped he might catch a glimpse of her, or of any other member of the royal family, but so far, he'd not had any luck. He had personally always fancied the youngest of the princes, Edward, born the same year as Michel. Surrounded by gay rumors as Edward was, Michel once had this crazy dream of meeting the prince and riding off into the sunset with him. He shook his head as he contemplated how preposterous the idea was to him now.

He rested his head in the palms of his folded hands, trying to relax. He'd been walking a lot and he was tired. A group of young people walked past him, almost tripping over his feet and momentarily blocking the sun. That alone had him look up at them, but it was the language they spoke that made him pay extra attention. He had never heard it before. It sounded strange, song-like, with ups and downs, like a rollercoaster. He couldn't put his finger on it, yet as he followed them with his eyes as they walked away, his gaze fell on a young man sitting to his right. He must've been around his age, several inches taller, and he had the most beautiful strawberry-blond hair, long curls framing his freckled cheek. Michel hadn't seen him from the front yet, but from the side, he looked very handsome and quite exotic. There were, of course, blonds and redheads in France, but he'd never seen anyone this tall.

He couldn't take his eyes off the guy, and after a while, the young man turned toward him, probably having felt Michel staring. They began to chat and instantly hit it off. The young man was from Norway, and he was in London for a couple of days to visit, just like Michel. His name was Haakon, which was a funny name, something he'd never heard before. "Oo-khón" was the closest Michel could approximate with his French accent. Apparently, he had been named after a former king of Norway, a hero of the Norwegian resistance against Nazi Germany.

It reminded Michel of his own family's history. Just like de Gaulle, Haakon VII had spent most of the war in exile, right here in London. What a coincidence!

Michel's gaydar had gone off straight away, but Haakon didn't seem to catch on, yet he gladly accepted the invitation to tag along to his hotel. Haakon's hotel room may have been closer, but he had a roommate, and given Michel's plans, he didn't need anyone interrupting them. They chatted the entire time on their way to Michel's hotel south of the Thames. Once in the room, he opted for a direct approach, given that none of the other, more subtle tactics had worked, kissing Haakon the second they walked through the door, eliciting a surprised response from him. But Haakon had caught himself quickly and instantly responded in kind. Their clothes flew all around them.

After their lovemaking, they lay in bed, Michel resting his head on Haakon's chest, listening to the steady beat of his heart accompanied by the rumble of the trains coming and going behind the hotel. "You know, very soon, we'll be able to take a train from Paris to London, rather than the ferry I'll take tonight. Our president, Monsieur Mitterrand, persuaded Mrs. Thatcher to build the Channel Tunnel. England will finally be connected directly to Europe." Michel was excited about the prospect. Haakon didn't say much but simply yawned and stretched out on the bed.

"You don't think this is a good idea?"

"I do. It's just not anything that will ever be of any use to me. I live in Norway. We'll always have to fly to England or take a ferry."

"I love to travel. And I love this city. London is so vibrant, so full of life. It is very different from Rennes. Do you like to travel? I wish I could see the world, you know? Backpack around the world."

"I do, too. I've been dreaming of seeing the world ever since I was a little boy. And I envy you. Soon you'll be in Paris, right?

Isn't Paris the most romantic city in the world?" Haakon sounded like he was parroting something he'd read.

"Yes, of course it is. It's the best city in the world!" Michel agreed. "I'm looking forward to living there, studying at the Sorbonne, enjoying life in Paris. Have you ever been?"

"No. This is my first real trip abroad. My parents are farmers. We've never had the time to travel far, as the animals always needed us. I didn't even visit Oslo until I was seventeen."

"Oh." Michel was surprised. He'd always had the impression that Scandinavians traveled a lot, like their Viking ancestors. Alas, this one had not.

"But yes," Haakon said, "I would very much want to travel. To explore the world, to see every last corner of Earth before I die."

"Well, when you come to Paris, you'll have a bed for sure. And you must come. You just have to visit me, d'accord? Are you hungry?"

Haakon nodded, and the two young men got dressed and headed out to a nearby pub for some traditional fish and chips— "The best in England," Michel had heard. They talked some more, and time seemed to fly by before it was time for Michel to return to his hotel and pack his bag. While he'd paid for two nights, his train was the last one to leave for Dover, where he'd catch the night ferry to Calais and then change onto a train to Rennes. Back home, he would more or less just pick up his belongings and move to Paris for his impending studies at the Sorbonne and hopefully a life very different from the one he'd lived around his parents. More men, more liberty!

They exchanged phone numbers and addresses, and Michel made sure to remind Haakon to be careful not to call him while he was still in Rennes. "I don't have a phone number in Paris yet, but please don't call my folks. They don't approve of me being gay, and I don't want to cause a stir needlessly. Plus they'd probably not be very kind to you." Just the thought of his parents made him sad. The past couple of years had felt like he lived in a gulag.

"D'accord? I'll write to you or call you once I have a phone in Paris. And you really must come and visit me. I insist!" He sealed his demand with a kiss, having to get up on his toes to reach Haakon's lips.

Haakon nodded and folded the piece of paper and put it away like a prized possession, or so it seemed to Michel. There was something about Haakon that intrigued him. His innocence and naivety? He wasn't sure, but it was endearing. He was so very different from all the other guys Michel had met and been with, maybe with the exception of Pascal, without any sense of duplicity. Most of the men he'd encountered had been older, some much older, but they'd also been so worldly, so confident of who they were and what they wanted of life.

Haakon wasn't like that. There was no subterfuge; there was no pretense. Whatever Haakon said, the way he looked, it was genuine. Haakon reminded him a little bit of Pascal, and for a moment the memories of his time with the latter in the military took hold again. But unlike Pascal, Haakon was not ashamed of who he was. He simply was a young man who loved other men. Michel didn't get the impression that Haakon questioned who he was, or why. He was himself, and that made him all the more attractive. Michel could've wrapped himself in Haakon like a warm blanket and never let him go. Alas, it was he who had to go, leaving Haakon behind in London to maybe, likely, never see him again. That's how one-night stands usually worked out.

Haakon accompanied Michel to the station, as far as he was allowed to without actually holding a ticket. They hugged but dared not kiss in public. Michel passed through the gates to the platform and got on board his train without letting Haakon out of his sight. He quickly found a seat, put his backpack away, and opened the window to see if Haakon was still there. He was, and Michel waved at him. Haakon waved back, and he remained there as the train pulled out of the station, heading south toward the coast of Dover. Michel watched as Haakon got smaller and smaller until the train turned a corner and he lost sight of him.

"Au revoir, a plus…" he said to no one in particular. He closed the window and sat down. Would he ever see him again? He hoped so, and for the first time in his life, Michel felt butterflies in his stomach.

MADAME CHARPENTIER

ICHEL, ARE YOU in here?" His mother had opened the door to his room and was peeking in.

"Oui, maman. I'm here, packing." It was the first thing he'd said to her in days. Since he returned from his military service, he had slept in his room above the garage but hadn't spent much time in the rest of the house. His father always left before he woke up, and his mom disappeared to morning Mass, midday Mass, or whatever Mass, was out in the garden or grocery shopping, avoiding him in any way she could find.

For her to show up like this was quite unexpected. Then again, he was about to leave the house for good in just a couple of days, and if it were up to him, he would never return. Maybe she felt that, too?

"Is there anything I can do to help you?" There seemed to be genuine care in her voice, and it caught Michel by surprise. He stopped what he was doing and looked up at her, really looking at her. Another thing he hadn't done in ages.

"Can we talk?" She approached him, putting her hand on his arm as if to make sure he wouldn't run away.

"Sure..." He didn't finish the sentence, wondering what she could possibly want to say to him, all of a sudden, after four years of avoiding him. She'd barely looked him in the eyes, and now she stood there, this petite woman, looking up at her taller son, seeking eye contact, he saw how much she had aged. Michel hadn't previously noticed the crow's feet around her eyes, the gray streaks in her hair, the sadness. His mother truly did look old, and tired.

She gestured for him to sit on his bed while she pulled up the chair from his desk, where Michel had spent countless hours doing homework in the years leading up to his baccalaureate. Finally, he was about to reap the fruit of that hard labor, to start a new life, far away from Rennes, the Church and its priests, his parents, the armed forces, and even Le Chat Noir. A fresh start. *My life is finally beginning.*

"Are you looking forward to Paris?" Her question interrupted his daydreaming.

"Yes, maman, I am."

"I'll miss you, son. These past years have been difficult, for all of us."

How to respond?

"And I want you to know that I love you, no matter what. I get that you are looking forward to being rid of us, and I understand that we have not been as supportive of your lifestyle as you would have wanted us to be."

Michel could see how difficult it was for her to talk about this, to even find the appropriate words, and he noticed the first tears appear in the corners of her eyes.

"I want to—no. I *need* to apologize to you, son."

Oh? He didn't want to interrupt her even though his body ached to reach out and hug her.

"I was talking to Madame Charpentier yesterday. You don't know her, of course, as you haven't been to Holy Mass for some time."

There it is—the familiar condemnation I recognize so well.

"She and her husband recently moved into the parish from the south, and we happened to sit next to each other. We began to talk after Mass, and it turns out that she and her husband have a son, too. He's a few years older than you."

Michel was curious as to where this was going but didn't say anything.

"Their story is similar to ours. They are a good Catholic family, making sure their children went to Sunday school, they always attended Mass, and they felt they were doing everything right. So when their son, Philippe, came out to them, they were devastated, of course."

Of course.

She took a deep sigh before continuing. "Anyway, Philippe was studying in Marseille where they lived at the time, and last year, he was accosted by a gang of people after visiting one of those clubs. Apparently, things got out of hand, and he got hurt very badly and eventually died from his injuries. Madame Charpentier told me that it broke her heart having to see him at the morgue, her baby boy, bruised and broken by the fists and boots of people who hated him, despite not even knowing him, just for what he was."

Who, maman, not what!

"You have no idea the things the poor woman and her husband had to go through. They got little to no consolation from their local congregation. They felt abandoned in their grief and finally decided to move away and start anew up north, which is why they moved here."

Michel was not surprised. *Been there, done that*, he thought. He had never told his parents about his own experiences with homophobia, knowing they wouldn't believe him, or perhaps couldn't. Would he be able to tell his mother now? Should he?

She wasn't done yet. "I'm just worried, my love. Are you sure you have to move all the way to Paris?"

So this is what she wants? Michel's hopes were dashed again. "Yes, maman! I do. You know as well as I do that no university here is as prestigious as the Sorbonne, and if me being beaten to death is your biggest fear, well, that risk is as big here as it is anywhere else, if not bigger given how narrow-minded people are around here." He was quickly working himself into a rage, "Just look in a mirror, will you? As you just said, you and papa haven't exactly been supportive of me. You two are exactly like madame Charpentier's congregation." Seeing his mother's face twitch at every word he said, he knew they had found their intended mark.

"Please understand, Michel. This isn't easy for us. We have been raised a certain way. We believe that certain values are non-negotiable. We can't just—"

Michel interrupted her. "Look, I'm not interested in a discussion about theology with my mother. Why do you think God made me gay if it wasn't his intention for me to be this way? Don't you think he has a plan, huh?" His voice was carrying, and his mother recoiled at the anger, the conviction behind it.

"But how can you be so sure you were born this way? How can you be so arrogant as to presume to know what plan God has for you? How can you be so sure this isn't a test put before you? To test your faith in the Almighty? Maybe you just haven't met the right girl yet? Maybe this is all just a phase? Or maybe you suffer from a mental illness? Maybe you could see a doctor? Monsieur l'abbé knows someone." She was pleading, and it also explained the letter he'd recently received. They'd never had this conversation before, but he knew it wouldn't lead anywhere.

"So you're telling me that if the right girl had come along, you'd turned out to be a lesbian?"

The slap across his face came unexpectedly and it hurt. His mother had never laid hands on him before. She'd always left that aspect of raising him to her husband. She said nothing else but got up and left his room. Michel resumed his packing, more resolved than ever to get out of Rennes. He thought of poor Philippe Charpentier and the agony of his death at the hands of those thugs, and he counted his lucky stars that he had survived his encounter with gay-bashing.

At least the Charpentiers had to face the harsh truth of their son having been murdered by the hatred and the poisonous words spread from the pulpit, sentiments they probably still shared. Why had they moved here to Rennes? Obviously, they still talked about their son, which he thought was brave. He decided to reach out to them, to learn more. It wasn't too difficult to find them on the Minitel, and he decided to walk over to their house.

PHILIPPE

THE NEXT DAY, after he was done packing, Michel took a stroll over to the Charpentier house and rang the doorbell. After a few moments, a woman, elegantly dressed in the black of a mother in mourning, opened the door. "Yes? How can I help you?"

"Madame Charpentier? I'm Michel St. Jacques. My mother told me you had met in church recently?"

"St. Jacques?" Michel could tell she was trying to connect the dots. Finally, after a few seconds, she seemed to remember. "Emmanuelle? Is that your mother? Is everything okay?"

"Yes, my mother is fine. Would you mind if I came in for a bit?"

She took a step to the side and gestured. "Not at all, please, come on in. I was just reading a magazine. I'm home alone. My husband is at work. Your mother was most kind to me the other day, welcoming me to the parish."

She showed Michel to their living room, where they sat at either end of the couch but facing each other. "Now, young man, how may I help you?"

"I know it's none of my business, but I was wondering if you might tell me about Philippe?"

The mention of his name visibly shook Madame Charpentier. Her shoulders slumped, and she dropped her head for a few seconds as if to gather strength for what was to come. When she looked up again, her eyes sought out Michel's, and she studied him intently. "You're like my son, aren't you? You're gay, too?"

"Oui, madame."

177

"Your mother didn't say. I take it they're not exactly supporting you, am I right?"

"No, madame, they find it rather difficult. I had a fight with my mother the other day after she told me about Philippe. My sincere condolences on the loss of your son."

"Thank you, young man. I appreciate it. But why were you fighting?"

"She tried to convince me to stay here in Rennes. She was afraid I might be beaten while in Paris. That led to a conversation about me not really being gay, and it all ended with a slap across my face."

"I see. Well, I'm sorry about that. And it pains me that your mother's heart wasn't in a place to understand the point I was making when we talked to each other. I still believe in God, and I believe he put Philippe in our path for *us* to learn a lesson, not for him to deny who he was. My son lived his true life, and I draw strength from the fact that he is back with the Lord in heaven. It was us, his parents, who did not pass the test. Had we supported him more, who knows, maybe this might all have never happened? But the Lord saw it fit to take our son from us to make a finer point."

She plucked a handkerchief from her dress and dabbed away a few stray tears that had broken through the dam of her eyelids, gently rolling down her cheeks. "You would've liked Philippe. He was such a strong person, undeterred by the many hurdles we put in his path, and I remember the smile on his face when he left our house that day, to go out with his friends. We knew, of course, where he was going, and we didn't approve of it, but he was a grown man and there was nothing we could do to stop him."

Michel sat quietly, listening to madame Charpentier and her sad story. He was impressed that she had managed to reconcile her faith with the loss of her son.

"After Philippe died, we met some of his friends, including a very nice young man he had been dating at the time. Philippe had never told us about him, and I can't blame him. It did take for him to be ripped from our lives before we realized our mistake. We never really knew our son. For a parent, that is the harshest of realizations.

"Alexandre and the group of friends that Philippe had been with that night helped us through the most difficult time of our lives. We met them at the funeral, actually, and while the priest hadn't said a word about how or why Philippe died, it was very obvious to everyone who was there. Rumors spread quickly, even in a big city like Marseille, and all our friends had abandoned us by the time of his funeral. It was a lonely service, just our family, but in the back of the church sat this group of young people, none of whom we had invited. They showed up for their friend, to honor him, and we could see how devastated they were. They were mourning in earnest.

"At the end of the service, Alexandre walked up to my husband and me, and he offered his condolences. It was the strangest of moments." Tears flowed freely down her cheeks now, as she remembered the day. "I was looking into the eyes of that young man, and I could see his pain. I could feel the hurt, his immense loss. I'm not sure if it makes any sense to you, but my husband and I had clung to doctrine for so long that we were unable to let go. We weren't grieving the loss of our son. We were ashamed of having to bury a gay man. We were ashamed of having failed as parents. The only thing we were grieving was our loss of face in the eyes of society, the condemnation of our friends, and we were angry at Philippe for letting us down.

"Then suddenly, we were looking into those eyes, and we saw someone who was genuinely devastated for having lost our boy, someone who had loved him with all his heart, unconditionally. Alexandre had loved Philippe, and he stood there, facing us, his soul bared, to offer us his condolences. I have never felt more ashamed in my life, and it was at that very moment that I felt that the good Lord had finally helped me understand. You should meet Alexandre. He's such an amazing human being. We are very close to this very day. He moved back to Algiers a few months ago after finishing his engineering degree. There was just too much that reminded him of Philippe in Marseille. I miss him dearly. In my heart, he's just like a son to me. I wish you could meet him."

"I am so sorry you had that experience, madame."

"So am I, but most of all, I'm sorry that we didn't get to have a better relationship with our son. He might still have been killed by those thugs, but at least he would have died knowing—" she put her hand on her heart, patting her chest "—you know, really understanding, feeling, just how much he was loved. That regret is ours to bear, and I wish it on nobody else, ever."

"I'm sure he knew you loved him."

"You're kind to say so, but it is one thing to assume and another one to know, to *feel it*. If you understand the distinction? From what Alexandre told us, Philippe didn't really know. He felt abandoned by us, his parents. And I'm not surprised he felt that way. Hindsight is a great teacher, albeit too late for us. But enough about me and my life! Tell me, how are things for you? Is there anything I can do to help? I don't know your mother very well, I've only just met her, and she seems very pious."

"Yes, that she is." Michel had to laugh at the term. His mother had always been that way. It was the best word to describe her, the first thing that came to mind when he thought of her.

"You see, young man, the sort of faith your mother grew up with is a two-edged sword. It provides an easy, convenient way to live your life as long as everything goes smoothly. There are rituals to deal with that which is commonly accepted in our society—birth, marriage, children, death. The Church will walk by your side as long as you stick to orthodoxy. But deviate from that and you're on your own. That is the flip side. Your mother will find no support from the Catholic Church. Therefore, she feels helpless and powerless, as she is not in control of things, and there is nothing she can do to change your ways. There is no ritual to help her, and no number of Hail Marys will make it better. I recall that clergy usually places the blame for everything that's wrong with our children at their mother's feet. How is your father dealing with it?"

Michel shrugged. "He's like most fathers I know. Absent. He never really played a part in my upbringing. He's not as religious as my mom. To him, it's more about sending the right signals to those he cares about. To his boss, his colleagues, his friends. I honestly don't know if he actually believes in God or not. I've never talked to him about these things. After I came out, he withdrew even more. He's barely home anymore. He works longer hours and spends his free time with his friends."

"Don't judge your parents too harshly. I know they love you. We loved our Philippe. Which isn't to say that I don't understand your point. It's just that you had no choice but to deal with it, while your parents were able to ignore it, push it out of their thoughts. Believe me, there will come a day when they will have to face their demons. I just hope you'll be around to witness it, to help them through it. But enough of these sad sentiments! Can I get you a cup of coffee? Or tea perhaps?"

"A cup of coffee would be great, thank you, madame."

"Oh, please, call me Louise." She got up and gestured for him to follow her. "What's next for you? You said you were going to Paris? To study?"

Michel trailed her as she walked into the kitchen to get some coffee ready. "Yes. My train leaves tomorrow."

"Where will you study?"

"I've gotten into the Sorbonne."

She looked impressed. "Congratulations! And are you moving there alone or is there someone special in your life?"

"I'm moving on my own." Triggered by her question, Michel thought about Haakon, the image of the young Norwegian clearly before his eyes, and the butterflies came back. Was he someone special in his life? Michel wondered if maybe he should tell Louise about him. Would his parents find out? Would she tell them? Could he trust her? He barely knew her.

181

"Something on your mind? I apologize if my question was cutting too close to home?"

"No, no, it's not that. There *is* someone, yes, but I'm not sure he qualifies as...special. I barely know him."

"Oh? That sounds like an interesting story." Louise smiled and handed Michel a cup of coffee. "Milk? Sugar?"

"No, thanks, I'll take it black." He shrugged. "I'm not sure if interesting is the right word. I was in London recently, just for a couple of days, and I met a Norwegian guy. We only got to spend one afternoon together, so it would be presumptuous to compare us to what Philippe and Alexandre shared."

"How can you be so sure? Only you know what you feel in your heart for this young man."

"That's the problem, though, isn't it? I don't know what I feel. I only know that I can't get him out of my mind."

"Will you see him again?"

"I would very much like that, but Oslo is so far away, and we are both poor students with limited means. I only have his address, but I did promise I'd write to him. So we'll see."

"So you should! Allow me to give you just one piece of advice if you will have it. Love, for all of us, regardless of what shape it appears before us, is like a rare and precious sapling. Once you find one, hold on to it, cherish it, and watch it grow into a marvelous tree. Care for it, and it will last a lifetime—and beyond if so you believe. Neglect it, and you will never know if or when another chance will be given, so don't let any opportunity go to waste. Give it your all, every time. Invest your heart and soul fully. That is the only advice I can ever provide anyone with ever again. I know that I wasn't the mother I should have been to my son, and I have learned my lesson the hardest way possible— having to stand next to an open grave and watch as my Philippe was lowered into it. It's a cliché, but it is not something any parent should ever have to go through."

"I will take your advice, I promise. Thank you." Michel saw that Louise had begun to cry again. He couldn't fully understand how she felt, as he had no children of his own. What did it feel like for a parent to bury their child?

"Was Philippe your only child?"

"No, we have a daughter, Danielle. She lives in Arles with her husband and kids. Being able to visit our babies now and then does help alleviate the pain, at least a little."

"I'm glad to hear that."

"Now, tell me, is there anything I can do to help? Do you want me to talk to your mother?"

Michel had to think about that. He wasn't sure his mother was amenable. "I think not. I mean, I can't forbid you to, I just don't think she'll be able to hear what you have to say. She certainly didn't understand what you told her after Mass last week."

"I shall be polite then. I quite understand. But please, young man, when you come back from Paris to visit, know you are always welcome here. I wouldn't mind if we stayed in touch, to see how things work out with your Norwegian young man."

"I'd like that, Louise. I'm just not sure when I'll next be back. Right now, all I can think of is getting out of this town."

Louise nodded. She understood.

ADIEU, MAMAN!

THE NEXT MORNING, Michel was ready to leave. He had given a lot of thought to the words Louise had spoken. He felt the greatest respect for her, the immense loss she and her husband had suffered, and the harsh lesson she felt they had learned from losing their son. He wondered how his parents would handle the same. Would they, too, see the light after it was too late? Would they, too, only then come to understand, really see him for who he had been? He pushed those morbid thoughts from his mind. Besides, there would never be an Alexandre at his funeral service. *But would there be a Haakon?*

Claude had promised to pick Michel up, and a small part of him looked forward to that because Giselle would also come, and they would take him to the station together. He had already taken his leave from his father, who had gone to work, bright and early, as always. The older St. Jacques had simply shaken his son's hand, wishing him a pleasant journey, good luck in Paris, and extracted from him a promise that he'd study hard. Then he had left without looking back.

Things had been weird between Michel and his mother after their recent conversation, even more so than before. After returning from Louise, Michel had wondered if maybe he should give it another go, but when he'd walked into the kitchen, he'd found a note from his mother to say she was at the rectory for some meeting with the priest. Michel interpreted that as a sign to leave things be.

184

At ten in the morning, the doorbell rang, and Michel opened it. His mother was in the back of the house, in the kitchen, preparing for lunch or slow-cooking a roast for dinner.

"Good morning, sunshine!" Claude beamed, as always, a cigarette hanging from the corner of his mouth, and, as always, Michel couldn't look away from those teeth, but for the first time, he told him so.

"You really need to have those teeth looked at."

Claude simply laughed and waved his arm to dismiss the idea as preposterous.

"Come on, you don't want to miss your train." He grabbed one of the heavy suitcases that stood in the hallway.

"Good morning, dear!" Giselle called from outside the door. "It feels odd being back here again. I will never forget my previous visit." She smiled sadly, clearly thinking back to the time she brought him home after he was attacked. "This occasion is so much more pleasant. Are you ready for your grand adventure? We're going to miss you so much." She began to cry.

Michel's mother appeared in the hallway. "Won't you introduce me to your friends?" she said, squeezing past Michel, noticing Giselle first. "Bonjour, madame. I'm Michel's mother, and you are?"

Giselle quickly regained her composure and dried off her tears. "Oh, we've met, madame St. Jacques, although it was only once and very briefly, about five years ago. Don't you remember? The night Michel was raped? I was the one who brought him home that night." Giselle stretched out her hand for a short handshake.

Michel's mother's expression was priceless. The blood completely drained from her face as she muttered, "Enchanté." She didn't, however, accept the handshake, and her arms seemed to hang lifelessly from her shoulders. Michel got the distinct impression it would be days before she fully processed what she had heard. It certainly added a new dimension to recent events and everything Louise had told her.

When Claude returned from the car and greeted her with, "Bonjour madame, how are you today?" as if it were the most natural thing in the world, Michel thought his mother might faint again.

To be a fly on the wall when the penny drops.

She said nothing, just stood there in the doorway to her house, staring at her landlord who had come to pick up her son to take him to the station. She didn't understand the world at all. It must have felt like she had woken up in a parallel universe where everything up was down, and everything in was out, a world where nothing she'd ever learned made sense anymore.

"Come on, kiddo. The trains don't wait for the likes of you here in France." Claude chuckled, grabbing the other suitcase and casually strolling back to his car, whistling a tune. "Have a great day, madame St. Jacques."

Michel pushed past his mother, who still stood immobilized, grabbed her arm for a squeeze, and wisely chose his words to say farewell. "Adieu, maman!" He gave her a quick peck on the cheek. Then he crossed the distance to the car in a few long strides and got into the back seat. Giselle and Claude also got into the car, and they took off for the station. Michel turned around one last time to look at his mother. She was no longer there; the front door had already been closed.

A TRAIN TO PARIS

THE TRAINS IN France were one of those things that every French person could be proud of. Michel had watched the opening of the first high-speed train line, the orange TGV from Paris to Lyon on TV, and it made his heart swell with pride. Yet from Rennes to Paris, there was no such thing—yet. His was just a regular train that would take him from the station in Rennes to Paris Montparnasse, from where he would have to take the subway to the Latin quarter and his small studio apartment. Of course, he hadn't told his parents how he'd managed to secure an apartment before even moving to the city.

Michel stood on the platform waiting for the train doors to open. He was eager to finally get underway. There were many feelings and emotions rushing through his body and mind. He'd taken his leave from Claude and Giselle at the main entrance. The last thing he wanted was for her to break down in tears when the train pulled out of the station. He knew he would. Claude and Giselle were sort of his adoptive parents, his chosen family, and leaving them behind was hard. So they had decided it was easier to say *au revoir* outside. Claude, practical as ever, didn't mind. It saved him the trouble of finding a parking space. They hugged, and Claude managed to slip a few large banknotes into Michel's jacket. "Just to get you started, kiddo. And if you ever need help with anything, you call, all right?"

For Michel, Paris had always been his holy grail. He knew that he'd find freedom there, that this was the only way to extricate himself from the continued pressure from his parents, to be able to live his life, his truth. The Sorbonne provided the only ticket out that would be acceptable to them, a university so prestigious that his parents' vanity vanquished any objections they may have had. Michel had put in the hard work and had finally reached his goal. Claude had been amazing. Not only did he encourage him to leave Rennes, despite losing his best friend, but he also helped Michel find an apartment in Paris, smack downtown, very close to the university. The man had connections everywhere and somehow had found a small rooftop studio with a very manageable rent. Michel didn't ask what strings Claude had pulled, or how.

Lost in his thoughts, for a while he didn't notice the young woman who had appeared next to him on the platform. Her auburn hair, cut very short, framed a pretty face with a scattering of freckles. She wore a large, straw hat, a thin, elegant scarf around her neck, a matching summer dress, and big black sunglasses. She was carrying two heavy suitcases, and when the conductor opened the train doors, she asked Michel for help, which was when he noticed her.

"Sure!" He smiled. "Why don't you get up into the car and I'll hand the suitcases to you? Mind helping me with mine as well?"

The girl nodded and climbed the couple of stairs up into the second-class car. There weren't many passengers waiting for this train, and they were alone at this particular door.

"By the way, my name is Gaëlle. I just came in on the train from St. Malo. I'm heading to Paris. You, too?"

"Yeah. I got a seat at the Sorbonne. You're from St. Malo? I was born there, but my folks moved to Rennes when I was young. What part of town did you grow up in?"

"In Paramé. You?"

"Paramé? So did I. That's interesting! What year were you born if I may ask? I'm a sixty-four myself."

Gaëlle laughed uncomfortably. "Didn't your mother teach you not to ask a girl about her age? St. Malo may not be that big a city, but it's still too big to know everyone. Are you looking forward to Paris?" She accepted the second of her suitcases from Michel who was puffing, as it was very heavy. He also realized she'd deliberately changed the subject and went along with it.

"What are you carrying here? Books?"

Blushing, she nodded. "I can't live without my books, but some of them are textbooks for my studies. I've been preparing for some of my classes."

Michel shook his head. He was looking forward to university life, but not so much the academic aspects thereof. He'd worked so hard to make it to the Sorbonne that he was a tad fed up with school and studying. It was the lure of gay life in France's capital that was beckoning him like a Siren call. Subconsciously, he knew he could easily get himself into heaps of trouble, even more than he'd ever been in here in Rennes. He had loved Le Chat Noir, but it was, after all, only one place, and the dance floor was rarely used, not to mention that everyone knew everyone else in such a small city. Paris on the other hand was an entirely different animal.

He heaved his suitcases up to Gaëlle and then climbed into the train himself. They put away their luggage in the vestibule. Theirs was not an open car but one with compartments, and they settled in the second one from the vestibule. It was empty and had eight seats, four on either side facing each other. They were alone for the entire trip to Paris, in time engrossed in discussions about growing up in St. Malo, the beaches, oysters, their favorite crêpes and galettes, the old town, and the excitement of leaving it all behind for Paris.

Paris.

In Michel's mind, the promise of Paris was growing by the hour. Everything about the French capital was larger than life: traffic, politics, history, food, music, literature, architecture, gay life, freedom.

Across from him, Gaëlle was staring out the window. They'd fallen silent as the train slowly began to pull out of the station. She hadn't taken off her hat or her sunglasses. *Odd.* Michel looked closer at the young woman, who was as tall as he was.

She was slim, wearing heavy makeup, at least as far as he could see, as the scarf and the glasses were masking part of her face.

"You never answered my question," she said, and Michel noticed her voice had taken on a deeper tone than before. She seemed to realize it, too, as she repeated herself in a somewhat higher pitch. "Sorry, I think I caught a cold the other day."

"That's okay! Aren't you hot, though, in that hat and scarf?" She blushed but slowly removed both garments, revealing her short hair and makeup that wasn't applied as carefully as he'd seen on other young women her age. Alas, St. Malo, as beautiful as it was, was a country town, and maybe Gaëlle wasn't used to wearing makeup. But what did it matter? She was a pretty girl, regardless.

"I'm going to study medicine. I want to be a doctor." The statement came out of nowhere, and again, her tone was deep though not unpleasant. That was when he noticed the Adam's apple in her throat, and the realization suddenly dawned on him: she was transgender.

"I'm gay," he blurted and tried to put on a smile, although he had no reason to fear anything from her. Gaëlle would be familiar with the likes of him.

"Ah, so you put two and two together," she responded, still staring out the window, avoiding his gaze.

"Sorry. I didn't mean to pry. I just wanted to assure you it's not an issue for me. How long have you been living as a woman?"

"An hour?" The sadness of that statement was not lost on Michel. "I changed after my train from St. Malo had arrived here in Rennes. I snuck into the ladies' room when no one was in there and changed. I had bought this attire and the makeup before leaving town." Gaëlle turned toward Michel, and he sensed the significance of the event, and of being able to tell someone without being judged for it.

"Wow, you're brave. I'm not sure I could do that."

"Well, you're not trans, so you don't have to." Michel felt the icy daggers in her voice but didn't think she'd meant it quite that way. This was clearly all very raw and new still. Michel couldn't blame her.

"I thought coming out was rough. My parents didn't take it well. I take it yours don't know yet?"

Gaëlle shook her head. "No, as far as they know, their son Gérard is heading to Paris to become a famous doctor as we speak. They have no idea that the next time they see their child, there'll be a daughter standing in the doorway."

"You're Gérard Martin? I remember you from school. You were in Miss Maurier's class, right? I was always drawn to you, but I was too shy to approach you in the schoolyard, and then we moved away."

Gaëlle nodded. "Gérard is dead, at least to me. I hope that's not a problem for you? I've been in touch with a psychiatrist in Paris who specializes in gender dysphoria. He's promised to help me, but I have to live as a woman first before I get to start the hormone treatment and have surgery."

"Have you always known?" Michel asked, instantly regretting his question. He hated it when people asked him that, even though he'd been asked the same by other gay people. "Sorry," he added before Gaëlle could even respond. "Stupid question! I mean, I've always known I'm gay, even if I didn't know how to label it or express it. I guess you have, too?"

She looked over at Michel, and he saw years of pain in those eyes. She didn't say anything, though, and went back to staring out the window at the landscape rushing past them. "You still haven't said what you're going to study at the Sorbonne," she finally said.

"I think I've settled for English, but I had originally intended to study law. I met someone." Michel thought about Haakon and their short dalliance in London a few days ago. He hadn't been able to shake him from his mind.

"He must be a very special boy for you to change your main subject," Gaëlle remarked shrewdly. "You're in love."

"You can tell?" He was astonished, but just then the conductor knocked on the door of their compartment and opened it.

"Bonjour. All tickets, please."

They both scrambled to get their tickets and handed them to the older man. He took Gaëlle's ticket first, punched a small hole in it with his ticket puncher, and returned it to her, smiling. "Merci, mademoiselle!" Then he holed Michel's ticket and returned it to him with a nod but no smile. "Enjoy your trip." He left them alone again and proceeded to the next compartment.

For a moment, silence reigned between them. "Can you tell that I'm in love, just from one sentence?"

She shrugged. "It's just a guess, based on the inflection in your voice and the look on your face. You clearly miss him, whoever he is. I hope I meet a guy like that someday." She blushed again and looked away.

Michel nodded. "I hadn't thought of it as love, you know? We only met for a short time in London. We had sex, dinner, and talked for a while. Mind you, that was great, and I have his address." He continued to retell the events of his encounter with the young Norwegian in London.

Now and then, Gaëlle would nod or ask a question, and when he was done, she put her hand on his knee and said, "You should write to him the moment you get to Paris. Don't let him slip away. Love isn't something that knocks on our door every day. For most of us, it's only once or twice in a lifetime, if at all. Don't squander the opportunity to find happiness. Because that is such a precious commodity for the likes of *us*." The way she enunciated that last word, Michel could physically feel her anguish at the life she was about to embark on and how challenging it would be. If he thought being gay was hard, how difficult must it be to be trans?

He couldn't even imagine what it must be like to live the way she had. Yes, he'd met a few drag queens and the odd cross-dresser in Rennes at Le Chat Noir, but they were all certain of their maleness. They might have tucked their junk away while on stage or at the bar, but once they walked into the darkroom, they all put it to good use. For someone like Gaëlle, every moment of her existence until today must have been a stark reminder of God's limitless cruelty. *Or maybe he was drunk at work?* The thought made Michel chuckle. He was not a believer, hadn't been for a long time, yet having been raised the way he had, God would always be a part of his thought universe, even though it was probably just a fluke of Mother Nature that some souls inhabited a body of the wrong sex. *Poor Gaëlle.*

"Funny you should say that," Michel commented eventually. "I had someone tell me something similar recently. Thank you."

They both fell silent and looked out at the passing landscape, leaving Rennes and their past farther behind, racing toward Paris, and the promise of a fresh start, a new life.

They kept talking about this and that, their expectations of Paris, life at the Sorbonne, and boys, and by the time the train pulled into the large station at Montparnasse, next to the skyscraper with the same name, the two had formed a bond of friendship, two Bretons in Paris. They took the subway from the station to the Latin quarter and discovered that Gaëlle's room wasn't far from Michel's apartment. It would be perfect.

Michel accompanied Gaëlle to her room because she'd asked him to. She was afraid that her landlord might not appreciate having a girl renting the room, but when they arrived, the landlady was thrilled that "G. Martin" was a girl, not a boy. "I've heard so many stories about what those boys do, and I wouldn't want all those nightly visits from women here."

Gaëlle was relieved, and when the landlady realized that Michel was not Gaëlle's boyfriend or lover, she invited him to stay for dinner. The start of their university time in Paris couldn't have been better.

FROM PARIS, WITH LOVE

RRIVING AT HIS studio after dinner with Gaëlle and her landlady, Michel unpacked his belongings. He had sent a few things ahead of time, and his landlord had already placed those boxes in the studio. Along with his clothes, the two boxes contained everything he owned. It wasn't much, but it was his, and it would be the start of a new life. Grown up and independent, except the monthly allowance from his parents to pay for room and board. He did, of course, intend to find work, but first, he needed to settle in and get his studies underway before he could even think about a job.

But even before any of that, after having unpacked with thoughts of Haakon on his mind, Michel sat down at the tiny kitchen table to write a letter. He had to dig deep into his high school English to formulate his thoughts to the young man he'd met for only a few hours in London just days ago. But he could put it off no longer. He had to write now.

Dear Haakon!

I hope you had a good stay in London after I left. It was great to meet you, as unexpected as it was. My stay was mostly over, and when I lay down on the grass outside the English Parliament, it was to reflect on my visit and ponder the future: Paris, my studies here at the Sorbonne.

When you came into view, my heart skipped a beat. No, it began to beat faster. I have never met anyone like you. You are so handsome, beautiful even. There is something about your face that just brings a smile to mine, and I feel as if time stands still when I look into your eyes. I wish we'd had more time together.

The one thing always on my mind from London is the time I spent with you. I just arrived in Paris today, and I have a few days to get settled before university starts. I'm looking forward to living here, getting to know the city, and making new friends. I already met a girl on the train today. Her name is Gaëlle and she's from my hometown of St. Malo. You'd like her. I told her about you, and she insisted that I write to you right away, and I couldn't argue with her. She's not the only one who thinks I should write to you. I also met a lady in Rennes who said much the same (long story). I shall have to tell you about her some other time. I'm very tired right now and will go to bed.

I really hope that you'll come to see me. I miss you. Please, Haakon, write back soon!

Bisous,
Michel

He put down the pen, folded the paper and put it in an envelope, added Haakon's address in Oslo, and then got ready to go to bed. In the morning, he'd need to find stamps; within him, the anxious wait for a response began, and he hadn't even posted the letter yet.

He had to wait nearly two weeks before he found an envelope with funny-looking stamps lying on the hardwood floor of his studio when he came back from a long day at the university. There were also some other letters, likely containing invoices and advertising along with flyers and leaflets. But Michel instantly spotted the small envelope with his handwritten name, a blue airmail sticker, and the capitalized word "NORGE" on each of the colorful stamps. It had to be from Haakon. He knew no one else in Norway.

He dropped his bag on the floor, kicked off his sneakers, picked up his mail, and rushed over to the small couch by the window. He jumped on it and gently tore at the envelope, trying to pry it open with his pinky. Inside, he found a couple of sheets of paper, lightly blueish with fine blue lines, and on them, neatly written text:

Oslo, October 1985

Dear Michel!

Thank you so much for your letter. What a wonderful surprise to come home after school to find your letter with the beautiful stamps waiting for me in my room. Mrs. Holberg was quite curious about you, and I had to tell her about meeting you. I didn't tell her everything, though. I'm sure you see why. I don't think she would understand this aspect of my life.

Life here in Oslo is calm. We've just had our first snow, and my days are all about university right now, but I think back on our time in London a lot. I can't wait to travel again, to see more of the world. Tell me about Paris. What is it like? I guess it's still warmer and you don't get much snow?

Yours sincerely,
Haakon

Michel read the letter several times. It wasn't very long, but he cherished every word on the loosely spaced two pages. Haakon's handwriting was very different from his, and as he re-read the words, he imagined Haakon reading it out loud, and he relished hearing his Nordic accent.

Haakon missed him but didn't say anything else about how he felt for him. Maybe it had been just a one-night stand for him. Maybe Haakon didn't feel what he felt. He'd have to find out, write back.

He lay on his couch, and he let his mind drift, and before long, he and Haakon were in his bed, making love. Michel quickly pulled down his pants and jerked off to this delicious fantasy, climaxing within seconds. He got up and hobbled to the bathroom to get cleaned up. He washed his hands and put his pants back on before returning to the couch to look at the remainder of his mail.

Later that night, after a quick dinner with Gaëlle and studying for a test the next day, he wrote Haakon a long letter, telling him all about his life in the City of Lights, Gaëlle, his studies, and how much he missed Haakon. He ended the letter not with kisses, bisous, as he had before, but with love. To Michel, it was a subtle suggestion that he felt something more than the formal sign-off Haakon had used in his first response, although he couldn't be sure that Haakon would understand. To end a letter with "love" in English was, after all, noncommittal, or so he'd heard.

Michel did miss Haakon, yet they were not in a relationship. There was no such concept for Michel. Yes, he dreamed of being with Haakon; his fantasies of sex with Haakon were most enticing and always a great source for masturbation, but to live with him, to settle down with the man? It didn't register in his mind, the concept was so alien.

At the same time, where did those thoughts come from? How was Haakon different from others? Michel recalled something Giselle had once told him about love: *picture yourself growing old with that person*. With Haakon, Michel could actually do that. He pictured them traveling together; he saw himself with Haakon on mountaintops in Norway, although he'd never been there and had no idea what they looked like, but they were both older.

He saw himself with Haakon sitting in rocking chairs, watching a sunset, surrounded by palm trees.

Had he fallen in love with the young Norwegian after just one day together? Was that even possible? To live a life in domestic bliss the way his parents were, or most other straight couples did, had never entered his mind before. Yet the mental images that Haakon evoked seemed to point to the contrary. He couldn't get them out of his head. As impossible and inconceivable as it seemed in reality, his imagination had gone there. Had meeting Haakon begun to heal his heart, providing him with the hope of redemption? Would he, in time, get over the monseigneur, forgive himself for Pascal? Was Haakon to be his savior?

Love—until now—had never been about playing house, but to catch a moment of intimacy whenever it was given, a soft kiss after a fuck in the darkroom with a stranger, a tender embrace from someone in passing, a pat on the shoulder or a kind and grateful smile after a blow job. It was all he had come to expect. No one he knew had ever known anything else either. It did not exist in the world they inhabited.

Somehow, being with Haakon was different, and for now, it was the perfect relationship, even though it wasn't one. *Yet.* Michel's heart already belonged to the young Norwegian, while his body continued to behave as if there was no tomorrow. There was no contradiction between his feelings for Haakon and having sex with complete strangers. On weekends, Michel and Gaëlle frequented the gay clubs in Paris, dancing, drinking, and enjoying the freedom of not being accountable to anyone but themselves. The two friends were close even though they rarely left the club together.

Michel would inevitably end up in the darkroom or bathrooms of wherever they were and mysteriously disappear while Gaëlle would find her clique, a tightly knit band of other trans women who looked out for each other and protected one another from those who might otherwise prey on them. To some men, young women who were perfectly coiffed, neatly dressed but "with a penis in their panties" were a prize too precious to pass up on, even if it meant disregarding their lack of consent. Too many young trans women had ended up raped, badly beaten into submission, at local Paris hospitals. Gaëlle was lucky to have found a band of sisters who would make sure they stayed safe, even in what was supposed to be a safe zone for their kind or on the subway home early in the morning.

This was a procedure that was repeated most weekends: dinner at Michel's apartment or a small bistro somewhere between Gaëlle's room and his studio, then they'd take the subway to whatever bar or club they were going to, where Gaëlle had arranged to meet her friends. They would share a drink or two until either her friends arrived or Michel found someone to satisfy his carnal desires and he'd disappear, sometimes coming back, sometimes with a grin on his face, sometimes a disappointed sneer, before vanishing again to prowl the dance floor anew.

1986

JUNE 22 – BIENVENU À PARIS!

*M*ICHEL HAD NEVER been more nervous in his entire life. He'd woken up long before the alarm he'd set went off, even though he'd been out late the night before. He was simply too nervous—and excited—to get any decent sleep. Today was the day Haakon would finally arrive in Paris. They had written to each other regularly and exchanged a few expensive, thus rare, phone calls. To hear Haakon's voice with its singing tone and that exotic Norwegian accent, even just to share the mundane aspects of their lives in Oslo or Paris for a few minutes, was like balm for Michel's soul.

Today, after lunch, Haakon's flight would touch down at Charles De Gaulle airport, and Michel needed to get ready to go and pick him up. There was no way he'd let Haakon come to town on his own, not that he wasn't capable of doing so. Michel wanted to maximize every moment they had together. Besides, what kind of host would he be? After a year apart—nine months and three days to be exact—Michel's longing to be with Haakon again was causing him physical pain, his body yearning to touch and be touched by him.

Given their limited financial resources, they'd be stuck in the city, taking the Métro or the RER to the outskirts on weekends or evenings. Haakon had willingly agreed to spend his summer vacation right here in Paris, sacrificing any other plans he might have had. However, Michel's semester wouldn't finish until July, so he had created tentative schedules for things they could do together and suggestions for how Haakon could pass the time while Michel was in school. In August, Michel would fly to Oslo to return the favor. There, it would be much the same, as

Norwegian universities began their semesters earlier, in mid to late August. This would be the best summer ever, of that Michel was sure.

He showered, had a quick breakfast, and then headed to the airport. So what if he was early? He could watch the planes come and go, and at least he'd be there when Haakon stepped out of the arrivals hall. To see him again...*heaven!* Michel could've crawled out of his skin. He could barely sit still in the train car.

Michel arrived at the airport shortly after eleven, a good two hours before Haakon's plane was due to land. It had most likely not even taken off in Oslo yet. Michel didn't mind. He'd never been at the airport before, this marvel of modern architecture. People poured through the circular terminal building, going up and down the escalators inside tubes seemingly suspended in mid-air, crossing the ring heading from one level to the other.

Michel passed the time walking around and taking in all the activity, pausing for a coffee at some point, and to check the arrivals board. When the SAS flight from Oslo landed, he watched it approach one of the outer satellites where it would dock. It was time for him to head over to the arrivals level, to wait outside for Haakon. The final thirty minutes of waiting were the hardest, as his longing had become unbearable. There was a constant stream of people emerging from the arrivals hall, but no Haakon. Every time the doors opened, Michel's heart skipped a beat, only to realize it was someone else.

Finally, the doors parted, and a tall young man came into view, holding on to an old-fashioned brown leather suitcase. He was at least a head taller than Michel, and his strawberry-blond locks and his freckled face gave him away instantly. Michel leaped to his feet and ran to him, hugging Haakon tightly.

"Bienvenu en France! Welcome to France!" He beamed, taking Haakon's suitcase to carry it for him. "I'm so happy to see you. How was your flight? Did you get to see the city on your final approach?" They took off toward the RER station back to the city with Michel chattering in nervous excitement the entire time, pointing out things along the way, especially once they transferred to the Métro at Châtelet–Les Halles. Haakon seemed happy to tag along, listening and taking in the scenery. He didn't say much.

When they arrived at the studio, Michel was bursting with emotions. He had wanted to kiss Haakon so badly at the airport but had refrained, as such displays of affection among Christopher's kind were very much frowned upon by the public. Once inside the apartment, he needno longer be afraid. They made love for a long time, not rushing, going again and again, from passionate and wild to more slow and deliberate lovemaking.

Michel felt at ease, cuddling up to Haakon as if the man would protect him from all evils of the world outside. He wanted to stay cooped up in bed, never letting go of the physical touch, the intimacy of skin against skin, but at the same time, he wanted to drag Haakon out on the town and show him the many great sights of Paris. In the end, their hungry stomachs decided for them, and they headed out.

Over dinner, Michel explained that Haakon would have to spend some parts of the days on his own. There were all the final exams at the end of the term to consider. Michel needed to keep his grades up, but he would try to spend as much time with him as he could.

Afterward, they took a walk down to the Seine as it was only a couple of blocks away, and Michel was dying to impress Haakon with the sight of the cathedral of Notre-Dame by night. As they approached the small island on which the cathedral was built, Michel's emotions got the better of him, and he took Haakon's hand in his. He was so madly in love that he could've yelled it from the rooftops, but Haakon's apprehension calmed him.

Michel shrugged and laughed. "It's love, you know?" Besides, there wasn't a soul in sight, or else Michel wouldn't have done it. At the same time, he felt bad for not giving Haakon the whole truth because it wasn't just any random kind of love. It was *his* love for *him*. Haakon had saved him, had reassembled his heart after all the events of the previous years. *Will he understand how significant this is to me?*

They found a spot near the wall surrounding the island and took in the sight of the magnificent cathedral, lit up by large floodlights all around. Michel could tell that Haakon was impressed. He leaned his head against Haakon's shoulder. He was happy. They were finally together again, and not just for an afternoon, but for several weeks.

Bliss.

He was surprised when Haakon began to speak of love and how you recognized it.

"How do you know that you're in love with someone? I'm not sure I've ever been in love with anybody before, and yet you're talking of love, we're holding hands, sitting here like this... Am I making any sense? I just don't know what love feels like."

When you can picture yourself growing old with someone, that's a sign of love!

Michel thought of Giselle's words and was suddenly aware of the significance the word love carried, what it could mean for them and their future. He assuaged Haakon, telling him that he wouldn't have invited him to Paris if he hadn't felt something strong, but they could take it slow, not label things needlessly. At the same time, he yearned to profess his growing love to his Viking, but he was afraid he might scare him away, and the fear of losing Haakon frightened Michel more than the idea of being in love. Haakon was not like Michel. His experiences had been very different; he'd lived a sheltered life and had not—as far as Michel knew—been through any traumatic events in his youth. He would need time to connect the thoughts in his mind with the emotions of his heart.

Yet as the days progressed and they fell into their routine— Michel going to school, Haakon discovering Paris, meeting up after lectures were over or tests completed, having meals together, making love, going out with Gaëlle or other friends— they established, without realizing it, a bubble of happiness and a little nest where their love could grow and be nurtured.

JUNE 29 – LOVE, OR IS IT?

*I*T WAS THE last Saturday of June. They had packed a picnic lunch and had ventured out to the Bois de Boulogne, a huge park in the west of the city, to walk, talk, and spend some quality time together. They found a spot to enjoy their lunch under a large, old chestnut tree and after eating, they relaxed awhile, Michel's head resting on Haakon's tummy when suddenly, Haakon professed his love for him and how afraid he was of going back to Oslo alone, being apart from him again.

"I don't want to leave you either. But why don't we enjoy our time and live in the now? Let's not worry too much about the future." Michel felt utterly betrayed by his lips for speaking those casual words, and ashamed for not having the courage to express the depth of his love for Haakon. Here they were, lying under this enormous tree that provided them shade and protection from a burning sun, and Michel remembered the words madame Charpentier had uttered about caring for the sapling tree.

Why was it so difficult for him to care for his sapling, to admit he felt the same way as the man on whom he currently rested his head? Why was he treating Haakon this way? It was a relief when Haakon held him tightly for several minutes as if the physical manifestation of his fears could tie Michel to him. To Michel, that hug meant the world, and he hoped that someday soon, his lips would do his heart's bidding rather than that of his troubled mind.

Was he afraid he'd scare him away? Or that mentioning the emotions by name might lessen them somehow? Michel didn't know, but for now, even though he loved Haakon with all his heart, the best he could do was show Haakon how he felt, until such time as he was ready to express it in words.

JULY 14 – I LOVE YOU!

ASTILLE DAY, FRANCE's national holiday, *le 14 juillet*, was a huge thing in Paris. The President himself attended the ceremony every year, with its enormous military parade down Champs-Élysées and air show. There were also fireworks and parties going on all around the city and the country to commemorate this important day of the French Revolution.

Michel was a proud socialist, and he hadn't been pleased with the parliamentary elections earlier that year. Even so, seeing President Mitterrand, his hero, oversee the parade in person swelled his heart with pride, and Michel wanted to share this feeling with Haakon. He had learned that Norway was ruled by a socialist government, under Prime Minister Brundtland, the country's first female leader. Haakon was rightly proud of his government and their high female representation, and it kept their conversation about politics going during the parade and later, in the evening, as they picnicked on Champs de Mars, waiting for the big fireworks at the Eiffel Tower to begin.

They had decided on a simple yet fitting meal of a baguette, hard-boiled eggs, vegetables, sausage, cheese, and a bottle of red wine from the Bordeaux region. They spread their blanket on the grass alongside thousands of other onlookers, families with kids, groups of friends, and other young couples like them, all camping out on blankets, eagerly awaiting the fireworks.

Haakon lay on his back, a glass of wine in one hand, his body propped on the other elbow while Michel rested his head on his boyfriend's stomach, as he often did, although rarely so in public.

Some people still reacted very negatively—and loudly—to seeing two men or women openly showing their love, but not tonight. Children ran circles around them and the countless other blankets spread across the huge open space leading up to the Eiffel Tower with tens of thousands of people waiting, eating, drinking, and enjoying their day off.

When the fireworks began, Haakon almost dropped his glass and admitted he'd never seen anything as spectacular as this. The entire Eiffel Tower had become part of the spectacle, and with every colorful ball of fire exploding around Gustave Eiffel's magnificent edifice, the crowd murmured in "oohs" and "ahhs," while the children watched silently with mouths wide open, and lovers held hands, expressing their love and wonder through the occasional gentle squeeze of fingers.

Like everyone else, Haakon and Michel were on their feet, with Michel in front, close enough for Haakon to put his arms around him. Michel rested against Haakon's chest, relishing the lemon and sandalwood scent of his boyfriend's cologne. Watching the display and being held by his Viking, Michel's heart exploded in fireworks of its own. Somewhere, deep within him, a geyser began to rumble, and as the final bursts of red, white, and blue light flashed around the Eiffel Tower, accompanied by loud bangs, that geyser erupted. Michel's head fell back onto Haakon's shoulder, and his lips finally formed the words he'd been struggling to find a few days earlier.

"Je t'aime, chou-chou!"

Yes, he loved Haakon, with every fiber of his being, and now he had told him so, his heart, mind, and vocal cords were finally aligned.

Haakon smiled, hugged him tightly, and kissed him on his forehead. "I know, babe, I know. I love you, too!"

JULY 19 – VERSAILLES

"LET'S HEAD OUT to Versailles today," Michel announced early on a Saturday morning. They were still in bed, having just made love, Michel as always cooped up against Haakon, seeking the physical closeness of his boyfriend. They had crossed that threshold without even realizing it. A few days ago, Michel had finally put into words how he felt, and their relationship had changed, albeit subtly. Haakon seemed more relaxed around him, less apprehensive and careful than before. Had the fear of rejection been so difficult to bear? Michel felt miserable about it and vowed to never keep secrets from Haakon ever again, most certainly not when it pertained to how he felt about him. No matter what the future held, he was going to be honest with his man.

The trip to Versailles took a while. They had to take a train and then walk through the village to reach Europe's most fabled castle. There were a lot of tourists, and Michel suggested they skip visiting the castle itself. "It's just glass, windows, gold, and endless corridors anyway. Let's go see the park instead." He led Haakon through the castle straight to the park, which faced away from the town. Haakon was impressed by the sights of it all, the enormous building complex finalized by France's sun king, Louis XIV, to reflect and showcase not just his personal power but the magnificence of the country itself.

"I'll have to show you our royal castle in Oslo," Haakon said with a chuckle. "It's minuscule by comparison, yet still one of the biggest buildings in downtown Oslo."

"Well, it's not just the size, chou-chou. You still have a king and queen residing in that castle. Ours lost their heads during the Revolution."

They walked for hours through the mazes and past the big ponds, admiring how the gigantic trees had been trimmed as if they were small, square bonsai. There were a lot of people in the park, too, but given its size, they never once felt crowded, and whenever they were completely alone, one hand would inevitably find another, fingers becoming intertwined as they strolled, happy together.

Now and then, they sat on a bench or found a quiet space under a large tree where they could just be. Michel felt a hint of sadness in his heart as he remembered that in a couple of weeks, Haakon would fly home.

"I look forward to visiting you in Norway," Michel said.

"I sure hope you do. I insist. After the time I've passed here, I'll be hard-pressed to show you as much as you have shown me. I'll have to talk to Mrs. Holberg first. I'm not sure how she'll take you staying with me, but I don't think it'll be a problem."

"I can always stay at a youth hostel."

Haakon laughed. "Yeah, right. No, that's not going to happen. Don't worry. Let's cross that bridge once we get to it. Given my landlady's travel experiences and the things she's told me, I'd be surprised if she has an issue with you staying for a few weeks. However, we may have to be a bit quieter."

"Very funny, chou-chou. As long as I'm with you, I needn't say a word."

"Aww, now that would be a shame. I want to hear you say it every day."

"Say what?" Michel teased, knowing full well what Haakon was angling for.

"Je t'aime!" Haakon replied in his best French.

"You do? What a coincidence. I love you, too!" Michel laughed and rolled on top of Haakon. "Tell me, chou-chou, how would you say 'I love you' in Norwegian?"

"Jeg elsker deg."

"Je t'aime." Michel bowed down and kissed Haakon. "I wish you didn't have to go home. I wish we could study at the same university."

"I know. I feel the same, but my French sucks. You know how the waiters always look at you when I try to order food. And with three words of Norwegian, you won't get far at the University of Oslo either, although I'm sure you'd make a lot of people happy with your I-love-yous."

Michel had to laugh. Haakon had changed. This was no longer the shy, introverted man who had come to Paris a few weeks ago. He was witty, funny, much more outgoing, and confident. To make a joke like that would've never happened in the first week of his stay in Paris, and Michel was proud of the influence he'd had on his boyfriend. He rolled off Haakon and put his arm across his chest, resting his head on Haakon's shoulder.

"Something on your mind?" Haakon asked.

"Life, and how we've affected each other. You've made me a better human being, chou-chou."

Haakon looked puzzled. "What do you mean?"

"I was just thinking about how safe you make me feel. Being with you is like being wrapped in a warm blanket. Safe. Cozy! My life hasn't been as sheltered as you've told me yours was. My parents, as you know, are very religious and staunch conservatives. I was only eleven years old when a priest abused me sexually."

"He *what*?" Haakon sat up straight.

"Let me tell you, okay? It's fine. He didn't do anything I wouldn't have done myself, given the opportunity. I was curious, and he helped me explore my sexuality. What I didn't understand at the time was that he was just using me, you know? He was much older, and he used his position to get into my pants. He didn't care about me, my needs, or my feelings. And he lied and threatened me to get what he wanted. Later on, during my school years, I basically became a slut, numbing myself with countless casual sexual encounters, trying to fill this void I felt within me. I completely lost control of that when I was in the army."

"What do you mean? Are you okay?"

Michel closed his eyes, then opened them again and looked straight at Haakon. "I am now, thanks to you. I won't bother you with the details, but I was in a very bad place for a while. Who knows where I'd be if I hadn't met you? For that alone, you have my eternal gratitude."

"But I haven't done anything. You've been in the driver's seat of our relationship from the first minute. Remember, it was you who reached out to me in London."

"The best thing I've done in my entire life," Michel responded. "I had no choice. When I saw you, I just knew I had to get to know you. I wouldn't have forgiven myself otherwise."

"I'm glad you did. I hadn't even noticed you until I suddenly had this strange sensation on the back of my neck—you know, when you feel someone is looking at you?"

"Yeah, I remember, and I'd been staring at you for a while before you turned around and looked at me. I was trying to get you to notice me." Michel laughed. "Seems it worked because here we are, together in Versailles, making plans for the future."

"What about the future?" Haakon asked. "What do you want to do when you're done with your studies?"

"Travel. I'd like to see more of the world. With you by my side."

"Sounds like a plan. Growing up, there were precious few opportunities to leave our farm in Røros. My mom took me across the border to Funäsdalen in Sweden a few times, but that doesn't count. You barely notice leaving Norway. The mountains look much the same on their side as they do on ours, and you don't even need a passport."

"It was similar for me. My parents used to vacation here in France. We'd pack our car and head out west to the Atlantic coast, or south to the Mediterranean. My trip to London was my first time abroad, ever. I haven't even been to Jersey or Guernsey before, and that's about the closest to a 'Sweden' we have in Brittany." Michel had to laugh at the comparison. He'd never been to any of the Channel Islands, not from Rennes either. Had he stayed in St. Malo, that would certainly have been a school trip one day, but from Rennes, they would visit Mont-Saint-Michel instead, to study the tide and the many ups and downs of Franco-English history. Michel tried to picture what Røros looked like, this mountain town where Haakon had grown up. But he failed miserably. His pictures of mountains usually amounted to images of the Alps, the Mont Blanc, or the famous Cervin.

"Do your parents know you're gay?"

"No, they don't. Not yet, anyway. I never got around to telling them. It never came up. The closest I ever got back home was jerk-off sessions with a friend from school. I doubt my parents even suspect anything."

"I'd love to see your hometown. I'm sure it's extraordinary."

"I'd love to show it to you. We could take the train to Bergen and board the Hurtigruten to Trondheim. It's the closest city to my hometown. From there, it's only a couple of hours by car. My parents could come to pick us up. You'll love Norway. It's such a beautiful country."

"You don't need to convince me. I will follow you to the end of the world and enjoy it, as long as you're by my side. I love you, Haakon Olafsen!"

JULY 25 – PARTING IS
SUCH SWEET SORROW

AFTER THEIR RETURN from Versailles, time seemed to pass by much faster, and the few remaining days ended almost as soon as they had begun.

It was the last night of Haakon's stay in Paris, and the mood at Michel's studio was somber. Where had the weeks gone? Undoubtedly, they'd had a great time together. While Haakon was nervous that he'd forgotten something to get him on his plane back to Norway, all Michel could think of was the empty weeks ahead before he'd rejoin Haakon in Oslo.

There had been a number of "finals" in the past days: a final visit to Notre Dame, a final dinner with Gaëlle, a final evening trip to the Eiffel Tower, a final climb up to Montparnasse and Sacré Coeur for the view of the city, and just now, a final round of lovemaking before they had to leave for the airport. To Michel, it seemed everything was final. It bothered him greatly.

He didn't want the moment to end and clung to Haakon's body as if it were a life raft in a stormy sea, but they both realized Haakon couldn't afford to miss his flight. Eventually, they got dressed and left the small apartment to head for the Métro and then transferred to the RER to the airport.

Once they were at the terminal, Haakon checked in for his flight, securing his coveted window seat. "I love to look out, to see the world disappear below me. You know, being up there in the air, looking down at the Earth is breathtaking. I can't imagine flying and not being able to look out the window to see anything."

"Duly noted. I'll make sure to try to get a window seat when I come to see you!" Michel chuckled, but inside him, a storm was raging, as he was falling apart over the fact that Haakon was leaving. "When is boarding?"

"In an hour. We can grab a coffee before I have to head to security."

"Good," was all Michel managed to say, his heart already breaking at the prospect of watching Haakon disappear through the doors behind which airport security lay.

They didn't say much as they sat there, nursing their espressos. Michel sighed heavily now and then, and Haakon finally commented on it. "Hey, don't worry. I'm not leaving you forever. We'll see each other again in a few weeks. Had I known how things would turn out between us, I'd have booked my flight later, but we didn't, did we?"

"I know, chou-chou. I know. Still...,"

Haakon put his hand on Michel's. "Can't we be grateful that we found each other instead? We have our entire lives ahead of us, long lives with travel around the world, long lives to love each other. What are two or three weeks apart compared to a lifetime together?"

Michel was fighting tears. "You're right. I can't explain it, but these past weeks with you have been the best of my life."

It was time to go. Michel accompanied Haakon as far as he was allowed, to a couple of tinted glass doors that were marked passengers only. Beyond the doors were security control and long corridors that led to the different gates.

Without warning, Haakon turned to Michel, gently grabbed his head with his hands, and kissed him. "I will see you in Oslo soon. I'll give you a quick call when I'm home, okay? I love you, Michel." Then he let go and turned around and walked away. The two glass doors parted, letting him through. Michel watched on as his tall, Norwegian boyfriend disappeared.

"I love you, too," he whispered as the doors closed again. Haakon was gone, and Michel could only go back home, to focus on his final tests, hoping for the coming weeks to pass quickly so he could re-join him in Norway.

The return journey to his small studio apartment left Michel empty. As he sat alone in his car on the RER back into town, he contemplated how much his life had changed after their chance encounter in London the previous fall.

Meeting the young Norwegian on Parliament Square had been life-altering in ways Michel hadn't fathomed at the time. Sure, there was this weird attraction of a kind he hadn't felt toward any of the other men he'd been with. Their sex that day had been incredible, and leaving Haakon behind in London had been difficult, not that Michel had understood why back then. In retrospect, he'd probably fallen in love with him at first sight. Unable to rebook his train ticket, he'd had no choice but to head back to Paris.

Haakon was the love of his life. He was sure of that now, and watching him go through security at the airport had been like having his heart ripped right out of his chest and torn to shreds. There was this childlike, naïve quality to Haakon, a purity Michel had never encountered before. Haakon always believed the best in people. There wasn't an evil bone in the man's body, and Michel worried that Haakon might easily be duped and used by others.

Indeed, Michel could've betrayed Haakon more than once. There were so many hot guys on campus, all those looks and glances in restrooms or the hallways of the Sorbonne, and Michel could have given in to his instincts. But for some reason, he couldn't. Whenever he was tempted to follow a guy for some quick relief somewhere, he'd see Haakon's face. One look into those innocent eyes, and Michel had no choice. Not that they were exclusive or anything. They hadn't even talked about it. No. Michel simply knew that if Haakon even heard of Michel being with someone else, the pain would be too much, just as Michel knew Haakon only had eyes for him.

How quickly his life had changed. These weeks of having Haakon share his studio, living side by side like a regular couple, had been very different from his previous stint of cohabitation when Claude had taken him in after he'd come out to his parents. Michel had no appropriate term for what they shared. It was as if they could read each other's minds; they finished each other's thoughts and sentences; grocery shopping and cooking were suddenly a lot of fun. Even the run to the laundry room wasn't the mundane chore it had once been, and doing the dishes, something Michel abhorred, became a game of who was faster: the one washing the dishes or the other one drying them. They'd laughed and tried to distract the other, and Haakon had inevitably won every time, regardless of whether he was handling the brush or the towel. A look, a smile, or a quick kiss would leave Michel utterly distraught and staring at his tall lover with his cute dimples and those adorable red-blond soft, long curls. Alone again, the love Michel felt became an ache, and he began to cry softly, staring out the window of his train to avoid making a fool of himself.

The sound of the voice announcing the train's arrival at Châtelet–Les Halles woke him from his reveries. Time to get off. He could've transferred to a Métro line, but he needed the fresh air and decided to walk the rest of the way, although he regretted that the moment he saw the cathedral's spires and the memories of his many walks with Haakon washed over him.

"I have to power through this!" he told himself, knowing he'd encounter memories of their time together in every corner of the city.

When he finally reached his apartment, the emptiness hit him hard. How would he go on alone, even if it was just for a few weeks?

AUGUST 2 – SYMPTOMS

ICHEL WOKE UP sweating, and his entire body hurt. He could barely get out of bed. When he finally managed to drag himself up and walked into the bathroom to relieve himself, he was surprised by how pale he looked and began to gently pat various parts of his body. The lymph nodes in his neck were swollen, and they were sore to the touch.

He got undressed and showered. Afterward, he felt a little better, but as he toweled himself dry, he noticed a weird spot on his arm that hadn't been there before. *Strange, I must've hit it on something.* He managed to eat a little, which didn't make him feel any better, but he had a paper to turn in, so he took himself off to school.

The next days were difficult, as his condition didn't improve. He wasn't hungry and constantly felt sick but put it down to the stress of getting through the finals and all the papers he'd had to submit. That was all behind him now, so why wasn't he feeling better?

Still, he was glad he didn't have to deal with what Gaëlle was going through, as she was smack in the middle of her psych evaluation to begin her hormone treatment. It was bad enough coping with the tests and the finals, but having your innermost thoughts poked and prodded just for some stranger to decide whether you deserve being who you already knew you were?

Michel had watched Gaëlle bloom over the course of the past year. Her hair had grown out, and she'd bought herself an entire new wardrobe with beautiful clothes that highlighted her femininity. These days, her makeup, heavy as it was, was flawless, and she was rarely misgendered. Her psychiatrist was now the only person standing between her and the operating theater. As far as Michel knew, so far, so good.

However, to get the surgery, Gaëlle had to prove she could "pass" as a woman. In that sense, it boded well that Haakon hadn't realized Gaëlle had not been born a girl. It wasn't until they'd spent an evening together, sharing a meal, that Haakon picked up on how she was taller and less curvy than most women and her voice was deeper—something that would be addressed as part of Gaëlle's treatment program, which, hopefully, she'd be allowed to begin within a month or two.

Michel wanted to support her as much as he could, but he needed to get well himself first. The one thing that meant the world to him was Haakon, and he wanted to see him again. That would heal him. They had spoken regularly on the phone, and Haakon said he was very much looking forward to Michel's visit. He just had to get over this thing, whatever it was.

SEPTEMBER 2 – A PHONE CALL

*M*ICHEL SO WANTED to travel to Oslo and spend some time in this exotic Nordic location, but he hadn't felt well enough to book a ticket let alone travel. A month had passed since Haakon had returned to Norway, and every day, Michel felt the memories of being with him fade further. He yearned to feel Haakon's touch, smell his scent, hear his laughter, so much so he sometimes wondered if his love had been replaced by longing, where one emotion began and the other ended.

Michel didn't tell Haakon how sick he felt, nor that he was getting worse, only that he'd arranged to see a physician later that week. He had no appetite and was losing weight rapidly. His throat felt dry, and his mouth was like parchment, with a disgusting sensation to it, as if stuff was growing in it. But what bothered him most was the cough and the strange purple rash on his arm that had not gone away.

They agreed that Michel would call Haakon after his doctor's visit, but somewhere deep within, Michel already knew something was seriously wrong. He wasn't naïve. He'd been around the gay community long enough to have heard about "it," this AIDS thing. He also knew what a positive diagnosis meant, and he desperately wished for Haakon to be with him, to hold his hand while he talked to the doctor. At the same time, he was terrified by the prospect—not for the inevitable death sentence but for fear of driving Haakon away. Michel wouldn't blame him. Who would want to be with someone who was dying? Who would want to be with someone who might kill you with a simple kiss?

SEPTEMBER 30 – FACING FACTS

*M*ONSIEUR?"

"Yes?" Michel opened his eyes. "Where am I?"

"You're in an intensive care ward at Hôtel-Dieu. You've been here for several weeks being treated for pneumonia—for a while we thought we would lose you. My name is Doctor Blanchard. I am the attending physician here at the AIDS clinic. You passed out in the middle of the street."

"Passed out?"

"Yes, somebody called an ambulance for you. How do you feel?"

"Dizzy. And my throat aches."

"That's from the ventilator. You were hooked up for two weeks. Have a small sip of water, but be careful, okay? Not too much at once." Doctor Blanchard placed a small glass to his lips and allowed Michel to take a sip.

"You said AIDS clinic? Is that what I have?"

"I'm afraid so. Your tests came back positive over a week ago. Not that we needed them. The lesions and the pneumonia were indicators enough."

Doctor Blanchard was all business. Michel couldn't discern any emotions in her voice.

"We don't have any contact details, and we need to inform your next of kin. Would that be your parents?"

"No, that's not necessary. I'm twenty-two next birthday. I make my own decisions."

"D'accord—but only for now. Is there anyone else we should contact?"

223

Michel had the distinct feeling this discussion wasn't over. The doctor wasn't satisfied with his reply. Then it registered what she'd said about how long he'd been there—*several weeks? Haakon!*—and Michel's heart began to race as he imagined the worry he'd caused him.

"My boyfriend, Haakon. He lives in Norway. I promised to call him after a doctor's appointment. Seems I missed that. Could you call him for me, please? He must be worried sick."

"I will." The doctor took out a notepad, and Michel jotted down Haakon's number. "And to confirm your identity. You are Michel St. Jacques, born October 4, 1964. Is that correct? We found a student ID card in your wallet."

"Yes, that's me. Am I dying?" The question just popped out of his mouth.

For the first time since she'd woken him, Michel sensed some emotion from Doctor Blanchard. "Yes, I'm afraid you are. We still don't know everything about the disease, and while some patients have survived for a year, sometimes longer, others wither away within months. It depends on how long ago someone's been infected, their immune system, et cetera. But let's not get ahead of ourselves. You've just come out of a tunnel, and you're a fighter, Michel! So for now, keep fighting, and do whatever you can to get better. I have lost so many already, I don't need your name on my list, too, okay? That is unless we can start a new list: survivors!" She put her hand on his shoulder and then left him to his thoughts.

Dying?!

He was numbed by the revelation. His life had barely begun, and now it was to end? How was he going to deal with this?

His thoughts drifted back to Haakon, and he felt the intense betrayal he was about to inflict on him. Not only had he failed to call, failed to travel to Oslo, but now he was dying. Helpless to stop himself, Michel fell into a dark rabbit hole of his own making, picturing Haakon having moved on from him after he'd betrayed him so completely. What else was his beautiful Norwegian to do?

OCTOBER 1 – REUNION

ICHEL FELT BETTER the second he saw Haakon's face hovering above his own. He hadn't even heard him walk in but woke to the soothing sound of his voice. It was the best day of his life, for sure, to see that beautiful face, although it was lined with worry.

"Chou-chou, why are you here?"

"Love, Michel. Because I love you..." Tears filled Haakon's eyes, and Michel wished more than anything he had the strength to sit up and kiss those tears away. Haakon had come back to him. He had not forgotten, and he had not abandoned him. Haakon was more faithful than Michel could ever have imagined.

"I've written to you, and I've called you many times, but you never picked up. I was so worried, Michel. I didn't know what to do, and I had no one else to contact. I never bothered to get Gaëlle's last name or address."

"Oh my God. I haven't spoken to her either. She probably has enough on her plate, what with her hormone treatment. I'm sure she went home to St. Malo for the summer and probably didn't even think about me. Try to reach out to her, would you? Her number is in the address book by my phone at the apartment. Are you going to stay there? How long are you here for?

"Shhh! Take it easy, Michel. We have time. I'm here now, for as long as it takes. I got on the first flight out after the hospital called. Mrs. Holberg paid for my ticket. She says hello, by the way. And she knows. It was hard to keep it a secret when the phone call kind of knocked me out of orbit."

225

"But promise me, you will talk to Gaëlle? I need to know that things went well with her and her parents."

Haakon got up and kissed him on his forehead. "Don't worry, Michel. Everything will be all right. I promise you. I'm so happy to see you again." He kissed him gently on the lips. "How are you feeling?"

"Well, look at me," Michel answered downbeat. "You do realize AIDS is fatal, right? You do have AIDS in Norway, too, don't you?"

"Don't say that!" Michel saw the different emotions—hope, sadness, fear, and desperation—dance over Haakon's face. "We don't know that yet. You will get out of here, and you'll get better, you just wait!"

Haakon knew what he was saying wasn't true. Michel could see it in his eyes. Sure, he may well get out of here, likely feet first, but he would not get well. That was not in his cards.

They only got to spend a few more minutes together before Haakon was ushered out of the room by Doctor Blanchard, apparently because she needed to test him, too.

It didn't dawn on Michel until later in the afternoon what the implications were if Haakon tested positive. *I might have killed my boyfriend.* Suddenly it went from the best day of his life to the worst.

OCTOBER 2 – PARENTS

ICHEL WAS PLEASED to see Gaëlle appear with Haakon the next day. They spent some time together, chatting, laughing, for a moment escaping the grim reality of his situation.

"I'm sorry, Michel," was how Gaëlle had begun their conversation. "I kind of lost sight of the world once I was approved for my hormone treatment. After the semester ended, I needed to confront my parents. I couldn't put it off any longer."

"Don't worry, girl. How did that go?" The effort of speaking made Michel cough, and Haakon handed him a glass of water.

"Better than I expected. My dad always wanted a daughter, and as far as he was concerned, they'd only ever gotten boys. Maybe it's because I'm the youngest of four siblings—that might have taken the worst of the blow out of it. I don't know. My mom cried, and I'm not sure she understands. She kept asking me if I knew what I was doing to voluntarily give up my male privilege." She laughed at that. "She doesn't see that I don't have a choice. She seems to think all I have to do is cut my hair, wipe the makeup off my face, put on a pair of jeans and a shirt, and everything will be fine again. She doesn't realize this is exactly what I've done for twenty years, and it never worked."

Michel sensed the sadness in her voice, and it must have shown on his face, as Gaëlle smiled weakly and patted his hand.

"She'll get there. The fact that my dad has taken it better will help."

"What about your brothers?" Haakon asked.

Gaëlle shrugged. "They don't care, perhaps because they already kind of knew, especially Armand, my youngest brother. He's only a year older, and I think he's always known. You know, the cliché of dolls versus cars? We were always very different growing up in terms of interests."

"I'm glad you had a good time in St. Malo," Michel said. "And I'm sorry you had to come back to this." He pointed at himself lying in his hospital bed.

"You always do like to be the main attraction, *non*?" Gaëlle joked, which made Michel laugh and, in turn, cough. Haakon hurried to give him more water, worrying over him like a mother hen, but Gaëlle's dark humor lightened the mood, and they continued chatting, completely losing track of time until they were interrupted by a quick knock on the door, which was opened without invitation, and a nurse appeared.

"Monsieur? I found your parents, and I have finally managed to talk to them. I spoke to your father this morning, and they are devastated. They will take the next train here to come to see you. Isn't that great news?"

In an instant, Michel lost it. "You WHAT? How dare you? I specifically told you *not* to contact my parents." He grabbed the glass from his nightstand and hurled it at the nurse, who fled the room.

Moments later, Doctor Blanchard appeared, looking particularly severe, and scolded him, but Michel didn't care. He needed to get out of here and nothing was going to stop him. Even if the hospital wanted him to stay, he'd demand to be discharged. He got out of bed and asked Haakon to get his clothes from the closet.

Doctor Blanchard protested, but she couldn't keep a grown man from leaving the hospital, which was exactly what Michel did, weak as he was. By the time they reached his apartment, he was exhausted and went straight to bed. They chatted for a while, and Michel suggested Haakon should fly back to Oslo. He felt guilty that Haakon was missing time at the university, away from his studies, but Haakon refused to listen, and eventually, the strains of the day caught up with Michel, and he fell into a deep sleep.

He awoke to find Haakon shaking him in panic, as his parents were at the door, demanding to see him. They had been to the hospital only to find him gone. Naturally, based on what the staff had told them, their next step after learning he'd discharged himself to go home, was to come here, to see him.

The coming moments, although the entire scene probably lasted less than ten minutes, seemed to drag on forever. His mom broke down in tears at the sight of him, which he'd seen for himself back in his hospital room. Pale, sallow skin, sunken cheeks from all the weight loss, and lesions on his face and neck. His father looked miserable, too, and his enormous mustache quivered with every word he spoke.

They barely acknowledged Haakon, who stood a short distance behind them, looking lost and confused while Michel's parents focused entirely on trying to persuade him to return to Rennes with them. For Haakon's benefit, Michel asked if he would bring some water for his parents, and Haakon left.

"Michel, please be reasonable. For once in your life, listen to your father."

"We've spoken to Doctor Blanchard. She says you'll only get worse, and there is nobody here to care for you. What will you do when you die?" His father's question wasn't unreasonable, but the implied answer was, at least to Michel, and he'd rather die alone in this room than in his childhood bed in Rennes.

"Come home with us, son. Let your mother take care of you in the comfort of your room. And please, help us avoid the shame you've brought upon us with this dreadful disease. What are people going to say when they find out?"

"Don't tell them then!" Michel said defiantly, instantly reminded of the story he'd heard from madame Charpentier about her journey after her son's violent death.

"What happened to you, Michel?" his mother asked, bewildered. "You used to be such a good son. I remember when the midwife placed you in my arms, your cooing, how eager you were to drink my milk. You were such a devoted son, but something changed. I don't even remember when, but I barely recognize you. You've become so hostile. Why?"

"See what you're doing to your mother?" His father was cracking up, too.

Michel contemplated his situation. It was dire. He knew he was dying. He could feel it. His time was running out fast, like water running through a strainer. When Haakon returned with the water, Michel told him what his parents had said. The two boys spoke English, which Michel's parents didn't understand. Michel desperately wanted to remain in Paris, and he wanted to be with Haakon, now more than ever, although he dared not ask him to stay, knowing the challenges the remainder of his life held in store.

Michel told his parents that he was staying put. He had to be true to himself, and leaving Haakon behind would not have been right, most certainly not after Haakon pleaded on his knees to be allowed to stay and look after him. The St. Jacques left without looking back. Michel was not surprised, but very sad, that they all had passed up on another chance at reconciliation, what was in all likelihood their last opportunity. He remembered Philippe and couldn't help but wonder if, like the Charpentiers, his parents would feel different about him after his death.

OCTOBER 11 – DYING

MICHEL WAS ANGRY. No, angry didn't do it justice, and before he realized just how upset he was, the vase shot across the room, crashing against the wall, leaving a pool of water, broken flowers, and a thousand pieces of glass strewn over the floor underneath a wet stain on the wallpaper.

"Michel! What's wrong?" Haakon flew up from the couch, dropping the book he'd been reading.

Michel fell to his knees, sobbing. "I'm fucking dying, that's what's wrong. For every day that passes, for every breath I take, I'm closer to my death, and I haven't even lived my life yet." Even to his own ears, his wailing sounded like that of a wounded animal. "What do I have to show for it, huh? In terms of a life? A closeted upbringing, sexual abuse in every sense of the word, no education, no accomplishments. Once I am gone, I'll not be remembered by anybody."

"That's not true. I'll always remember you. I'll always love you."

"Oh, fuck off, Haakon. You know what I mean. What have I ever done with my life? Nothing! Zero, zilch." Michel's anguish turned to anger. "How long have we known each other? A couple of months? Do you really know me? Do I know you? It's not like we're engaged or anything. You're just another one-night stand in my never-ending stream of bad decisions." Michel knew that one of the many men he'd encountered over the years must've infected him, and chances were that he'd passed it on to others as well, beyond Haakon. He didn't want to think about that.

231

To really, and fully, accept that piece of information would've broken his heart all over again.

"Now you're not being fair. I'm here, am I not?" Haakon had unexpectedly raised his voice to match Michel's. This was a fight Haakon wasn't backing away from. It was their first.

Michel looked up in surprise. There was something in his boyfriend's eyes that he couldn't quite pinpoint, but it made him reconsider what he'd intended to say. All he could muster was, "I'm sorry. I shouldn't direct my anger at you. It's not your fault after all. It's just so frustrating. Dying, you know?"

"No, I don't know. Not yet anyway! I'm still waiting for the results of my test. So who knows?" Haakon added with emphasis, "Maybe we'll be together again before you know it."

Michel stared at Haakon blankly, having nothing left to say. He didn't know if Haakon was accusing him of murder, simply stating the truth, or in fact, trying to console him. Whichever it was, Haakon seemed to get that he'd not been very clear.

"Look, I know you don't believe in any life beyond this one, I just..." He didn't say anything else either. Instead, he crossed the distance to Michel, sat down next to him, and held him as Michel began to cry again, letting out the sorrow over his all too short life.

***

The coming weeks were difficult. Michel's general condition deteriorated from day to day, as his body was attacked and ravaged by any and all infections in his vicinity. But he fought valiantly for every single moment he had left, relishing the time he got to spend with Haakon, the occasional visits by Gaëlle, and the little things in life, like walks in the neighborhood, a cup of coffee, a croissant, or a hug. Sometimes he managed to venture all the way down to the Seine, sitting on the bench near Notre Dame where he had professed his feelings for Haakon the very first time. It wasn't far, maybe a twenty-minute walk, but in his condition, it was a stretch.

The results of Haakon's HIV test had come back, and they were positive, too. *I have killed him!* But no vases flew across his apartment after they'd received the news. While Haakon had acted bravely and had not shed a single tear at the announcement, for Michel, knowing he had infected Haakon was worse than dying himself.

Had the news been any other, Michel would have wanted to fight on, to stay alive in the hopes of a miracle cure, to be with Haakon for as long as humanly possible. But after the conversation at the hospital with Doctor Blanchard, who coolly insisted on a list of all sexual contacts Haakon may have had since he contracted HIV, Michel resigned himself to his death. Why fight on? Why struggle? What for? To see Haakon get sick? To see him develop sarcomas? Get pneumonia? Never-ending diarrhea? Skin feeling like parchment? To feel pain in every part of his body? No, Michel was done. He wouldn't witness a death he had caused, not Haakon's death. He couldn't.

That was the day Michel stopped fighting his AIDS.

By the end of the month, he felt so bad that the hospital demanded to readmit him. But Michel had no trust left, and despite Doctor Blanchard's insistence, he refused to go back. Haakon supported him, knowing that Michel was too stubborn to give in. Michel felt miserable putting Haakon through the extra pressure of caring for someone as sick as he was. Yet Haakon never complained, not once.

The man was a miracle, and he was his. Michel had killed him, even though the bullet would reach its target months or years after he himself had passed away, his corpse rotting somewhere in an anonymous grave. For the first time in his life, Michel had something he truly cherished, someone he'd have given his life to save, and instead, he'd take Haakon with him. There was just no way he could live with that. He wouldn't have to for very long. The guilt ate away at his soul as fast as the virus ravaged his body.

NOVEMBER 2 – PAPEETE

*H*AAKON, ARE YOU ready?" Michel peeked into the living room of their tropical island cottage. After their round-the-world trek, they had found a new home on the island of Tahiti, of all places. Michel chuckled at the memory. *If you'd told me this when I first met you, I'd have called you mad.* "I'm ready. Just putting on my shoes." Haakon sounded tired. He'd suffered a stroke a couple of years ago and had slowed down considerably. They were both retired. Michel was no longer teaching French, and Haakon, who had written articles for travel journals around the globe, had to put that aside to concentrate on his rehabilitation. He'd recovered enough to live an independent daily life, but that was it. They both enjoyed their walks into Papeete, to visit their favorite bar with friends, drink a glass of beer, and eat a small meal before shopping for dinner and heading back home again to their cottage in one of the valleys leading into the town.

They'd been a couple for decades, inseparable since their reunion in Paris in 1986. After getting his degree, Michel had first moved to Oslo, to get to know Haakon's fabled and exotic home country. They lived there in Haakon's apartment near the Royal Castle for a short time before they moved north to Haakon's farm in Røros. After several long, cold, and dark winters in the mountains of Trøndelag, Michel couldn't stand it any longer, and they decided, having saved as much money as they could, to finally fulfill their common and long-held dream of a backpacking trip around the world.

It had been an amazing time: traveling through Europe, into Turkey, on to Egypt, India, down to Malaysia, Singapore, and from Indonesia to Australia, and to New Zealand. It had been exhilarating, and educating, and they had cherished every second of it because they had each other to share all those incredible moments. By the time they'd reached Auckland, money was running out, and they booked a working passage on a freighter headed to the many island nations in the South Pacific with much-needed supplies. They spent months hopping from island to island, the names of which inspired many childhood dreams: Samoa, Bora-Bora, Tahiti, and Fiji.

It was during that time they fell in love with the simple and relaxed lifestyle of the Pacific Islanders, their welcoming smiles and their open hearts. It was a far cry from the hustle and bustle of the city life of Paris or Oslo. Here, different values seemed to matter in the pursuit of happiness. It wasn't the next step on an endlessly ascending career ladder or the never-ending hoarding of possessions. They cherished the islands for their natural beauty, climate, pristine waters, clean beaches, and tropical forests.

When they reached Tahiti, and its capital Papeete, they decided to set down roots, and given Michel's French citizenship, being allowed to stay was easy enough.

They first lived in the city, in a tiny studio apartment, working as teachers by day, surfing and enjoying life at night and on weekends. They didn't have much money, but they had each other, and it was all they had ever needed.

Haakon's stroke had come quite unexpectedly. It had been a hard blow, and Michel was afraid he'd lose him. At their age, both having turned seventy a few years ago, they had talked about the end of life, how they wanted things to be arranged. They were very much aligned on their wishes: cremation and scattering the ashes at sea. A simple get-together with their local friends was all they envisioned.

Still, it was one thing to plan for the event, to discuss it in theory, sitting on their porch in matching rocking chairs in the afternoon sun. It was an entirely different beast to be sitting on a hard plastic chair in a cool, sterile hospital room, the love of your life hooked to life support in his ICU bed, with seemingly countless sensors attached to and cables running from his frail, thin body as the ventilator pumped air into his lungs. That had been a nightmare. When Haakon had woken up, suddenly, after four days of unconsciousness, hanging on to life by a thread, Michel had lost it, finally acknowledging how close he'd come to being a widower. The nurses rushing in were confused as to whom to assist at first.

It had taken many months of rehab before Haakon was allowed to return home to continue a slow and arduous journey back toward a nominally regular life. Finally together again, they adjusted their circumstances to the "new normal," which was much slower than it had been before. But they managed, and they enjoyed taking it easy, approaching each day as it came along, no demands, no expectations, just the two of them.

After they'd returned from the city, exhausted from the hustle and bustle of it, they'd opened a beer and sat on the porch to watch the sun set. They had a great view from their front porch, covered with a typical palm-leaf roof, just like the rest of their house.

Today was no different. The walk had been tiring, and Haakon sat in his rocking chair, looking out over the valley, the town, and the sea. Michel went inside the house to grab them a couple of beers and returned to the porch.

"Here you go, chou-chou!" He handed Haakon his bottle. "Santé!"

"Skål!" Haakon responded, raising his bottle before taking a swig. "We have lived great lives, haven't we?"

"We have, Haakon, and they're not over yet."

"I'll drink to that!" Haakon chuckled and raised his beer again, taking another drink, his thoughts elsewhere.

"You know," Michel mused, "a friend of mine told me once, a long time ago, back in Rennes, that I'd know I was in love with someone when I could picture myself growing old with that person. And here we are, still together. I didn't fully understand what she meant back then, and I certainly never would have believed anyone if they'd predicted this future for us. But I sure do believe her now."

"I love you, too, babe. She must have been a smart person." Haakon looked at Michel, smiling indulgently. He'd heard the story many times before...

Michel woke up as Haakon gently shook him. "Babe, are you dreaming again? You were talking in your sleep."

NOVEMBER 8 – WALKING
ALONG THE SEINE

ICHEL HAD GOOD days, and he had bad days. He slept a lot, often dreaming, sometimes having nightmares. Most of the days were miserable when his AIDS kept him from leaving his bed, except to possibly hobble to the bathroom, or be carried there by Haakon, to relieve himself. Even that was increasingly impossible which is why he'd begun to wear diapers. He hated it, and he despised having to put Haakon through it. The stench coming from his nether regions whenever Haakon had to change a soiled diaper was sometimes so bad that Michel wanted to die, right there and then. The shame was the worst part, and it was only the—much worse—thought of having all of this done by his mother instead, the complete loss of dignity it would've involved, that allowed him to cope. Haakon's stoic personality was a great help, too. He never once complained, flinched, or said a word in these situations.

Thankfully, not everything was bad, and there were still days when he could get up, wash himself, let Haakon shave him, and even get dressed for a meal at the table. Sometimes he even had a really good day, when all the stars seemed to align in a heavenly symphony and allow him a few hours of respite, a glimpse of a humane life. Michel was under no illusion that it would last, and the terms "normal" or "regular" certainly didn't apply. There would be no more lectures at the Sorbonne, no more drinks with friends at a local café, no more nights of dancing at a club, no more sex with Haakon, and most importantly, he never knew how long it would last.

He didn't understand why it happened nor could he predict when it would, but those few hours gave him a chance to recapture what little humanity was left within him, provide Haakon with a brief respite, and allow them to be a young couple in love. Well, almost.

Today was such a day, and when Michel woke up, he felt different. He had a bad urge to go pee and, without thinking, got out of bed the way he'd done ever since he was a child. It wasn't until he felt the diaper around his waist that he remembered everything was not as it always had been. Haakon stirred in the bed and turned around but didn't wake up.

Michel tiptoed to the bathroom to relieve himself, taking off the diaper and throwing it away. It was unused. Unusual but most welcome. A smile greeted him when he saw his reflection in the mirror. He didn't dare to shower because this feeling of strength might disappear again at any moment with overexertion, but he used a washcloth lathered up with soap and warm water and washed his face, ears, armpits, chest, and private parts. It was chilly in the bathroom, yet he relished the sensation of cold on his skin, feeling the goose bumps forming after the moisture evaporated.

It saddened him to look at his bony frame, gray skin and dull hair draped over his skeleton, barely any muscle tissue left and no fat. He'd lost so much weight in the last couple of months, he looked like a walking corpse. *What does Haakon see in me?*

He shaved and applied a little aftershave moisturizer. It felt like a once-in-a-lifetime luxury, the faint scent of Kouros on his face and neck. It had been a present from Claude, at a time when Michel couldn't have afforded it himself.

Returning to the main room, where Haakon was still asleep, Michel went over and kissed him on the cheek, waking him up.

"Good morning, chou-chou! Did you sleep well?"

"Michel!" Haakon shot up. "Are you okay?" Confusion and fear flashed across Haakon's features as he tried to shake the sleep from his body.

"I'm fine." Michel smiled and patted Haakon's face. "I'm well, actually. I thought we could go for a walk and grab some breakfast? I don't know how long this will last, but I'd hate to spend one of my good days in the house. Do you mind?"

Haakon's unspoken response—the love in his eyes, the joy of seeing Michel up and in front of him, mixed with the fear that it might not last, *could not* last, and the sorrow—made Michel's heart ache. How did he deserve this man in his life? Had Haakon not been on his side when his parents had suddenly shown up, he'd most likely never have left his loft above his dad's garage again. His parents would've never have allowed him out in public, looking the way he did, afraid of the shame he would have brought upon them. But thanks to Haakon's heroic decision, here they were, and Paris beckoned, if only for a little while.

"Of course, babe. Just give me a couple of minutes for a quick shower. I feel filthy."

Michel looked after the naked form of his man disappearing into the bathroom, his beautiful shape, his strawberry-blond curly hair, his stunning ass, his hairy legs, and his lean body. Suddenly his throat felt dry, but for once not due to the ulcers in his mouth. He quickly dismissed the thought. He did not have the energy for sex, and they hadn't been intimate since Haakon's return. It just wasn't in the cards, not for him, ever again.

When Haakon reappeared a couple of minutes later, a towel draped around his waist, Michel sat fully dressed at the small kitchen table, admiring the beauty of the only man he'd ever truly loved, and he remembered again Giselle's wise words: "love is when you see yourself growing old with that person." That image of the two of them as old men sitting in matching rocking chairs, holding hands, had first appeared in his mind on the train ride from London to Dover over a year ago. Since then, it had reappeared in his dreams regularly. Alas, it was not meant to be.

He could still conjure the image to appear whenever he wanted, even in an awakened state—the porch, the rocking chairs, the palm trees—but he didn't need to imagine. He knew how much he loved Haakon. He felt it deeply. He had grown up and had come to realize how very different he was now compared to the boy Giselle had known.

Watching Haakon drop the towel and bend over to pick up his underwear gave Michel pause. *My man is so beautiful, and I so want to be with him.*

As if sensing Michel's eyes on him, Haakon turned around, asking, "Are you okay? Are you sure you're up for a walk?"

"Yes, absolutely! Hurry up, chou-chou." Michel smiled back, feeling the warmth of his love spread across his entire body.

His next thought was different, as was so often the case these days. There was his love for Haakon, and how lucky he felt for having met him, contrasted with the pain of his disease, his looming death, and the futility of it all. It had all happened so fast, and Michel understood now, having learned enough about HIV over the past months, that he had no one to blame but himself. It was his lifestyle, the choices he had made as a youth, the endless hours spent in the darkroom at Le Chat Noir, the anonymous fucks with countless, faceless men.

Michel had long ago come to terms with never knowing who had infected him; nor would he ever know if he'd passed it on to anyone apart from Haakon. He could, in fact, have infected dozens of others. He remembered the accusatory glares from the nurse in charge of compiling the list of people he had been with. She'd given up after a few minutes because Michel couldn't tell her. He'd mentioned Claude, of course, their stupid one-time thing after his eighteenth birthday, and he felt terribly guilty that he had not been emotionally capable of contacting his friend after his diagnosis. At the same time, he was afraid he'd learn he'd effectively killed Claude, too. Or had it been vice versa? Who knew?

He did, of course, realize he was responsible for passing it on to Haakon, and it was his greatest regret. *I've killed Haakon, the best thing that's ever happened to me.* If there had ever been a red thread in his life, it was that he would eventually destroy any and every good thing that happened to him. He'd lost his puberty to the monseigneur; he'd lost his innocence to Bernard. He'd lost Pascal because of his horniness, and he was about to lose his own life because of his promiscuity. Even beyond his own life, he would cause havoc for his parents, Haakon, and his friends.

"Are you ready?" Haakon's voice yanked him from his dark thoughts.

"Yes, sure!" He got up and put on a coat and a pair of comfortable walking shoes.

They left the apartment together and stepped out into the street. The air was chilly; fog had nestled in across the entire city, and even though it was mid-morning, streetlights were still on, casting a strange glow around them. Michel hooked his arm in Haakon's, for support and to be close to him, as they began a slow stroll down toward the Seine. The river crossing the city had always had a strong pull on Michel, and he remembered taking Haakon there on their first evening together. How much had changed since then.

After a good forty minutes or more, they reached the riverbanks, dammed up on both sides inside the city, and they crossed Petit Pont to reach the island, Île de la Cité, home to the cathedral of Notre Dame. At this time of year, there were few tourists, and Parisians went about their weekend business. Nobody cared about the two young men strolling over to a nearby bench for a short rest.

"Do you remember?" Michel asked, resting his head against Haakon's shoulder, as he so often did, enjoying the physical proximity, soaking it up like a water-deprived plant.

"Yes, babe, I do. I asked you about love. How could I ever forget? I realize now that I loved you already. I just didn't know it then. I couldn't see it, even though it was right there in front of me."

Michel lifted his head and planted a kiss on Haakon's cheek. "That makes two of us. I'm sorry that I ruined everything. I'm so very sorry."

"Don't be, babe. It's hardly your fault. This is a virus, and that's what viruses do. They spread to survive. How were you supposed to know it was spreading? Nobody knew. I certainly don't blame you. I never could."

"Thank you for saying so, chou-chou. I wish it were that simple. I guess all the years of Catholic indoctrination have taken their toll on me. Feeling guilty is my go-to position, my life's default. I don't know. The only thing I do know for certain is that I love you. You're the single best thing that's ever happened in my life. And I don't know how to repay you." He began to cry. "I know I won't be able to…"

"Michel, babe! Listen to me." Haakon turned to face him and took both his hands in his. "I love you. And because I love you, I want to be with you, no matter what. You don't owe me anything because you have given me the most valuable gift any man could ever ask for. Your heart. I never thought it possible that anyone would ever love me. Let's not waste this day worrying about what-ifs or wallowing in guilt. Let's just be a regular couple in love, on a walk in the most romantic city on Earth. Shall we?" Haakon got up and pulled Michel to his feet. "Where to next?"

"Let's go to Île Saint-Louis. I've always loved that little island." Michel grabbed hold of Haakon's arm again, and together they strolled past Notre Dame toward the smaller of the two islands that once formed the Gallic settlement of Lutetia, and what was later to become Paris. The fog was still heavy, effectively dampening the noises of the large city, casting every street in dull, subdued light.

They walked mostly in silence. Michel didn't know how to show Haakon how much he loved him and how grateful he was for the sacrifice his Norwegian Viking had made by staying with him these final weeks of his life. Yet he also understood that Haakon knew. He didn't see it as a sacrifice. If Michel had interpreted his words correctly, for Haakon, it was an act of love. *For better or worse.* It filled Michel with a sense of peace, to know that he, too, was loved, unconditionally.

They crossed Pont Saint-Louis and walked the entire length of rue Saint-Louis en Île, moving over to rive droite and continuing on the main boulevard toward Place de la Bastille where they stopped for a meal. The walk had exhausted Michel, and he needed to rest.

"Would you like to go home?" Haakon asked.

"No, let's have a coffee and something small to eat. It's so nice to be out and about. I don't want to go home yet. Who knows when I'll be able to get out again?"

The waiter was a handsome young man, and he served them swiftly and politely. They had been to other places where the service sometimes seemed forced, as the general public had learned enough about the disease that many were scared of catching it, but not enough to know they were not at risk. Not from dishes, a handshake, or the simple physical proximity to someone with AIDS. Still, people like Michel were largely shunned by others.

"Have a good day." The young man smiled as they left. "And get well soon."

"He's family," Haakon murmured. "We got lucky."

Michel didn't answer but agreed, of course. He wanted to go back to the river and had steered them toward City Hall when Haakon stopped.

"Hang on for a second, I'll be right back." Off he ran, back to the square behind them. Michel's eyesight had not been improved by his disease, and he found it difficult to focus on anything beyond ten or twenty feet away, thus didn't see what Haakon was up to.

When he saw a horse-drawn carriage approach, he instinctively took a step back against the wall of the nearest building. Then he saw Haakon beaming from the carriage.

"Let me help you up!" The carriage came to a full stop in front of him, and Haakon jumped down.

"But we can't afford this!" Michel protested.

"Don't you worry about it. Do you want to save up for heaven?" Haakon teased and helped him climb the two steps up into the carriage. The driver helped to drape a couple of thick blankets over Michel's thin frame and off they went. Haakon had arranged for the carriage to take them to the Trocadéro, along the river, to enjoy a different view of Paris.

Michel squeezed Haakon's hand under the blankets, happy. "Merci, chou-chou. What a wonderful idea. I love it."

Feeling the wind blowing gently across his face, listening to the trot of the horses' hoofs on the pavement, the cars passing them, Michel enjoyed taking in the scenery, knowing this would likely be the last time he'd ever do anything like this.

He'd been to see Doctor Blanchard just a couple of days ago, and she had not been very hopeful about his prospects and had once again urged him to come back to the hospital for proper, professional palliative care. His hand firmly placed in Haakon's comforting grip, he'd refused, but he knew he had weeks at most, maybe just a few days. He pushed the thoughts from his mind, focusing on the now and the beautiful man sitting next to him, enjoying this ride like a child, grinning happily, pointing out fascinating details on facades, the odd cargo ship on the river, and happy couples walking along the Seine.

When they reached the Trocadéro, they sat on a bench overlooking the river with the magnificent Eiffel Tower rising and disappearing into the fog on the other side of the Seine. They could barely see the first level; that was how low the fog descended. Michel was fatigued and soon asked Haakon to call a cab to go home. He began to feel an all too familiar pain in his abdomen and could barely sit up straight. Haakon rushed to get him home.

Back at their studio, Haakon helped Michel lie down on their bed, undressed him, and made sure to tuck him in properly. "Can I get you a cup of tea? Some broth?"

"No, thanks, chou-chou. I just want to rest a bit. Can you stay with me?"

"Sure." Haakon lay next to him.

"Can you do me a favor?"

"Anything." Haakon's eyes resembled those of a puppy, eager to please his master.

"Could you get undressed and get into bed with me?"

Haakon looked puzzled but did as instructed. Shedding his clothes, he climbed into bed, naked, and scooted up to Michel, who was lying on his back. He put his arm around him and kissed him on his cheek. "Like this?"

"Merci, chou-chou! I wanted to feel your skin one more time."

***

Haakon stayed in that position until he was sure Michel had fallen asleep.

NOVEMBER 29 – A GLORIOUS DAY

TODAY IS A beautiful day. I feel so much better. My mouth doesn't feel like raw meat for the first time in weeks, and the sarcomas aren't giving me any trouble. Outside, the sun is shining at last. The temperature is supposed to reach 15°C, and Haakon made us breakfast. He went down to the local bakery for fresh croissants, as a treat, and I managed to eat something without throwing it up again. I've asked him if we can take a taxi to the Trocadéro, to get some fresh air and see the Eiffel Tower from that bench we found a few weeks ago. I didn't get to enjoy the view then. Maybe I'll be strong enough to walk a little.

He said yes, my brave man. He's so good to me, always looking out for me, caring for me, doting on me. I'm so lucky to have him. I feel so sorry for him. I know my time is quickly running out. I can feel my body giving up. I haven't had the courage to tell him. I just can't do it. He's always so brave, so optimistic, so hopeful. I can't bring myself to break his heart. Poor chou-chou!

He's just now calling a cab. I need to go. It's going to be fun. I love him so much, my Viking. Jeg elsker deg, gutten min. I think that's how they say it in Norway.

PRESENT DAY

MON BIJOU, BRITISH VIRGIN ISLANDS

*H*AAKON GENTLY CLOSED and put down Michel's diary. Tears were running down his cheeks. Suddenly his whole body shook, and he began to sob uncontrollably.

Jeg elsker deg. I love you. On his last day, Michel had professed his love one last time, in his mother tongue. It meant the world to him.

The memory of that day in Paris was overwhelming. Michel's passing, the difficult days and weeks that followed, and how Michel's death had pushed him straight into the arms of Charles...

Charles.

And here he was, in Charles's former house, this Caribbean paradise. Michel had been dead for decades, yet somehow, that wound had never healed. Reading about it made him relive all those memories of having to empty the small studio apartment ahead of Michel's parents' arrival, making sure anything racy would not be found...and saving this journal.

He never learned what had happened to Michel's body, except that it was returned to Rennes. Undoubtedly, his parents buried him there. But what about his friends? Did Giselle, Claude, and Antoine ever find out? Were they able to attend the funeral?

He could ask Gaëlle, but they had lost touch after he'd gone on his travels. Given that her medical transition hadn't begun when he'd left Paris, and with the complexities of changing names and all the legal implications, who knew if he could even track her down?

He looked out to the sea, still as calm as it had been a few hours earlier. *It's getting late. I need to get inside and check the forecast.*

Haakon got up and walked into the house. There was no word yet from India, so he typed another email to Nidhi, asking her to expand her search to also include one Gaëlle Martin, last known address in Paris, ca 1986. *Talk about finding a needle in a haystack.*

He checked the latest weather forecast: for now, it seemed they might get lucky. The hurricane had begun to shift ever so slightly on a more northern trajectory and might completely miss the islands if it continued on this course, instead heading toward northeastern Florida and Georgia. But it was growing in size and would still affect Mon Bijou. Time to get cracking and prepare. It was, after all, better to be safe than sorry.

***

Haakon spent the next day with Rose and Ansel, making sure the island was ready to be hit by the storm, regardless. They had stayed in touch with the home base in Bangalore and had managed to change the flight arrangements for the kids. They'd be picked up the next day and flown back to India, straight from Tortola, on a chartered flight. It would be a week earlier than planned, but hurricane season was unpredictable, and nobody dared take any chances.

There was no news on the other front, and Nidhi apologized. With Nanju, her husband, in surgery in the hospital and Mahender still on route, she had to prioritize the repatriation of the kids. Haakon understood. "It's okay. Forget about it. I'll do it myself. I have plenty of time, now that everything is arranged for the kids and the bungalows are all boarded up."

After dinner, Haakon logged onto Facebook and searched for Gaëlle. Most people were on there these days, so why not her? He found a handful of people matching her name on the site, and he was able to exclude most, as they were either too young or couldn't be her judging by the profile picture. But there was a Gaëlle Oberhausen who looked familiar. Maybe she had gotten married? There had to be a reason why the algorithm had included her in the search results. Haakon looked at her profile and her details, which were sparse but informed him this "Gaëlle Oberhausen" did indeed live in Paris. Could it be her? There was only one way to find out. He sent her a brief message:

Bonjour!

This is Haakon Chitragar, formerly Olafsen. I'm not sure if you remember me, for two reasons: either you are not the right Gaëlle Martin I am looking for, or you might have simply forgotten about the events of 1985/6 and our common friend Michel St. Jacques.

Either way, a response would be greatly appreciated.

He sent it off and called Mahender.

"God morgen, kæresten min!" Haakon's heart skipped a beat when he saw his husband's face on his phone's small screen. Mahender always greeted Haakon in Norwegian, a token of his great love for him. "I miss you! I just got home a couple of hours ago." It felt good to hear his voice, to see him.

"Good! Thanks. You? Have you heard from Nanju?"

"He's fine. I got a text from Nidhi a while ago. He's out of surgery. Everything went well. He'll be out of the hospital in a few days. He got lucky with nothing but a couple of broken bones and no internal injuries. How are things on the island? Can you already feel the effects of the hurricane?"

"The waves have picked up a bit and so has the wind. But it's still mostly sunny. I don't expect to feel the real effects until the day after tomorrow. By then, we'll all have left."

"I can't wait to see you again. These past two days have been lonely without you."

"About that," Haakon said cautiously, "I'm not coming home. At least, not straight away."

"Oh?" Haakon wasn't entirely sure if Mahender was curious or worried.

"I need to go to France first."

"France? How come?" That was definitely curiosity. They had been a couple for so many years now, they trusted each other implicitly. There was no reason for subterfuge or jealousy.

"Well, it's a long story. Do you remember Michel, my first lover? Remember how we went to Paris on our first trip together? After Charles's death?"

"Sure, I remember it fondly. You showed me the bench where Michel passed away. How could anyone forget such a tragic memory?"

"I came across his diary yesterday and spent the day reading it. Not just the last entries, few as they were, about us and his final months battling his HIV, but the entire diary from when he was a child. I got to know a whole other part of Michel—his childhood, his youth—and there are some questions left that I would like to get answers to."

"What are you talking about, dear?"

"Well, for one, I've never been to his grave, but also, there were other people in Michel's life, important people who meant a great deal to him. I want to see them—if they're still alive. Tell them about him, maybe learn more about him? Get closure? I've already fired off a message to someone we both knew back then in Paris."

"May I join you on this quest?"

Haakon knew Mahender would accept a "no" from him if he wanted to do this on his own. "You just got home. Are you sure you want to get on the next flight out again? I'd hate to do this to you, nanna bangaru."

"Don't worry about me. I'll wash my underwear and be on my way out again." Mahender had the weirdest sense of humor. "Luckily, the European flights don't leave until after midnight, so

I have all day to do laundry, check in on Nidhi and the office, and visit Nanju at the hospital. So if you'll have me, I'd like to come, to be by your side on this journey."

There was no reason to do this alone. They were a team, and if he had his husband by his side, things would be easier, regardless of what they found.

"I'd love it if you were with me. I'm flying out to Paris tomorrow. I'll send you my flight schedule and what hotel I'm staying at. See you in a couple of days then?"

"Another adventure! This is so exciting! I can't wait."

"Nanna bangaru, thank you, for everything."

"I love you, too!" Mahender smiled happily, and then the line disconnected.

Haakon booked his flight to Paris and a room in a nice hotel in the Latin quarter, then sent everything in an email to his husband before going for an evening swim. The sea had begun to shift, and the waves were getting bigger. Nothing spectacular yet, but it made swimming difficult, and after a couple of mouthfuls of water, Haakon cut it short and went back inside the house. He went to bed early, excited for the next day and his flight to Europe, to hopefully find the answers he was yearning for.

GAËLLE

WHEN HE WOKE up in the morning, he noticed the notification on his phone. Someone had sent him a message. It was Gaëlle. He'd found the right person.

Bonjour Haakon!

You have no idea how happy I am to receive this message from you. I was afraid you had died, too, after your diagnosis, especially after never hearing from you again. How are you? Your last name sounds Indian? And your profile says you live in Bangalore? Seems you're living the life of travel after all!

Bisous, Gaëlle!

Haakon looked at the timestamp and figured the message had been sent shortly after she'd woken up. Given the time difference, he decided to try the bold thing and call her, and after a few signals, his call went through.

"Haakon? I can't believe it's you! It's been so long."

"I know. I feel bad for not having been able to stay in touch through all these years, but I forgot your address and so I couldn't write, and to be honest, my life after Michel's death was chaotic. You wouldn't believe half of it if I told you. But I have something to share with you, and I think I'll need your help."

"Oh?" Gaëlle sounded worried. "You're not sick or dying, are you?"

Haakon laughed. "No, not at all! I just wondered if you might be interested in joining me on a small quest back into the past? I'm about to leave my house and take a flight to Paris. I'll be there early tomorrow morning."

"*Color me intrigued. Any details?*"

"Of course. I stumbled across Michel's diary the other day here in the house. And I read it, from cover to cover. I'd never done that before. I only ever read the passages from the time when I knew Michel personally. The end, you know? But there are some people mentioned in the diary. Some very important people, it seems. Do you remember how Michel didn't want his folks to take him home to look after him? And how he panicked at that prospect? And how they dragged his body back to Rennes without ever letting us know or inviting us to the funeral?"

"*Sure,*" Gaëlle said.

"Michel didn't grow up in a vacuum, but he had friends back in Rennes. People who meant the world to him. There were two in particular who functioned like a second set of parents for him. So I wondered if you might join me on a journey of discovery to see if any of them are still alive? Maybe help bring them some closure, too? For all we know, they never learned of Michel's passing. If his parents were true to form, they might not have announced it in public, you know?"

On the other end of the line, it sounded as if Gaëlle was crying. "*It brings up a lot of memories from back then. Of course I'll join you on your quest. I'll put in for a short leave of absence at the university. You fly in tomorrow, you said? Where are you staying?*"

Haakon gave her the details, and they agreed that he would call her once he and Mahender were installed, to meet up for a drink at her house to make plans.

"*Haakon, thank you so much for reaching out to me. It means the world. I've not thought about those days in quite some time. After I met my husband, I drifted away from club life and most of the friends I once held dear. Time can drive an enormous wedge between people, and I'm glad I get to overcome this one. Michel was such an important person in my life back then."*

They hung up, and Haakon finished packing before overseeing the final evacuation of the island.

The kids left on a ferry right after breakfast, straight to the airport on Tortola, accompanied by their camp leaders, both Indian and local, while Ansel and Rose stayed behind with their team to look after the island's infrastructure. Haakon's flight was later in the day, straight to New York, from where he would catch the overnight flight to Paris. He was looking forward to enjoying a final couple of hours alone in the house after all the hustle and bustle with the evacuation, although he couldn't find any quiet given that the winds had begun to pick up, and the boarded house made him feel caged.

Then there were all the thoughts of Michel, Paris, Gaëlle, and the mysteries that lay ahead. In the end, he called Ansel and asked the team to take him to Tortola earlier.

RETURN TO PARIS

*G*AËLLE, YOU LOOK amazing. How have you been?" Haakon was stunned when he saw his and Michel's old friend. Last he'd seen her, she was still pre-op, having barely begun her hormone treatment, a girl unsure of herself and her place in the world. The Gaëlle in front of him was a stunning woman in her mid-fifties, with her auburn hair set up in a chignon bun, wearing a formfitting Bordeaux knee-length red dress and matching high heels. She was a towering figure.

Haakon and Mahender had been invited to her apartment in the Latin quarter, a stylish high-ceilinged condo meticulously decorated with tasteful fin-de-siècle furniture.

"You seem to have lived a good life so far?" Haakon commented after having been shown into the living room.

"I'm not complaining. My husband Georg and I are doing well. He's an executive in the aerospace industry and travels a lot, and I teach right here at the Sorbonne. You could say I never really left university, although that is not entirely true. Georg and I lived both in Hamburg during the nineties and in Toulouse for a few years. We only came back to Paris five years ago. But do sit down and let us catch up."

"You were studying medicine back then? Are you a doctor?"

"Yes, and no. I have a PhD in medicine, but I'm not doing clinical work. Michel's death had a deep impact on me, and I ended up specializing in virology. I was with the Pasteur Institute for a long time until we moved, and upon our return to Paris, I took up teaching again, here at the Sorbonne, where it all began. I'm helping shape the next generation of virologists.

Given recent outbreaks of Ebola, Zika, and obviously the COVID pandemic, we need more virologists to help us fight whatever next crawls out of the woodwork."

"I'm impressed," Mahender said. "I can't wait to hear more. We have a special program at our center to inoculate the children we rescue, but it's a constant uphill battle."

They sat on the couch in the living room, which overlooked one of the neighborhood's major arteries, rue Monge, with a beautiful small park across the street. Gaëlle offered them drinks.

"Mahender, we have never met before, so I'm not sure what I may offer you. A cognac? A glass of Bourgogne, or maybe some Champagne? Haakon? I barely remember what you were drinking back then. Mostly beer if memory serves me right? Would it be preposterous to suggest we open a bottle of Champagne to celebrate our reunion? Is that okay with you guys?"

Haakon and Mahender both agreed. If ever there was a Champagne moment, this certainly qualified as one.

"We may not have met in real life, but I still feel like I know you, Gaëlle, as Haakon has mentioned you from time to time. We haven't spoken a lot about his time here in Paris, or Michel, probably because he doesn't want me to feel like a second choice or his fallback guy, but I don't remember a single conversation about Michel where your name wasn't included. It is a privilege to finally meet you in person."

"Why thank you, Mahender! Sadly, there is no way I can reciprocate the compliment. All I know is that the two of you are married, which I gathered from Haakon's Facebook profile. I'm sure there's a story worth telling behind it?" Gaëlle seemed sincere, and as she passed Mahender on her way to the small bar in the corner of her living room, she smiled at him and gently squeezed his arm with her immaculately manicured hand.

Over the next hour, they caught up, each telling the other how their lives had been after they had gone their separate ways back in 1986. Gaëlle had focused on her studies and her group of trans friends, but she'd never been as close to any of them as she'd been to Michel.

"You know, truth be told, I was in love with him. Madly even. I never told him any of this, of course. And he never knew, as far as I know, but he was the first person to accept me for who I am. He was, in fact, the first person to ever meet the real me. This was way back when we first met on the train to Paris. He never questioned that I was a girl, even though at the time, I hardly presented convincingly with my cheap dress and haphazardly applied makeup. I'd changed into my one and only dress in the restrooms at the station in Rennes after getting off the train from St. Malo. Michel was so nice to me, and I fell for him. I fell hard." She chuckled at the memory. "But since he was gay, there was little interest on his part. It was a very one-sided affair." Her smile turned to sadness, and Haakon suddenly saw a lot of things from back then in a new light. The way she had helped him, accompanying him to the hospital, etc., and never once asked for anything in return.

"I had no idea, either. I'm so sorry for having been so blind."

"Oh, don't be! I mean, I knew that it was a crazy endeavor for a woman to fall for a gay man. And it wasn't the first time that happened in human history if I may say so. Luckily, about five years after my transition, I met Georg, the love of my life."

"Tell us about him."

"Georg was born and raised in Stuttgart. He studied engineering, and for some reason, he always had a bit of a love affair with anything and everything French. I guess there are opportunities for men like him in our day, what with the EU and all. His career brought him to Paris early on, and we stumbled across each other in a grocery store, not too far from here." Gaëlle threw her arms in the air. "A stroke of good luck. For some strange reason, he fell in love with me. He's one of a kind, my Georg. You'd like him."

"Won't we meet him?" Mahender asked.

261

"Not in the next few days, I'm afraid. He's on a business trip to Japan. But I've let him know about your arrival, and I'm sure we'll make it happen one day soon. I understand you live in India, right? He has a lot of business all over the country, so I'm sure we'll make the trip soon."

"That would be amazing. We would love to have you as our guests."

"So tell me." Gaëlle turned her attention on Haakon. "What is it you wish to accomplish on this trip?"

Haakon told her about Claude, and how he had helped Michel secure the apartment in Paris, and their friendship stretching back to when Michel had only been fourteen years old. He told her about Giselle and Le Chat Noir and how important both had been for Michel as a youth.

"Wow," Gaëlle was stunned when Haakon was finished. "That is quite the story. I have always contemplated going to Rennes to try and find his grave, but I never got around to it." She looked down to the floor, as if ashamed. "I have no real excuse for never having done it, but life kind of happened, and for every year that passed, it became less acute, less pressing, and after a while, it was but a distant afterthought. Does that make sense? And to be honest, Mahender, just like you feel that maybe Haakon didn't tell you everything about Michel or didn't talk often about him to protect your feelings, it was much the same for me. I sort of buried that part of my life because I was afraid it might make Georg jealous, although I'm certain he'd love to know. Silly, right?"

She picked up her glass and held it up. "Let's toast to our friend Michel, and the adventure ahead. May we find the answers we seek! Santé and welcome to Paris, my friends!"

They toasted and continued to chat for hours until Gaëlle's phone rang. She excused herself to answer it, and Haakon and Mahender could make out that she was speaking to her husband. She spoke a funny combo of French and German which Haakon barely understood. He'd never studied German in school, and Mahender understood neither language.

She came back after ten minutes, apologizing. "I'm sorry, my friends. That was Georg, calling me from Tokyo. He knows I usually retire around this time of day, and so he gets up early to make sure to wish me a good night. He's quite the gentleman."

Mahender looked at his watch. "Oh dear, it's past ten p.m. Have we been chatting away for four hours?" The others laughed. "We should leave you be, so you can get your beauty sleep. We can catch up more tomorrow because I'm sure we're also both jet-lagged, albeit from different directions. Lunch perhaps?"

"That would be great. I have lectures until noon, but any time after that would work. Would you like me to pick the place and send you the address?"

Haakon mock-bowed. "By all means, you're the local. We trust you implicitly." He kissed her on her cheek, three times, as had always been their custom, despite a thirty-five-year hiatus, and Mahender did the same.

PLANNING

So, TELL ME, Haakon, what's the plan? I can't wait to get going." Gaëlle seemed giddy with excitement. They had enjoyed their lunch and time had passed quickly.

"I'd say our first stop has to be Rennes. Maybe check in with City Hall and their records department to see if we can learn anything about Le Chat Noir, Giselle, and Claude? I'd also like to see if we can find Michel's grave. That would mean a lot to me."

"Agreed." Gaëlle nodded. "Since Le Chat Noir was a bar, it needed to have a liquor license from the city, so that should be easy enough to find out. And they should also still have the addresses of the proprietors. You said you couldn't find anything on Google?" Haakon shook his head. "That doesn't surprise me. We mustn't forget that their generation wasn't much for the internet. If it was still the 1980s, we'd have found them on the Minitel, but alas… Based on what you told me Giselle and Claude will be in their eighties, and if they moved, or if they have passed away, we'll need to dig locally. We can leave tomorrow if you like. I have already alerted my staff that I'm taking a few days off to look after some personal matters. My research assistants are covering for me."

"I'll get us the train tickets and book a hotel. Looks like this is really happening." Haakon beamed, squeezing Mahender's hand. "Rennes, here we come."

RENNES

THE TRIP FROM Paris to Rennes on the TGV Atlantique was comfortable and quick.

"I remember a time when this would take a lot longer." Gaëlle recounted the story of her trip with Michel to Paris, back in 1985. She shook her head. "Then again, we didn't mind. We were heading for the great big adventure that was adult life. I mean, it could've taken ten hours and we'd still have loved every minute of it. Besides, I quite enjoyed getting to know Michel." She blushed at her final remark.

They had booked their rooms at the Balthazar Hotel in downtown Rennes. Arriving just before lunch, compliments of the French railway company's high-speed train, they had the entire afternoon to check in with City Hall to find answers.

"Non, madame," the young clerk said after Gaëlle had asked about the bar. "Le Chat Noir went out of business back in 1990. There was a fire and the entire building burned to the ground."

"Do you have an address for the owner from back then? A clue as to where we could find her?"

"You mean madame Montand?"

"Yes, I believe so. Giselle Montand?"

"Just a moment, please." The clerk began to type on his computer. "I'm not supposed to hand out this information. May I ask why you are looking for madame?"

"It's a bit of a long story," Haakon said. "A friend of ours once lived here in Rennes. He passed away in 1986, but in his diary, he mentions being friends with Giselle and her ex-husband,

265

a Claude Montand. We're trying to find out if they're still alive. Get some closure."

The clerk's eyes widened. "Claude Montand as in the real-estate magnate?"

"That one, yes!" Haakon confirmed. It had to be. "Do you know him? Is he still alive?"

For a moment, they were all hopeful.

"Everybody in Rennes knows about Claude Montand," the clerk said. "He was famous! But I'm sorry, he's been dead for ages. He died from AIDS. That was quite the scandal here in town back when it happened." The clerk looked at Haakon and Mahender. "I'm family, too. It was a dark time for the LGBTQ community in Rennes. When he died, people freaked out. His tenants all feared that he had somehow infected them. It was insane, and our kind was persecuted for years. People talk about him to this very day. I'll see if I can find an address for madame Montand."

He disappeared for a few minutes but returned all smiles. "You are in luck. I found her. Madame Montand lives in Brest. Here's her address. She moved away from Rennes shortly after the fire." He handed them a piece of paper with an address written on it.

"That makes sense," Haakon said pensively. "I recall one entry in Michel's journal about Giselle making a trip to Brest. If I recall, she grew up there and traveled back to see her estranged family."

"You've been most helpful, sir, but might we trouble you with one more question?" Mahender asked gently. "Their friend Michel is most likely buried here in town. Can you see where?"

"Sure, we have that information on file. What's his name and dates of birth and death?" The clerk typed on his computer, opening up a different registry. Haakon and Gaëlle looked at each other.

"His name was Michel St. Jacques," Haakon provided, "and he died November 29, 1986, in Paris. He was born in 1964, on October 4. I have no idea what his parents' names were or anything like that. I forgot to bring the diary. I think their names were mentioned in it. It's still at the hotel."

The clerk smiled and made a dismissive gesture. "That's quite all right. I have more than enough information. Thank you. And here we go, here he is. He's buried in the Cimetière du Nord, section ten. Let me write down that information for you. His parents are buried in the same plot. It's a family grave. Just a moment, please."

The clerk busied himself to get everything on paper for them, and as they took their leave, he added, "My sympathies for your loss. I was born twenty years after monsieur St. Jacques and never really experienced the AIDS crisis firsthand, at least not the way it must have been back then. I can only imagine what an earth-shattering loss it must have been."

THE GRAVE

*N*OW WHAT?" MAHENDER took a deep breath after the successful but short visit to City Hall. "Do you want to go see him now, or would you rather wait until we come back?"

"We have plenty of time now. I don't see what we have to gain by waiting. We can head out to Brest after breakfast tomorrow. Besides, it makes no difference to Michel, does it?" Haakon looked at Gaëlle.

"No, I agree," she said. "We're here. Let's pay him our respects."

They took a cab out to the city's northern cemetery and—using the instructions and a map they'd been handed—quickly found the right section of the cemetery. They roamed the rows, looking for the grave of the St. Jacques family.

"Here, guys, I think I've found it," Mahender suddenly called out. "It's right over here."

Haakon hurried over to a grave site with no flowers. There was a simple granite cross with a white marble figure of the crucified Christ instead of a headstone, and the slab covering the grave had three names engraved on it. Mahender read them out loud:

St. Jacques
Michel 1964 – 1986
Edmond 1934 – 1990
Emmanuelle 1939 – 2014

That's not a whole lot of information, Haakon thought. The engraved letters of Michel's name had eroded and were partially overgrown with lichen, as they had been exposed to the weather and elements for a long time. It made him sad to see it and drove home the point of the passage of time with particular finality. There was nothing to indicate any sort of emotion on the stone, and that probably affected Haakon more than anything. No indication of love, loss, or sorrow. It was the saddest gravestone he had ever seen. On the other hand, it was indicative of how Michel had described his family on the pages of his diary. To the bitter end, Jesus on the cross was more important than the bond of family.

Gaëlle came up to him, tears streaming down her cheeks, and put her arm around him. "You okay?"

Mahender took Haakon's hand.

"Yeah, I'm okay. It's just mind-boggling to finally be standing here. I'm not even sure what I expected if that makes any sense. Yet being here, it feels so empty. I lost him thirty-five years ago, and I have often thought about different what-if scenarios. Now I'm here, standing in front of his grave, and all I feel is nothing. Emptiness!"

"It's okay, Haakon." Gaëlle was drying away her tears. "It's okay. You have mourned him for all those years, again and again, every time you had to think back to those days in Paris, as Michel got weaker and weaker, the hospital visits, dressing his wounds, feeding him, cleaning him, washing him, losing him, and finally, for good measure, being robbed of the chance to bury him, to say farewell. You had to be so brave, so strong. Give it time, my friend. The emotions will come back to you."

Next to Haakon, Mahender squeezed his hand. "I agree with Gaëlle. Would you like to be alone with him for a while? Maybe you, too, Gaëlle? I can wait over there by the bench. I don't mind."

Gaëlle looked at Mahender and nodded. "I think I'll join you. Now that I know where his grave is, I can always come back to visit him. I'll bring Georg along next time around." The two left Haakon to reflect.

"Thirty-five years, babe!" Haakon finally said once he was alone with Michel. "And here you've been all this time. I'm sorry I haven't been around." He crouched and put his hand on the gravestone, tracing the letters of Michel's name with his index finger, caressing every single letter.

"I've missed you so much. You have no idea. That day, when you died, after the ambulance picked you up, I wasn't allowed to see you again. I wasn't allowed to ride along in the ambulance. I had to take a taxi to the hospital, but they wouldn't let me near you. They wouldn't let me see you. I couldn't even say goodbye, I wasn't allowed to. They just sent me away."

He fell to his knees and began to sob, as the memories and the pain of that fateful day washed over him anew, how he'd been sitting on that bench across from the Eiffel Tower, the city at his feet, and the weight of Michel's dead body against his. The desperation, the fear—no, the panic—of not knowing what to do. Finally, a passerby had noticed his circumstances and had run to a nearby phone booth to alert the authorities.

They had come quickly, blue lights, sirens, and all, and around Haakon, still sitting on the bench, still holding Michel, a small group of onlookers had gathered, staring, pointing fingers, chatting amongst themselves. Nobody offered their help, nobody dared to approach them. Michel looked frightfully pale, his cheeks sunk in from the weight loss in the wake of his disease, and that scared people off. Even when he'd still been alive, he had looked dead. That had been the case for quite some time, which is why he'd normally worn sunglasses and a cap whenever he'd left the apartment, which had been less and less frequently in those final weeks.

But that fateful Saturday, he'd been upbeat and wanted to go out to enjoy the bleak November sun. Haakon had never known why. Had he been done with his life? Had Michel suffered enough? Was he ready to go after seeing his beloved Paris one last time?

Je t'aime! Those had been his final words. Haakon pictured that moment of that day so long ago, before the mayhem, their final tender moment, both professing their love to each other.

"I guess you were ready to let go. I just didn't see it. I'm so sorry. And I know now that you couldn't express it any other way. I missed you so much, Michel. So much. Life has been good to me, you know? I've had some difficult years, especially in the beginning. I met this man, a rich Englishman, shortly after you died, and while he enabled me to travel the world, he also brought more darkness into my life than I ever imagined possible. When he died, I inherited his money, and Mahender—my husband—and I, we have put it to good work, to redeem some of the evil he did. We rescue street children in India. It's difficult, hard work, but very rewarding. You'd be proud of me.

"Michel, I still miss you so much. But I'm happy. I really am, and I'm glad I came here today. We will head on to Brest tomorrow, to find your old friend Giselle. Hopefully, she'll have the answers to the questions we have about what happened after you left Rennes. Your diary left some things unclear." He got up, brushed off his jeans, and wiped the tears from his cheeks. He looked over to the bench where Mahender and Gaëlle seemed to be ready to jump to action at any moment. He smiled at them bleakly before turning to the grave one last time, touching the slab with the names tenderly.

"Thank you, Michel, for walking into my life, and for teaching me what love is. Thank you for everything. Rest in peace, my love!" He turned around and walked toward the bench where Mahender and Gaëlle were waiting for him.

BREST

*M*ADAME IS TIRED, so I ask you not to stay too long." The young nursing assistant led Gaëlle and Haakon to the room where Giselle was staying at a local nursing home. Mahender had not been allowed to join them inside, as the care facility judged that three visitors at one time would be too much for the fragile old woman.

"Madame Montand? Are you awake? I have a couple of visitors for you. Remember that I mentioned they were on their way from Rennes?"

A thin voice responded from the bed. "Ah, yes. Please show them in, and please open the window. It feels so hot and stale in here. And would you help me sit up? I'd like to be able to see them properly as we speak."

As frail as Giselle might be physically, she has a strong will, Haakon thought, watching from the doorway as the young woman first opened a window and then moved over to the bed to help Giselle sit up.

Gaëlle was the first to enter the room and approach the bed. "Madame? My name is Gaëlle Oberhausen-Martin. I used to be a friend of Michel St. Jacques way back during our university days. This is Haakon Chitragar, Michel's partner at the time. May we speak to you for a moment?"

"But of course, dear. Please come in. I could barely believe it when Bernadette told me about you. A visit, and one from the past at that? I don't have many of those these days. Visits, I mean. You bring news about our dear Michel? I knew he was dead. I recall seeing the obituary for his father in the paper. St. Jacques is such an unusual name. Heart attack, apparently! He wasn't even that old, the poor soul.

"I took it upon myself to visit the grave, out of curiosity, and that's when I saw Michel was already buried there. It broke my heart, as you can imagine, even though part of me expected as much, given we never heard from him again, particularly after Claude had gotten sick. But there had been no news at the time, no obituary, nothing. I think his parents just buried him quietly, afraid people would find out their son was gay. When did you say he died? I have forgotten. My apologies!"

Haakon approached the bed. "Madame. It is an honor to meet you. I wanted to personally thank you for being such an important figure in Michel's life, and for all the help you gave him when he was young. You and Claude feature prominently in his diary, and you were a most important part of his formative years. To answer your question, he passed away in 1986, barely a year after he moved to Paris. Complications from AIDS."

"As I suspected. We lost so many good people, it was carnage, really. I lost countless friends at the time, and there was nothing we could do to stop it. But we never heard anything from Michel after he left for university, and I didn't really blame him. His youth had not been easy, especially not around his parents."

"We heard yesterday that Claude was dead. My condolences, madame."

"Yes, along with half the gay men of that generation. I'm just glad Antoine didn't experience any of it."

"Antoine? The older gentlemen who rescued Michel off the street? What happened to him?"

"The old coot suffered a stroke a few weeks after Michel moved to Paris. He never woke up again. He was lucky because in 1985, things began to deteriorate rapidly. Claude died in 1988 after having been sick for over a year. He was unable to look after his finances, and when word spread he had AIDS, people turned against the gay community and Le Chat Noir. He had been such a prominent figure in Rennes, and he made everybody notice the epidemic.

"The bar became an important place to disseminate information about AIDS and HIV. We closed the darkroom in 1986 and turned it into a place where the local gay association could distribute information, do HIV tests, and so on. But people saw us as the root of all the evil. One day, someone threw in a Molotov cocktail and the whole place burned to the ground. We were lucky to get everyone out in time.

"It was bad, and my insurance didn't cover a rebuild. The city refused to grant me a new license, and in the end, I left town. After losing Claude, I didn't have the strength to continue the fight on my own. Besides, my parents were getting old and needed help. I moved back here, to Brest, and I've never returned."

"I'm so sorry to hear that," Haakon said. "I don't mean to be nosy, but I wondered what happened to Claude's fortune. There's a post in Michel's diary about Claude wanting him to take over and run the business rather than giving it to the government since he had no natural heirs." Haakon pulled out the diary and read the passage to Giselle.

"Yes, I remember Michel mentioning that to me once. You must understand that Claude had been very generous, probably far too generous, for far too long, giving money to people who didn't deserve it. There were quite a few who took advantage of his generosity. And to be honest, he had no nose for business. He squandered most of it on lovers and people he liked, like Michel and his family. I'm not sure that the picture Michel paints in his diary is accurate. He was, after all, just a teenager back then. By the time Claude passed away, most of his real estate had either been sold off or wasn't of much value, due to his reputation and due to his AIDS.

"To speak of a fortune would be an exaggeration. And yes, he died without ever writing his will, so it all ended up going to the state, whatever was left. He was a stubborn mule, that one. He always thought he'd have more time, putting things off to another day. I wasn't involved in his finances, so I don't know much about them, but the nurses who looked after him at the end must've cost a pretty penny. I doubt the government could've built any monuments with what was left." Tears appeared in Giselle's eyes. "Tell me about Michel. Tell me about the life he lived in Paris, and about you."

Gaëlle went first, retelling the story of how she'd met Michel at the station in Rennes as they both embarked on their journey to university, his ready acceptance of her, their friendship, while Haakon filled in with how they'd met in London, and how he'd eventually visited Michel in Paris the next summer for a few weeks, and how he'd rushed to return to his hospital bed after he'd fallen ill.

All three of them cried when Haakon told them about Michel's final moments on that bench in front of the Trocadéro.

"Merci, mes amis. Thank you so much for telling me. I have wondered so many times what had happened to Michel. He was special to me. I was unable to have children of my own due to a mistake I made in my youth. So I took on all the strays Antoine brought me, providing them a safe space, a place where they could be themselves. Michel was always my favorite. Thank you for letting me know that he didn't die alone. Thank you for being there for him. But above all, thank you for loving him." She looked up at Gaëlle. "And thank you for your friendship."

"Thank you, madame, for taking the time to answer our questions. Is there anything else you would like to know?"

Haakon smiled at the tender way Gaëlle held Giselle's hand. The old woman's once-red hair was white, brittle, and unmanaged, but her eyes still sparkled behind a thin veil of tears. She must've been formidable in her prime. Just like Gaëlle.

"Ma fille, thank you, I am tired, and I need to rest now. You have answered all the questions I had, thank you. I don't have much time left on this Earth. I look forward to meeting them all again—my parents, Claude, and Michel. Whenever the good father decides it is my time, I will happily join them." She closed her eyes and took a deep breath.

"Time to go," Gaëlle whispered and got up. She walked over to Haakon and hugged him. "Did you get the closure you were looking for?"

They left the room, looking back one last time at the old woman, who had already fallen asleep. They told Bernadette that they were done and that madame was sleeping. Before the young nurse rushed off to lower the bed again to allow for Giselle to sleep more comfortably, Haakon gave her his card.

"If there is any news about madame, or if she needs anything, please let me know. I would appreciate it. I understand she has little family left."

"She has a niece and a nephew here in Brest, as far as I know. They never visit. I'll let you know if anything changes. Au revoir." Bernadette took the card and walked away toward Giselle's room.

MICHEL

WELL, HAAKON, THAT was quite the trip. Are you satisfied with the answers we found?"

Mahender smiled at his husband as the plane carrying them home climbed higher and higher after takeoff from Paris. They had returned from Rennes the day before after a short stop there to make sure Michel's name on the headstone would be properly cleaned and refreshed, and that a bouquet of twenty-two red roses be placed on his grave every year on his birthday. Back in Paris, they had taken their leave from Gaëlle, but not without her assurance she would come and visit them soon. Georg, her husband had already scheduled a trip to Delhi, and she promised she'd tag along, and they would make a detour to Bangalore to visit them and the Center for Fallen Angels.

Haakon took Mahender's hand and squeezed it. "It's been quite the trip, nanna bangaru. And yes, I am content with the outcome. While there will always be a part of me that wishes Michel were still alive and by my side, his death nudged me in the direction and onto the path to ultimately meet you and pursue the amazing life we live today. So please don't be jealous. You know I love you more than life itself, but Michel was my first real love. And I guess our first love always holds a special place in our hearts."

Mahender lifted Haakon's hand toward his lips and kissed it. "My beloved Haakon, so pure of heart you are. I know how much you love me, and I would never be jealous of your past. I believe that Michel is with you, right now, alive, right here—" he pointed to Haakon's chest "—in your heart. Cherish the memories you shared. As long as you honor him, Michel will always be a part of your life. He'll always be a part of you, and that is exactly as it should be. That is the most important thing. You wouldn't be you if you didn't feel exactly the way you do."

Haakon closed his eyes, still holding Mahender's hand, mulling over his husband's words. He let his mind drift and found himself back in London, in the fall of 1985, on his first-ever trip abroad, looking into the eyes of a young man around his age, handsome, with relatively straight, short, dark-brown hair and lively hazel eyes, smiling intently at him.

"Salut, I'm Michel, and you are?"

THE END

ACKNOWLEDGEMENTS

It's the same story, at the end of each book: to say thanks, and I believe I've also used the term "it takes a village" more than once. Because it is true. How often have I been told by people that "writing must be lonely!" It's usually given as a statement, not a question. And yes, my writing process is rather solitary. However, once the manuscript leaves my laptop as an attachment in an email to my publisher, that's when the collaboration begins, and a long process where I often marvel at the result: the editing, the typesetting for the printed book and the ebook, the proofreading, the creative process around the cover design, with separate versions for all three types of publication: electronic, printed, and the audio version.

So first of all, my thanks to my extraordinary editor, Debbie McGowan, for her knowledge about commas and em-dashes (and then some), and her indulging my quirks every so often. Working with you is one of the many blessings of writing, and for every book, I learn and hopefully improve my work. My thanks to everyone at team Beaten Track, for proofing, beautiful typesetting, an amazing cover design, emotional support, and for putting up with all the strange requests we authors put before you.

At this point, I'd also like to say thanks to my voice, the astonishingly talented and kind Michael Bakkensen, who has narrated several of my books, including the stories of Haakon and—now—Michel. He brings the most subtle of nuances to the narration, puts all his own emotions and passion into every chapter, and I couldn't be happier with the outcome. Thank you!

A special shout-out to my dear friend Tracy Willoughby, who's proofed the audio versions of the last three of my books, including Michel, diligently and patiently, listening to hours and hours of audio to find even the slightest errors.

Those of you who follow my work know how important covers are for me, and what a harsh judge I am when it comes to great cover design. Finding the right angel was amazingly easy, thanks to the power of the internet. Securing the rights to the image was a different story, and I want to thank Agostino Kranhold from photo studio Shootingstar in Wuppertal, Germany, for going above and beyond and taking the picture you see on the cover, from just the right angle, thus capturing the entire emotional spectrum of the grieving angel. Dankeschön!

The creative process of this novel has been very different from previous books. The pandemic had shaken my creativity to the core, and for the first time, I've relied on notes and an outline of sorts. But in the end, the bulk of the story came to me in just ten short days, when Michel finally decided to talk in the fall of 2021. This all made the editing long, and arduous. Another first: the story got longer the more I edited, as I felt I had to clarify, explain, and expand upon some of the early scenes.

Because it's been so long in the making, I've also been able to share and read snippets of text to some of my best friends, to gauge whether or not I had struck the right balance. Thank you for indulging me! To see my husband's teary eyes when we talked about his impression of the story told me everything I needed to know.

I have never felt less certain about a story, likely because I've never worked for so long on a single manuscript. I need to thank my family for the patience they've shown, as I would suddenly leave them alone to write down an important scene that came to me—another first. Noise-canceling headphones on, I was able to disappear into a world long gone.

As I close out this project, I am holding everyone who's helped me very close to my heart in eternal gratitude. Michel is now yours, too, and I hope you will love him as much as I have for the past eight-plus years!

The author

GLOSSARY

Below is a glossary of all non-English terms that appear in this novel. While many of the French words/phrases are commonly used by English speakers, one cannot assume that everyone will understand their meaning.

We decided to write non-English words in plain (non-italic) text throughout the novel. This is to avoid misinterpretation of italics as denoting emphasis.

French:

abbé	priest
adieu	farewell (literally "to God!")
au revoir	good-bye, literally: until we meet again
a plus	until the next time (informal)
bienvenu en France	welcome to France
bisous	kisses
bonjour	good morning
cahier	notebook
c'est la vie!	that's life!
Centre pénitentiaire	detention center
Cervin	Matterhorn
château	castle
chéri(e)	darling

chou-chou	term of endearment
clochard	bum, homeless person
cul	ass
d'accord	all right / okay
détente	relaxing tensions
Diabolo Menthe	Green-colored French drink made from lemon soda and mint syrup
Enchanté	A pleasure to meet you
Gai Pied, le	French gay magazine of the 1980s, founded by Michel Foucault
intra muros	inside the walls
je suis	I am
je t'aime	I love you
Le Chat Noir	The Black Cat
les flics	the cops
Liberté, Egalité, Fraternité	Liberty, Equality, Brotherhood (French national motto)
madame	madam, mrs
mademoiselle	miss
ma fille	my girl, my daughter
maman	mom
merci	thank you
mes amis	my friends
Métro	subway
Mon Dieu!	Oh my God!
monseigneur	honorific title in the Catholic Church
monsieur	mister
non?	right? (literally meaning: no)

Olympique Marseille	Local soccer team of Marseille
oui	yes
Palais du Parlement de Bretagne	Palace of the Parliament of Brittany, seat of the appelate court of Rennes
papa	dad
pédé	faggot (condescending)
RER	commuter trains in and around Paris
rive droite	the right river bank (of the Seine)
Saint / St.	saint, holy
salut	hello
santé	health, also cheers!
SIDA	AIDS
Stade Rennais	local soccer team of the city of Rennes
toilettes	restrooms
14 juillet	14th of July, France's national holiday

Norwegian:

jeg elsker deg	I love you
god morgen, kæresten min	good morning, my dearest
gutten min	my man/boy
skål	cheers

Kannada:

nanna bangaru	my treasure/gold (term of endearment)

ABOUT THE AUTHOR

Photo: Alina Oswald, New York

Hans M Hirschi writes hopeful character-driven stories where ordinary people have to deal with unexpected situations making the spectrum of queer lives visible to a wider public. There's a reason why he's been dubbed The Queen of Unconventional Happy Endings.

He lives in the Gothenburg archipelago with his husband, son, and pets. When not writing, he works as a learning and development executive and VIP tour guide.

Visit Hans online at: www.hirschi.se

285

BY THE AUTHOR

Adult Fiction

Novels

Family Ties

The Opera House

Living the Rainbow – A Gay Family Triptych
(includes *Family Ties, The Opera House,*
and *Jonathan's Hope*)

The Fallen Angels of Karnataka

Willem of the Tafel

Spanish Bay

Ross Deere – Handy Man

Last Winter's Snow

Disease

Matt: More Than Words

Michel – Fallen Angel of Paris

The Jonathan Trilogy

Jonathan's Hope
Jonathan's Promise
Jonathan's Legacy

286

Short Stories

Shorts – Stories from Beneath the Rainbow

Clara
(part of the *Never Too Late* anthology)

A Christmas Miracle
(*The Opera House* short story)

Young Adult Fiction

The Golden One

Blooming
Deceit
Reckoning

Children's Fiction

Valerius and Evander

The Dragon Princess
Felix and the Orphanage

The Vampire Who Lost Her Fangs

Non-Fiction

Dads – A Gay Couple's Surrogacy Journey in India

Common Sense – In Business & Life

BEATEN TRACK PUBLISHING

For more titles from Beaten Track Publishing,
please visit our website:

https://www.beatentrackpublishing.com

Thanks for reading!

www.ingramcontent.com/pod-product-compliance
Lightning Source LLC
Chambersburg PA
CBHW011452170626
46814CB00009B/3025